OF BELLS & THORNS

of BELLS and THORNS

Valentina Cano

REUTS PUBLICATIONS

Cover design by Ashley Ruggirello
Edited by C.M. Spivey, Kisa Whipkey
Book design by Ashley Ruggirello

Electronic ISBN: 978-1-942111-29-0
Paperback ISBN: 978-1-942111-30-6

REUTS Publications
www.REUTS.com

For Carabosse.

ONE

MY DRESS CRINKLED AS I SHIFTED IN THE PLUSH carriage seat. Still not accustomed to the layers of heavy cloth, I made much more noise than was absolutely necessary. My hand slipped into my gown's pocket, a pocket I had especially made, and wrapped around the rose. The one that never seemed to wilt, that never crumbled under my touch, that always greeted me with its scent.

And its thorns.

"Damn," I gasped, bringing my finger to my lips.

"Anne, do you think you could manage to keep your expletives to a bare minimum when we reach the hotel? We'll be thrown out otherwise, and I don't fancy spending another night in the cold."

"I'll certainly try."

"Good."

August put down the book he'd been absorbed in for the majority of the trip and looked up at me. He shook his head and smiled. The gesture made his thin face even thinner, and all I wanted to do was press a pastry on him, or a thick scone with a glob of Devonshire cream on it.

It had been two months since Rosewood Manor had burnt down, and he was as insufferable as ever when it came to his health and well-being. He still waved aside food as if reading alone could keep body and soul together. The cough was gone, at least, swept away like fog when we vanquished the wraith, but his leg still hurt him when the weather was wet, as it was most days this spring season.

One of my corset stays dug into my ribs as the carriage jostled, and I wriggled to shift it to a more bearable location. I'd worn corsets for many years, but none of them as intricate as the one I wore now, and certainly never as tightly laced. When the woman at the shop had wrapped me in it, I had almost fallen in a swoon of skirts. I had adjusted, somewhat, to the tightness, but I still had to pause to catch my breath at inopportune moments. Scrubbing floors or carrying chamber pots up and down seemingly endless stairs would have been impossible wearing this. I groaned and shifted in my seat again.

August chuckled.

"Does my discomfort amuse you?" I asked, lifting an eyebrow.

"You look positively miserable, Anne."

"If you had to wear all this fabric, it would not be so entertaining, I assure you."

He reached out, wincing slightly as he moved his weakened leg, and smoothed a bit of cream lace on my new, China blue bustle skirt. "Perhaps, but it would not look nearly as pleasant on me as it does on you." His hand lingered on the fabric just a second longer than necessary, causing a flare of that strange heat created by the combination of our two innate abilities. After a second more, he removed his hand.

My cheeks warmed with the compliment, rare enough from August's lips. Most of the time, he noticed his surroundings and the people in them only when they were on fire or touching things they shouldn't, the latter sin of which I was very much guilty. And the former . . . well, that was the reason we were headed to London.

Rosewood Manor was now no more than a patch of raw ground on which roses had bloomed with astonishing speed. We had gone to see the grounds one more time before we took the carriage to London, and I had gasped at the sight of the bushes. I suppose I should have been used to it by now, what with everything that had happened, but the plants had tripled in size. They bloomed with such fervor it was frightening. Their thorns were thicker and sharper than ever before, and the scent coiling off their petals was enough to make me feel faint. Even August was taken aback for a moment before shrugging off the effect.

Although I'd known that the destruction of Rosewood Manor would have no real impact on August's wealth, I hadn't expected to see him so freed by its loss. I had expected him to somehow mourn his childhood home and all the memories in it, but I saw him smile more now than ever, as if his shackles had been loosened. Which, I suppose, they had. After not setting foot outside the manor's grounds in five years' time, he was now traveling toward London.

With me.

I cleared my throat.

"What are we going to say when we get to London?" I asked. It was a question I had pondered all of last night, as I lay in one of the lush rooms of a manor an hour away from Rosewood, whose master had kindly provided us with lodgings. We were limited in options when it came to explaining why we traveled together without the usual trappings propriety demanded. I couldn't very well say I was his maid, not when I traveled without female chaperones, and he wouldn't need a maid at all, but a valet. Someone like my father to ensure his clothes were cleaned and pressed, and that he lacked nothing else in the way of comfort.

To that end, and apart from my having lost all my worldly belongings in the fire, August had taken me to be fitted for the clothes I now wore, along with another three full sets of bustles, corsets, skirts, and chemises—all of them of the highest quality, the likes of which I had only learned to button and lace from the outside.

"It is a concern, but I have been thinking of a solution," August said, and frowned slightly. "The ideal situation would be to say that you were my sister, or perhaps a cousin, but in London's finest hotels, I'm afraid that will not work without a chaperone. At the very least, you would have a lady's maid with you to help you in and out of your various outfits."

My cheeks warmed again. Despite everything we had experienced together, it was challenging to put aside not only August's status, but the liberal way he spoke of things which are not usually spoken of in mixed company. Such as dressing and undressing.

I looked down at my hands, gathering the courage to say the words. To ask about an idea that had been pulsing in my mind from the moment August had mentioned this trip to London. There would be no better time to speak about it than now.

"What about Elsie?" I began. "She's not a lady's maid, but she—"

"No, Anne."

I glanced up, frowning.

He sighed. "What would Lady Caldwell say if I showed up on her doorstep and asked for another of her maids? There would be too many questions, too much fuss about the manor and my family. About you." He shook his head. "And the last thing I want to do is place another innocent person in Lily's path."

I slumped back, the weight of his words heavier than all the cloth I suffocated under. Until now, when August had shattered the possibility, I hadn't realized how much I had hoped I could call Elsie to my side. It had been easier to tuck away my grief at being separated from her when my life had been in danger, when my days had been filled with hours of trying to snuff out candles without moving.

But August was right. I couldn't put her in danger.

No. Once we'd found Lily and brought all of this to an end, once August's life and mine had settled into some kind of normalcy, I'd allow myself to see both her and Father again. Until then, I couldn't risk their company.

If I'd needed any further incentive to speed our search, that would have been more than enough.

I leaned forward again. "Fine, no Elsie, but how will we find a chaperone?"

"Ah, well, I was thinking that we might not need one at all. Unless, of course, you feel uncomfortable traveling alone with me. If that is the case, we can arrange for someone." He looked directly into my eyes and cocked his head to the side, like a bird.

Was he daft? Had I not already spent days alone with him and a bloodthirsty wraith? I had entrusted my reputation and, more importantly, my life to him once before, and I saw no reason not to do it again.

"For Heaven's sake, August, I think I can manage. You forget that all I need to do to incapacitate you is kick your walking stick away." This was not entirely true anymore. He had lost most of the limp and had regained function in his leg, little by little losing the need for the carved cane he had used for the past two months.

He lifted an eyebrow. "I see. Well, then you will have no trouble at all with what I have in mind."

I shrugged. "If it will help us begin searching for Lily, then I am sure I will not."

"I think you should become Lady Grey."

He said it so simply that I didn't gather the full meaning of his words for a few seconds. When the reality of his suggestion finally reached me, I could do nothing but sit there and blink at him in utter confusion. To my consternation, all I could think of was that one moment in Rosewood Manor, when he had knocked on my door and taken me into his arms. The moment neither of us had spoken of or alluded to since. It had been two months of skirting around that kiss, dancing around it as we planned the trip to London, our eyes meeting in awkward glances that ended with one of us turning away. There was so much I wanted to know about him, but my courage failed me when it came to August Grey.

"Anne?"

His voice brought me back, and I realized I was still staring at him. I looked down at my lap. "You mean, pretend to be your wife?"

I felt the weight of his eyes as he watched me as intently as I'd watched the candle flame he'd taught me to snuff out with my powers.

"It is the only way I can devise that will allow us to remain a duo without creating gossip. It is a peculiar notion, I know, but it won't be so different from what we have done already. You have already spent a night in my chambers, if you recall."

There was a familiar edge to his voice, flinging me back to the first time I met him by that cursed black fountain. I knew him better now, however, and would not allow his sarcasm to provoke me.

"I don't know how to behave like someone of your station," I said. "I can barely dress like one, so how am I expected to go unnoticed as a fraud? As soon as I step into the first ballroom, everyone will know that I belong there only with a feather duster or a serving tray in my hands."

The discomfort this thought caused me was surprising. I had never felt the need to belong in the higher classes. On the contrary, despite all the work I shouldered, I felt rather fortunate to belong to an industrious class that could accomplish things throughout the day, and not to one that could be brought to hysterics by a streak of dust. Things had changed, however. I was no longer content with just following orders, not now, not after everything I had seen and found out. Not after realizing how I felt about August.

When he spoke next, all the sarcasm had seeped out of his voice. "You are a hundred times better than any of them. Than any of those fancy women in ribbons and silk who simper through afternoons doing nothing but gossiping. You are much better than the men with their cigars and brandy, endlessly congratulating themselves on their wealth."

His distaste for his class struck me for what felt like the thousandth time in the past two months. As he'd recovered from his wound, I'd seen him interact with people from his station for the first time—for the first time that wasn't in a memory, at least—and while he'd been perfectly cordial on the surface, there'd been a simmer of laughter in every word he'd said. I'd caught his half-smothered sighs of boredom as we spent evening after evening sitting and speaking of horse races, and I'd even seen him roll his eyes at our host when the man's back was turned. I couldn't understand it. Not really. It was one thing for me to feel that way, to find men like Lord Caldwell—men who required a collar to be starched *just so* or it wasn't worth wearing—or women like Lady Caldwell—who needed her smelling salts if a bit of mud so much as neared her shoe—ridiculous, but August? He'd been raised among these men and women. What could have possibly turned him against them to such a degree?

I watched him as he glanced at the greenery we galloped through.

"No, you will never fit into their circle," he said, after a moment of silence, "but never doubt that it is because of your virtues, not your faults."

Although his words warmed me, there was a darkness threaded through them that I didn't understand. A bitterness that reminded me too much of the despairing young man I had thought I'd helped free.

After months in the countryside, surrounded by trees and the ever-present roses, the smell of London was a shock. The first thing I did as I opened the carriage window was sneeze. *Had there always been this much dust in the air?*

The city was warmer than when I left it, and the sun's heat brought a miasma of unpleasant scents that I must have smelled every spring and summer of my life, but yet had passed unnoticed until now. A splash of mud against the carriage's side provided the perfect excuse to close the window again.

"Did you miss it?" August asked as we jolted past Trafalgar Square, busy with people.

"I don't know." And I didn't, really. London had been my home since I was born, but I felt somehow distant from the city and its rumble of life now that I was within it once more.

Rosewood Manor had left its mark on me, that much was certain.

"I am not very fond of the city, myself," August said with a shrug. "Never really took to its hectic pace."

That was shocking, considering how difficult it was to keep August still for more than an hour.

"And, of course, after everything that occurred with the Brothers, I had hoped never to step foot within its borders again." He turned away from me and gazed out the window. "That is why I'm certain Lily is here."

"But wouldn't people recognize her? She did live most of her life in London."

August shook his head. "Her father was abominably strict with her. The only times she was allowed away from her private quarters was when I escorted her to the theater or a ball. She had not been presented into society because the Master did not believe in the trifles of that world, so even attending events such as those drew many glances."

I frowned. A young woman of her position and wealth not introduced into society? It guaranteed that she would be an outcast for most of her life, unmarried, without connections, isolated in the bustle of London.

"I don't understand. Why would her father do that to her when he had the means of doing otherwise?"

"I've wondered about that myself," August said. "At the time, though, I was content enough to bask in the knowledge that the Master had chosen me to be his daughter's escort." Bitterness crept into his voice, coiling around each syllable. "That it would help me advance in the Order."

I was about to ask more when the carriage slowed, and then stopped.

"We're here," August said.

I looked out the window and gasped. We were at the grandest entrance in all of London, one I had passed only a handful of times while on errand for the Caldwell household.

"*The Salisbury*," I said in an awed whisper. Nerves fluttered up and down my spine at the thought of stepping foot through its ornate entrance, let alone through its interior. Dukes and duchesses walked the Salisbury's floors, slept in its beds, not parlor maids.

I couldn't do this. It would have been difficult enough to play a lady in some of the smaller hotels, but I couldn't pretend I was something I wasn't when I was surrounded by all the glitter of the most luxurious hotel in London.

I turned to August to tell him this and found him watching me carefully, one eyebrow lifted in expectation. He was daring me to say something, to cower under the opulence in front of me and allow the gulf of position that had divided us when we'd first met to grow once more. After all that we'd been through, I could not allow that.

I swallowed my words, along with my fear, and reached for the grey silk gloves resting next to me on the seat. "Give me a moment to slip them on, or I might cause some old duchess to faint at the sight of my bare hands."

August's thin lips curled into a soft smile and he nodded.

I had helped Lady Caldwell into innumerable pairs of gloves, but had never worn any myself, so getting used to the constricting slipperiness would take some time. When I was done, I reached for the carriage handle, but August lifted a hand, urging me to wait.

Not two seconds had passed under the pretense of being a Lady and I'd already forgotten that they didn't open their own doors. How was I ever to convince anyone that I belonged here?

A man dressed in a beige vest and trousers, and a deep blue, double-breasted coat with the hotel's curling *S* embroidered in silver over his heart approached the carriage and opened the door.

"Welcome to the Salisbury, Lord Grey, Lady Grey." He bowed deeply from his waist in a crisp manner that told of hours practicing in front of mirrors. He then stood straight once more, clicked his heels together like a soldier, and extended a gloved hand in my direction.

Swallowing back nerves, I leaned forward and took hold of the offered hand. The corset cut into my ribs and stomach as I shifted my weight in an attempt to stand. I made it only about an inch off the carriage seat before landing back down with a swish of fabric. My mouth opened immediately, an apology ready, but I clamped it shut again as I caught August's glance. Ladies did not give excuses for their behavior.

Right. I cleared my throat and avoided looking up at the man outside the carriage. I knew how many hours of work he still had left before he could retire to his chambers for the night, and here I was, wasting his time with my clumsiness.

With my free hand, I gathered as much of my skirts as I could without it becoming indecent, took a deep breath, and girded myself for the pain of the corset's stays digging into my skin. I shifted my weight again and allowed the momentum to carry me, and the pile of fabric swathed around me, out of the carriage.

There was a moment when I thought I would snag my new shoes on the dress's bustle, and would end up in a most embarrassing position in front of the Salisbury, but I managed to right myself without so much more than a slight hesitation.

"Lady Grey," the man said with a small head bow that made my cheeks burn, and released my hand, turning to offer it to August.

August waved away the offer of help, alighting from the carriage on his own. Only the small twitch of his mouth betrayed a wince of pain in his leg as he stepped down onto the stone entranceway.

There was a flurry of bird-like movement behind us as a group of young men hurried to remove our luggage from the back of the carriage. The impulse to walk over to them and collect my own piece of luggage was stronger than I expected. But it was chased away a moment later, when I recalled that it wasn't my mother's case they carried. That had burned at Rosewood Manor, as had everything else I'd ever owned. No, my new luggage was comprised of a valise, two hat boxes, and a trunk full of all the petticoats and dresses I'd acquired in the past two months. Each piece cost more than I'd ever spent in my seventeen years on this earth, and together, it was much more than I'd be able to carry on my own.

August cleared his throat lightly next to me, drawing me out of my thoughts and back to the present. He offered his arm, curving it into a dark wing, and I swallowed as I realized what was required of me.

I slipped my gloved hand through the opening and placed it lightly on his arm. Even with the dampening layers of fabric between us, I still felt the warmth our touching produced. It was like a muffled flame. It wasn't unpleasant, though I knew the sensation would grow the longer we stayed like this. The anticipation of pain was most likely the cause of my tumbling heartbeats. Nothing more, nothing less.

"Lord Grey, if you would come this way, please." The hotel's employee motioned us toward the gilded doors of the Salisbury, which opened seemingly of their own accord from the inside.

August took the first step, for which I was profoundly grateful, and I moved with him. He walked as slowly as he could without calling attention to himself as I adjusted to the weight of the clothes. It was like walking in layers of fabric that had been drenched in the Thames.

"Are you all right?" he asked, softly enough not to be heard in the noise of efficiency around us.

"Yes. Do all lady's clothes weigh this much?"

He chuckled. "I'm afraid so."

We stepped through the doorway and into the grandest room I'd ever been in. Neither Caldwell House, with its rich furnishings and porcelain figurines, nor Rosewood Manor with its size and striking beauty, had prepared me for the glittering sight before us.

I'd never been in a hotel before, let alone one like this, so I'd had no real idea of what to expect. I feared I would lose my limited self-possession if I looked too closely at any one thing around me, yet I could not tear my gaze from the beauty of the foyer.

The floor alone, sculpted of speckled marble, was enough to leave me as wide-eyed as any country maid. The room was enormous, with high ceilings and a large glass cupola in the center that flooded the place with London's afternoon light. The walls were a deep burgundy brocade that could have made the room oppressive without the natural light cascading from above, but which provided a sense of warmth in the spaciousness instead. There was an ornate golden mirror which, while not as beautiful as the one August had enchanted at Rosewood Manor, was still a splendor to look at. It was spotless, and I was sure someone had slaved over it earlier this morning. The mirror was hung behind a carved and massive wooden desk that sat at the far end of the room and had been polished enough to almost function as a mirror itself. How many hours had it taken to achieve such a glow?

A few other people drifted through the foyer, mostly well-dressed women sipping from delicate china cups. They wore what I imagined were the latest fashions, in an array of colors that made me cringe at my own outfit until I remembered that I wasn't dressed like I had been at Caldwell House or Rosewood Manor. My dress was as beautiful and as well-crafted as any of theirs. Visually, at least, I looked like I belonged within these walls.

As we walked by, some of the women shifted their attention from their teacups or lazy fan movements to watch us. Their collective gaze was strong enough to send a wave of nerves bubbling in my stomach like a teakettle. I had a vision of my heels catching on the hem of one of my dress's many layers and being propelled across the shimmering marble floor to land with a reputation-shattering crash.

It was absolutely ridiculous that, after fighting a wraith and all its horrors, I would be so frightened of these colorful beings who had been born to walk with ease in rooms like these.

As if my thoughts had fluttered out into the open air for everyone to see, August tucked his walking stick under his free arm and, with one graceful move, placed his gloved hand on mine, which still rested on his arm.

The weight of his hand, along with the familiar warmth, bolstered my frayed nerves. I shouldn't have needed his reassurance, but I did.

A man approached us from behind the ornate desk and bowed his head slightly before speaking. "Lord Grey, what an honor to have Your Lordship at the Salisbury. I could hardly believe it when I received notice of your imminent arrival." He bowed again.

He had a bald patch at the very top of his head, reminding me a bit of a type of monks I'd seen when I was younger. The light from the cupola bounced off whatever pomade he'd applied to his hair and scalp that morning, accentuating the bare spot.

"Mr. Rushworth, it is a pleasure to be here," August said with more sincerity than I expected. "May I present my wife, Lady Grey?"

Hearing August call me his wife was a shock, even if I'd been expecting it. My heart couldn't help but trip over itself with yet more nerves.

Mr. Rushworth's eyes turned to me and a smile as bright as the foyer lit his face. He bowed deeply, from the waist this time. "It is an absolute honor, Lady Grey. Lord Grey mentioned that he would be traveling with a lady, but I hadn't imagined it would be *his* lady. And a ravishing one at that."

I did the only thing I could think of. "You are too kind. It is lovely to be here in your hotel, Mr. Rushworth."

I hoped my voice didn't betray how nervous I was at the possibility of being spotted as a fraud. I had been raised among ladies and lords, and my mother had been a lady's personal maid, but the way I spoke, everything from my accent to my choice of vocabulary, could betray me at any moment.

Mr. Rushworth's smile widened, and he nodded to August as if nothing at all were amiss. I exhaled with relief.

"If you will come with me, Lord Grey, I will show you to your chambers."

"Of course," August said, and gave my hand a squeeze.

Mr. Rushworth led us down a glittering corridor, gilded with what appeared to be designs in gold leaf, and toward a peculiar pantry-like structure along one side. It had a set of intricate doors that were crafted of carved wooden panels and thin, elegant iron bars displaying curlicues of every design. Flowers and birds adorned the center of the doors, as well as the iron dome that enclosed them.

I'd never seen anything like it, and for one confused moment, I thought this might be a water closet, though it would be the strangest one I'd ever encountered and one that I would feel not at all comfortable to use.

As we neared, the doors opened, as if by their own design, and I held my breath. Had August done that? Did Mr. Rushworth know about his special abilities?

But once the doors were fully open, they revealed a man in a blue and cream uniform with a small hat on his head. He bowed to us and stepped aside to allow us to enter.

"This is our famous 'ascending room,' as our patrons like to call it," Mr. Rushworth said. "Its official name is a lift, but I prefer the former. It is more romantic."

An "ascending room." I'd never heard of the like. How could a room "ascend," even one as small as this one? I looked at August, who had pure curiosity written all over his features.

"This was not installed the last time I stayed here," he said.

"You are quite right, Lord Grey. It is a new addition, and one we are very proud of. And, of course, it means that neither you, sir, nor your lovely wife will have to worry about climbing up or down stairs during your stay at the Salisbury. We are the only hotel in all of London—and, dare I say it, all of the empire—to have such a device."

I couldn't hold my tongue any longer. "What do you mean by 'ascending room'?"

"Let me show you, madam," Mr. Rushworth said, smiling. "Please, if you would step inside." He extended a hand toward the open iron doors. "I can promise you it is perfectly safe."

I wasn't frightened. It was just a room—one that must have been a nightmare to clean, with all of its carvings and crevices, but just a room, all the same. Still, my curiosity would not have allowed me a moment's rest if I didn't see what the all fuss was about, so I stepped forward, withdrawing my arm from August's support without realizing it. I was so accustomed to doing things on my own, to walking unaccompanied, to not being offered help of any sort, that it was an automatic gesture.

Mr. Rushworth's widened eyes told me that this was an action not usually seen in this level of society, however.

"How does this contraption work, then?" August asked quickly, masking my apparent unseemly eagerness with his. Biting down an apology, I took his arm again.

"Jonathan, here, will demonstrate," Mr. Rushworth said, and motioned to the young man with the peculiar hat as he closed the metal doors and enclosed us in the room. "He has been expertly trained in operating this lift."

"Sir, madam," Jonathan said. "First is the selection of the floor you wish to go to."

"Their chambers are on the last story," Mr. Rushworth said.

Jonathan pressed a button with a golden number five on it.

Five stories! I'd thought the hotel was large, but not as large as that. Five stories of floors to sweep, curtains to dust, furniture to polish—and I very much doubted the maids were allowed to use this "moving" room.

"Then you turn this here," Jonathan said, and took hold of a large lever attached to a round base on the floor. He moved it until it rested in the opposite position to what it had been.

The floor beneath us shifted. No, that was wrong, not the floor, the whole room. The noise of gears filled the space around us, and the hallway of the hotel disappeared in front of my eyes as the doors, as the entire room, rose.

I held my breath and looked up. It was dark above the cupola, as if we'd just been plunged into night. How could we not crash into anything, rising this quickly and with what I imagined was significant force? I expected to hear the screech of metal against plaster at any moment. But light flooded the moving room again as we passed another hallway and kept rising.

"Isn't it a wonder?" Mr. Rushworth said.

"It's magical," I said.

"Indeed." August squeezed my hand.

The moving room stopped, and Jonathan pulled open the doors with a small, cleverly concealed lever.

"This is the fifth story, and we have arrived without having to catch our breaths," Mr. Rushworth said with a chuckle. "I cannot imagine that human invention will ever surpass this ingenious mechanism. Thank you, Jonathan. Please wait here while I show His Lord and Ladyship to their chambers."

He led us out into a hallway papered in egg-yolk yellow that was a bright contrast to the richness of the foyer below. The color had a sudden, immediate effect on me, bringing a smile to my lips and a wave of cheeriness to my mind. I couldn't imagine anything horrible occurring inside these friendly looking corridors.

"Here we are, then," Mr. Rushworth said, stopping by a set of cream-colored doors with golden door handles. "Our best chambers." He turned the handles and opened the doors to one of the most beautiful rooms I had ever seen.

It was all sunlight. Even the foyer, with its cupola, felt like a cavernous space when compared with this sitting room. It had an entire wall of windows. They stretched from the wooden floor to the sconces on the ceiling, flooding the room with the light and sights of London.

Two large sofas in the same shade of friendly yellow as the corridor's walls sat before the windows, along with two sitting chairs in a mossy green that perfectly complemented the bright tones. A large clock ticked cheerily against one of the far walls.

If I had a home of my own, one that I could decorate at will, this is what it would look like.

I turned to August to find him looking at me, his thin lips curved in a half-smile.

"This is the sitting room, of course," Mr. Rushworth said. "Through those doors are your personal chambers. One for Lady Grey, and one for you, sir." He cleared his throat and lowered his voice, as if to keep what he said next from the prying, nonexistent ears around us. "Will Lady Grey be requiring a maid?"

I opened my mouth, ready to say that there was no need, when I suddenly remembered the face Lady Caldwell made the one time a woman of breeding had stayed as a guest at her home without a lady's maid. She had looked as if she was about to fall over in a faint.

I swallowed the words back and nodded, instead. "Yes, I will. Thank you."

Mr. Rushworth bowed his head. "I have arranged for some tea and refreshments to be brought up, as I am sure you must both be parched from the journey, and your bags will be brought up momentarily. In the meantime, is there anything else you require?"

"I think you have covered everything, Mr. Rushworth. Diligent as always," August said.

"Thank you, sir. I will leave you both to rest." He turned to me and bowed at the waist. "Madam."

He placed the room's heavy key on a peg near the entrance and slipped out, closing the door softly behind him. I sighed with relief. Now I could be as clumsy and awkward as I wanted without sparking off gossip or strange looks. At least until the refreshments came.

"This will do, I suppose," August said, motioning at the room around us.

"Do? It's incredible. So full of light!"

I walked toward one of the large windows and stared out at a view of London I had never before seen. Roofs of all sorts crowded around each other in a way that should have looked disorganized, but which was actually quite captivating. I couldn't see the street from the window because of the smaller buildings that blocked the way, but it made me feel as if London were just mine and August's, on display for us and us alone.

I felt him draw near, his energy, the opposite of mine, pushing and pulling at me like the Thames lapping at the shoreline.

"This will not be easy," he said.

I nodded, though I wasn't sure if he meant the search for Lily, my pretending to be a lady and his wife, or the two of us revolving around each other the way we had been since that last night at Rosewood.

I didn't know how to ask for what I wanted, how to bridge this strange divide that separated us in awkward silences. All I knew was that the memory of that one kiss haunted me as much as the wraith had haunted Rosewood Manor. What I wanted, more than anything at that moment, with the sunlight strong enough to warm away the bone-deep memory of all those frozen weeks, was to press myself against August's chest and have his arms enfold me in their warmth.

His breathing sped up behind me, and for an instant, I thought that he would come closer, that we would end this strangeness between us.

But then he cleared his throat and backed away.

I closed my eyes.

He was right, this wasn't going to be easy.

TWO

"ONCE MORE."

"August, I'm exhausted."

"What you are is out of practice."

I couldn't argue with him on that, even if I could have managed to find the strength to do so. I hadn't exactly had a lot of opportunity to use my powers since we left Rosewood Manor. Apart from exerting them on August himself when he'd refused the morphine and laudanum the doctor had prescribed for his leg and the pain had become too great to allow him to sleep, my abilities had languished with disuse. As had his.

Not that anyone would be able to tell from the energy that now radiated off him. Ripples of it gathered all around him.

"Can we not do this tomorrow?"

With no more warning than the twitch of an eyebrow, August flung all of his coiled power at me.

I guess we were doing this now.

I called on my abilities, but my mind and body were sluggish, the skills I'd chiseled into shape to fight the wraith had dulled. Not completely, I knew that, but enough to allow August's considerable powers to slam right into me.

I yelped, a whip of fire striking my entire body.

"You're not focusing, Anne. Remember, Lily is many times stronger than I am. Between the two of us, we might have a chance, but not if you cannot pull your weight."

A flare of irritation lit in my mind, allowing me to gather my scattered powers into something I could wield.

I shoved back at his energy, as if I were pushing closed a damp, swollen wooden door. "It's funny you say that, because I don't recall you pulling your weight with the wraith. If I remember correctly, you were unconscious through most of it."

He smiled and flicked a finger at me, along with enough power to force me back a step.

Right, well, that was enough of that.

Shifting one leg forward to stiffen my stance, I thrust my hands in his direction. The pressure around me eased, unraveling like torn silk, and the chandelier above us gave a crystalline whimper. It was now August's turn to stagger back.

Sudden silence descended on the room, and it took me much too long to realize why.

I frowned. The clock had stopped ticking.

"Now, I could be wrong, but I think I just grounded Mr. Rushworth's clock," I said.

August's laughter was like a splash of cold water, sending a chilled ripple down my spine.

Turning around, he walked to the wall behind him and pressed his ear against the clock's thick wooden torso. "I think you're right, Miss Tinning. We've been here for barely an hour and you've already caused trouble. Honestly."

"Well, I wouldn't have done that if you had left me well enough alone."

He waved my words aside. "But this is new. You haven't done this before."

"No."

"You're accessing more of your powers." His eyes glittered as he stepped away from the wall and walked toward me. "We should try—"

"We should try nothing. I am tired and hungry, and there's a perfectly lovely pot of tea cooling on that table. I am going to sit right there and eat some of those cucumber sandwiches, and you can battle the wall, if you like. Or you can join me like a civilized person."

Without waiting for a response, I walked to the small table between the two sofas, onto which a maid had placed our tea half an hour before.

August gave a sigh that better belonged on a stage and followed. He slumped down on one of the sofas, shoving to one side the mound of ornamental pillows that someone had spent quite a lot of the morning arranging.

Pursing my lips at the untidiness of it all, I spooned a generous amount of sugar into each of the two cups and poured the tea. The amount of gratitude I felt at it still being warm was shocking.

I held out a cup to August and, when he accepted it from my grasp, sat down with mine.

We ate and drank in silence, both of us wandering our own paths.

I tried to turn my thoughts away from Lily, but they kept returning to her, to what harm she might be planning for us right now. To how we could possibly find her before that harm could befall us.

"You are sure she will be in London?" I asked and took a sip of my second cup of tea.

"No, of course I am not sure, Anne, but it is the best I've got. After years of living like a prisoner in her father's home, the last thing I imagine her doing is retreating to somewhere in the countryside to hide." He sat back and sighed. "When I knew her, she was hungry for life, for the city and everything it had to offer. It is not even a question of means, because her father left everything to her. She could be anywhere in the world, but with the hate she has for me, and now for you, I do not think she would wander so far as to miss the results of whatever further destruction she might have in store for us."

I frowned down at my cup. "That is all well and good, but London is a huge city. Where do we even begin searching for her?"

"I don't know." The frustration in his voice was palpable. "She had no family other than her father, and no one she spent any time with who was more than just an acquaintance."

Despite what she had done to us, it was difficult not to feel at least a bit of pity for her. Lily's life, regardless of her wealth and status, had lacked even Mary's rough, motherly influence or Elsie's affection. I had grown up in a kitchen, my every minute dedicated to serving other people, but my childhood had held more warmth and freedom than hers.

Even August's part in her life, the way he had used her to gain favor in her father's eyes—I had seen the destruction it had brought to her mind. I had seen it all with my own eyes. And I knew the way the guilt of this and everything that had followed had eaten away at the young man I loved, which is why I looked away from August as I spoke next.

"Were there any locations that she liked to go to with . . . with you?"

"The theater, as I showed you in my memory. Covent Garden sometimes, in the morning for the freshest flowers. Once in a while, her father allowed her to join us for dinner at his favorite restaurant, the Royal Café." He sighed. "We can try at all of those places, of course, and see if anyone has seen her, but I don't think she would be so obvious."

I shook my head. "Neither do I, but we must begin somewhere."

"I suppose so. If we at least had the painting of her you found at Rosewood Manor, we could show it to people at the theater or restaurant. As it is, we'll have to be as accurate as possible with her description."

Although I didn't say so, it was easy to describe her: she was the most beautiful woman I had ever seen.

A knock on the sitting room door dispelled Lily's image from my mind like a breeze tearing away at smoke.

"Enter," August said.

A young woman, no older than I and perhaps even a few years younger, entered the room. She wore a dark dress with a crisp white apron and white lace cap. But neither her youth nor her dress were what struck me. It was her resemblance to Elsie.

She had the same broad shoulders, the same straw-colored hair, even a similar collection of freckles on her nose and cheeks. Her face held the same round innocence. Her cap, too, so clean and stiff, and slightly askew.

"Pardon me, my lady, that I did not come sooner. I was just now made aware of your request for a lady's maid."

It felt like someone had clenched a fist around my heart. Every memory of Elsie, my sister in everything but blood, came back to me so sharply that I feared I would be ill.

I looked up at August, who watched me carefully. He made a slight motion with his head, indicating that I should speak.

Taking a deep breath, I did my best to steady my voice. "Do not trouble yourself. I was not in need of assistance."

August cleared his throat, giving me another significant glance.

"Uh . . . however," I said, "please remember to be punctual the next time you are required."

The words felt like needles in my mouth, but I knew from experience the way a real lady would speak to a delayed maid.

"Yes, madam," she said and bowed her head. "Would Her Ladyship like assistance dressing for supper?"

Was it suppertime already? I glanced at the window, noticing for the first time how the sun had lost its grasp on the day, how shadows had taken over most of the sitting room. Without lamps lit or sunlight streaming in, it felt less like a hotel room and more like a home. I realized then that I had spent at least two hours alone with August in the most companionable manner. As if I had been doing it my whole life. It was shocking to think that, until to seven months ago, he had been a complete stranger.

"Would you like to go somewhere for supper?" he asked softly. "It seems that I lost all track of the time."

"So did I. But, to be honest, I'm not very hungry after all of this," I said, motioning to the remnants of the scones and sandwiches. August had had two scones with cream and preserves, which was more than he usually ate at most meals. I did not doubt that he shared my sentiment.

He nodded. "We'll stay in, then."

"It's all right," I said to the young woman still waiting by the door. "You can retire for the evening."

She blinked a few times. "Doesn't Your Ladyship need me to help her undress and turn down her bed?"

Damn. She was right. I'd forgotten that women in my supposed class did not undress on their own, something I would have remembered very quickly when I tried to undo the laces on this unfamiliar corset, tied at the back instead of at the front.

"Oh, of course. The trip has addled my brain," I said and stood. I ensured that my feet were untangled from the heavy skirts and walked to the door that led to my own bedroom.

The cases of new clothing had disappeared from where one of the hotel attendants had left them, just inside the door. The maid who had brought us our tea had spent a good half hour hanging everything up in the large armoire standing in one corner of the room, so that, when the young woman opened its doors, all my new clothes hung perfectly straight and at the same distance from each other. It would have taken precise care to achieve that result. I couldn't help but admire that kind of dedication.

The young woman held up one of the two sleeping gowns I now owned. Neither of them was as delicate as the one August had given me at Rosewood Manor, but they were still of the finest quality.

"This one, madam?"

"Yes, thank you. What is your name?"

"Eustace, madam."

I smiled at her. "Beautiful name."

"Thank you, madam." She placed the sleeping gown carefully on the bed, making sure that no wrinkles formed on any part of it, and folded her hands in front of her.

It took me a moment to realize she was waiting for me to turn around.

I had never been a personal lady's maid, like my mother, so I'd had no real idea of what having a maid to help me undress would entail. At Caldwell House, Elsie had helped me if I encountered a particularly stubborn knot at any point in my undressing ritual, but as a rule, maid's clothes were designed to require no assistance stepping in and out of them. No complicated laces in the back, no heavy skirts to step into, just clothing that could be slipped on and off in a hurry.

Feeling as out of place as I had felt the first time I stepped into Rosewood Manor, I turned around.

Eustace's fingers were nimble and strong as they carefully lifted the fabric and slipped the dress's top layer off of me.

"There's a rose in one of the pockets," I said. "Could you remove it?"

"Of course, madam."

She gently pulled out August's rose, as fragrant and fresh as ever, and placed it on the dressing table. Just seeing it put me at ease.

The corset laces came next. And as she pulled on them and undid the knots, my head began to feel weightless with the surge of air.

My vision clouded. Two hands steadied me.

"Madam?" Eustace said.

"I'm all right. Just a bit tired, that's all." My face warmed as I said the words. I knew what she'd be thinking, how ridiculous it was for me, in my supposed idle station, to claim to be tired when she was the one who'd been working since the sun's break. How many times had I rolled my eyes at Lady Caldwell's sighs of exhaustion when she returned from an evening at the theater?

Eustace said nothing, as expected, and continued pulling layers and layers off me, setting each one on the bed to hang or fold. I shivered as she slipped the nightgown over me and smoothed it out all the way down to my feet. Just in time, too, because I couldn't find the strength to stay upright for another minute. I truly hoped that I was simply tired from the travel and afternoon's exertion, and was not about to catch cold.

"Would madam like to sit so I can unpin her hair?"

"No, that's fine, Eustace. I'll do it myself." I knew that this was not usual, that ladies did nothing on their own if they could avoid it, but having her unpin my hair was an excess I could not imagine allowing myself. Now that my torso was free from the corset and my arms free from the layers of heavy cloth, I could do my toiletries myself.

She nodded and began meticulously hanging and folding the clothes on the bed. It took her at most a couple of minutes, which I had to admire. I wouldn't have known where to begin.

When she'd finished, Eustace turned in my direction, though her eyes were locked firmly on her folded hands. "Is there anything else, madam?"

"You can retire," I said with a smile. "I imagine it has been a long day for you."

Eustace looked up for an instant in surprise. The resemblance to Elsie cut through me again. "Yes, madam."

"Go rest, then."

"At what time does madam want to breakfast and dress tomorrow morning?"

Bloody hell, I'd forgotten about that, as well. I should have asked August at what time he would prefer to begin the search, but if I stepped into the sitting room now, in my sleeping gown, poor Eustace might suffer an apoplexy.

I went through some rough calculations in my head. If I wanted to breakfast at seven thirty, Eustace would have to rise at five thirty, or thereabouts, depending on the other duties she had to perform. Much too early. Although I couldn't imagine myself sleeping past eight, I would not want anyone rising before dawn for me.

"Eight thirty, then," I said. She would be able to sleep at least one more hour, which would ease some of my guilt.

She did her best to hide her surprise, but it was written clearly on her face.

"Yes, madam." With a small curtsey, she slipped out.

I exhaled with relief. My first experience as a lady with a personal maid and she hadn't run out of the room screaming, "Impostor!" She had found me odd, yes, but I'd known odd lords and ladies, including the one in the very next room. That was the advantage of being part of that station, I supposed: no one dared question your actions, no matter how bizarre.

Speaking of which . . .

I opened the bedroom door and leaned out of the doorway. August still sat on the sofa, his eyes lost in thought.

"Is a manservant coming up?" I asked.

He blinked away the film of thoughts blurring his eyes and turned his gaze toward me. "Not unless you require one."

I fought the urge to roll my eyes. A straight answer every once in a while wouldn't bring about the end of the empire.

"You don't need any help?"

"I lived without a manservant for years at Rosewood; I'm fairly certain I can survive without one tonight."

I could have mentioned that he hadn't had a somewhat injured leg at Rosewood Manor, but I was too tired to argue.

I stepped out of the room, feeling oddly nervous standing before him in just a sleeping gown. Logically, I knew that August had seen me in this state of undress before, but it was different now, in this situation that lacked the urgency created by life-and-death circumstances.

"I told Eustace to come help me dress at eight thirty tomorrow."

He nodded. "All right. That should give us time to have at least a cup of tea before beginning our search. She went to fetch fresh water for us." He cocked his head to the side. "What are you doing?"

I looked down at my hands, which were busy fluffing one of the sofa's ornate pillows. I hadn't even realized I had picked it up. With a sigh, I returned it to its spot. "Habit, I suppose. It's hard to break after more than a decade."

"Well, you will no longer have to worry about any of that."

He said it as if it were obvious, but it wasn't for me. Yes, right now I didn't have to worry about a maid's duties, but what would happen after we found Lily and did what we could to stop her from cursing us again with something worse than a wraith? I couldn't keep pretending to be something that I wasn't. Neither a lady nor a wife, but stuck in some sort of limbo. I loved August, and I would do anything I could to keep him safe, but I didn't have the foggiest idea what the future held for us.

This was neither the time nor the place to bring all of this up, however. We still had a daunting job ahead of us.

I nodded toward my bedroom door. "I'm going to retire. And you, my good sir, should do the same. We have an exhausting day planned tomorrow."

"I will, in a few minutes."

I knew what that meant. He would probably still be perched on that sofa when I walked out of my room in the morning.

Short of physically dragging him into his chamber, for which I did not feel inclined, there was nothing I could do. With a shrug, I walked to my bedroom door.

I was about to close it behind me when he spoke again.

"Anne, may I make a suggestion?"

He was asking permission? "Of course."

"Don't get too friendly with the maid. It could complicate matters."

I poked my head out. "That's a bit rich, coming from you."

His eyebrows lifted and a smile broke through his lips. "Touché."

"Goodnight, August."

"Goodnight."

THREE

THE DAY COULD HAVE STARTED BETTER.

The coach we had hired to drive us around London did not arrive on time, and when it finally did, the coachman smelled like the inside of a wine bottle. Mr. Rushworth sacked him on the spot and went into a frenzy of apologies that forced August and I into the street to avoid further bowing and lamenting.

"We'll just hire a cab," I said. "It's early enough that we will not have long to wait."

The other option was the underground Metropolitan Railway, which had been finished half a decade ago and which I'd never had the chance to ride. I wasn't sure if there were any terminals nearby, though, and walking for more than a couple of streets in this torturous corset was still beyond my ability.

"Yes, I imagine that is the best choice." August looked down the street as if expecting a hansom cab to appear out of the thinning fog, summoned by his proclamation.

"We'll have to walk at least another street away from the hotel to hail one," I said. "I doubt regular cabs are allowed near a place as fine as the Salisbury. Especially since they have their own hired coaches to take guests to and fro."

"Hired coaches with drivers prone to drink," August said under his breath. He sighed. "Fine, if not here, then where can we find a cab?"

"Follow me," I said, and turned to walk down the street.

"Lady Grey," August said, a ribbon of amusement woven through his voice. "Are you not forgetting something?"

Bugger. I had indeed forgotten that I was a married lady now, someone who would rather languish in her bedchamber than venture anywhere without a male arm to lean upon. I walked back to August, whose lips were curled in a smug smile, and placed my hand on his curved and waiting arm.

"Can we go now?" I said.

"But of course, madam."

"It must be so dull to be one of these high class women," I said as we started down the street toward the nearest intersection. "Always having to wait on their husbands."

"I don't imagine it is any worse than having to spend the entire day scrubbing floors."

I frowned. "No, but it is different. A maid, strangely enough, has more freedom. They're restricted by their masters or mistresses, of course, but not by a social code that must be observed at all times, or risk expulsion from society. When I worked at Caldwell House, I heard Lady Caldwell mention all manner of faux pas by this or that woman, practically banishing them from her drawing room for wearing the wrong shade of green or not holding a dessert spoon properly. It must be exhausting."

Not to mention the clothing they have to wear, I thought as I tried to catch my breath. I'd almost told Eustace to tie the corset a bit looser today, but had balked at the last second. She already thought me peculiar. I didn't need to add more wood to that fire.

"You're speaking to the wrong person about this, Anne," August said. "It's been many years since I have been a member of society. I'm as uncomfortable with all this nonsense as you are. Would that we could walk down the street as we would prefer, would that we could wear what we liked, speak as we liked, and that you wouldn't have to pretend to be something you are not. Everything would be much, much easier."

I smiled. "I know. It is not as bad as I paint it, though. Pay no mind to my chattering."

"It is never chatter, and I always mind what you say."

My heart hitched for a moment, but I didn't have time to think about his words, because right then, I spotted a cab at the corner of the opposite street.

"Look! A cab." I lifted my hand in the air to draw the driver's attention. He spotted me quickly and clicked at his horse to get him moving in our direction.

"Mornin'," the man said, hopping off his raised perch at the back of the cab with surprising agility, considering he looked to be no younger than fifty years. "Where can I take Your Excellencies this fine day?"

I gritted my teeth at the ingratiating tone of his voice.

"Good morning," August said, and from his own voice, I knew that he did not appreciate the overly servile greeting, either. "The Lyceum, at the Strand."

"Of course, sir." The man bowed low and motioned to the cab with a sweeping arm.

August glanced at me, giving me my cue to step onto the vehicle. This meant releasing his arm and taking the cab driver's hand, which I would have rather not done, but which could not be avoided.

In no more than a couple of minutes, we were both seated inside the snug of the cab, the driver guiding the horse away from the curb and right into the morning traffic. While the coach I had taken to Rosewood Manor had provided a few jolts as well, it had cushioned most of the common potholes and other disturbances on the road. Not so with the cab. I could feel every stray pebble under the wheels as we lurched toward Wellington Street at Westminster.

We'd chosen the theater first because it would be open at this time of day, unlike the restaurant in which Lily had dined with August and her father. The less time we wasted in finding her, the better. Still, I couldn't help but despair that we hadn't chosen the Metropolitan Railway instead. The cab might have been more expeditious, but I had to think that the Railway would have been more comfortable.

"What will you say if someone recognizes you?" I asked softly, so that the driver could not hear us. Not that there was much chance of that with the various noises swooping by outside.

"I doubt anyone will. I've only been to the Lyceum twice, and both times with Lily. If someone does recognize me, I'll just say that I've been traveling. People are so wary of being trapped in an endless conversation about travels that they won't pry any further." He shrugged. "It will be the most natural thing in the world to ask about an acquaintance after being out of England for so long. Ah, yes, we've arrived." His eyes shifted to the building looming over his side of the cab.

There was a shift in the vehicle's center of balance as the driver jumped off his seat and appeared at August's side.

"Here we are, sir. The Lyceum." He murmured something else, which I assumed was the cost of the ride, and moved back so that August could step out of the cab. The exchange of shillings was done so smoothly and with such grace that I only caught a flash of coins as the driver tucked them into his pocket.

I bit back a smile. Whatever August said, he was still a lord—by habits, if not choice. I took his offered hand when he gave it and this time, climbed out of the cab without tripping. Improvement.

The Lyceum had seemed impressive the few times I'd seen it in the past, and it continued to be so now. It must have received its own scrubbing recently, because it was whiter than I remembered. None of its six Greek-style columns had stains from accumulated coal dust, standing radiant, instead, in the early morning light. I had never seen it at night, lit up from the inside as it would have been when August and Lily visited, but I could picture it. If it looked at all like I imagined, it would be a stunning sight.

Together, we walked toward the carved entrance as the cab pulled away.

The door, which we hadn't been able to see from where the cab left us, was barred. Two planks of raw wood, jarring against the building's whiteness, created a large cross which stopped us midstride.

"What's this now?" August asked.

It was peculiar, no question about it. I'd never seen the Lyceum closed, let alone barricaded in such a crude fashion.

Curiosity got the better of me, and I slipped away from August's warmth, moving toward the door.

It was impossible to see through it, though it was mostly glass on a sturdy wooden frame. The panels were stained, fogged over as if smoke had gotten inside the very panes, and scratches ran like veins throughout. Some were superficial, but others looked deep enough that a small tap to the glass would have been enough to shatter it. The fine hairs on the back of my neck rippled with a sudden chill.

"Something awful happened in there," I said when August reached my side.

"I feel it, too," he said. "But when did it happen? It couldn't have been recent, yet the cab driver didn't mention that the theater was closed."

I shrugged. "That doesn't mean much. He just wanted his fee and was probably afraid that if he told us the theater was closed, we wouldn't need his services anymore."

Although I said this casually, the dishonesty of the driver's actions rankled. I understood what it meant to have to earn your keep. But just because we were members of the working class did not mean we had to be untrustworthy to make a living. I would not have been at all surprised to find the man waiting around the corner to see if we needed a ride back to the hotel so he could earn his fee twice.

"What now?" I asked.

August turned away from the door. "I would like to know what happened here, but I haven't the slightest idea as to whom we should ask."

I turned toward the street, as well, and in an instant saw exactly the person we should ask.

"Do you have five pence?" I asked August.

"Of course." He pulled the coins out of his vest and placed them in my hand.

"Wait here."

He frowned. "Where are you going?"

"To get the information we need."

I hurried across the street, a blasted difficult effort in my gown, which became quite a bit heavier when I drenched the hem in a puddle of mud. I must have looked like I'd lost my senses, because the boy I approached took a step backward.

"Ma'am?"

He couldn't have been more than ten or eleven in age, and there was a good chance he was younger than that. His face was smudged with dirt, as if he had made a half-hearted attempt at washing his face and had succeeded only in spreading the grime around instead. In his hands was a pile of newspapers called the *Daily Mail*. How he'd managed to carried them all, being as scrawny as he was, I had not the vaguest idea.

"Want to buy one, ma'am?" His voice held disbelief. This had to be the first time a woman not dressed like a maid had ever gone near him of her own impulse.

"Actually, I was wondering if you knew what happened to that building." I pointed to the theater.

His face lost its surprise and closed itself off like a curtain drawn over a window.

"I'll give you five pence if you tell me."

The boy's eyebrows leapt back up into life. "It was a fire, ma'am. A small one, but it burnt some of the inside." He lowered his voice into a substantial whisper. "A person died, ma'am. They're fixin' it up to look like new, but it ain't open yet."

So that explained the unblemished white façade.

"What started the fire?" I asked.

The boy shrugged as much as he could with arms heavy with newspapers. "Don't 'ave no clue, ma'am. It was all sudden-like durin' a play. It stopped all on its own, too. People said it was real mysterious."

A sudden thought made me hold my breath, as if a hand had closed around my heart. "Do you remember when this happened?"

"About a month ago, ma'am," he said, shifting his weight from foot to foot. I wouldn't be able to hold his attention for much longer.

"I want you to think carefully. This is really important. Could it have been two months ago?"

He shrugged again. "Suppose so, ma'am. It was a Saturday night. I know that because I was carryin' the 'eavy editions for Sunday mornin' when someone told me about the fire."

I swallowed. Two months ago, both my life and August's had been shaken on a Saturday night, and Rosewood Manor had burnt to the ground. It could be nothing. It could just be a coincidence. But if I had learned anything in my time at the manor, it was that I should listen to my instinct, and right now, this didn't feel like coincidence.

"Could I have my five pence now, ma'am?"

I nodded and extended my hand. "One more thing," I said before I released the coins. "Have you heard of any other strange fires around that same time?"

The boy frowned. "You mean other than this one and the one at the Royal Café?"

My eyes widened. The Royal Café.

"It 'appened on the same night, which was buggered strange, if you ask me," the boy said. He cleared his throat. "Pardon the language, ma'am."

I did my best to smile despite the chill that had wrapped around me on this sunny spring day.

"Would you like a paper, ma'am? The quicker I sell them all, the sooner I can go home."

"I don't have any more money."

"The paper is three pence and you gave me five, so that means . . ." He trailed off, his eyes focusing on something over my shoulder.

I turned and saw August walking toward us. His leg was bothering him today; no one would have noticed by the way he walked, straight and steady, but I could tell by the way he pressed his lips together, making them thinner than they naturally were.

When he reached us, he nodded at the boy and pulled some more coins from his vest.

"Here," he said. "Go have something substantial for lunch."

The boy's eyes were as shiny as polished silver as he took the offered money. "Yes, sir."

He took one of the newspapers out of the pile wrapped in twine and handed it to me with a nod. "If you need me, ma'am, my name is Tim. Timothy, really, but I don't know 'ow to write the rest of it. You can find me about these areas most days, or over by St. Paul's."

"Thank you, Timothy," I said. "I will keep that in mind the next time I need some information."

"It was a pleasure to meet you, Timothy," August said, making the boy's face redden to an alarming degree before he headed off to find other clients.

I turned to August. "That's quite a change."

"How do you mean?"

"Well, I can remember very clearly the first time you spoke to me, and it was nowhere near as cordial as that."

August cocked his head. "If I do remember, I had just saved your life. That wasn't cordial enough for your taste?"

I laughed. "Fair enough, I suppose." I lifted the newspaper. "Are you at all interested in this?"

He smiled and took the newspaper from my gloved hands. He glanced at it and his brows creased. "Anne," he said.

"What is it?"

He held the paper up so I could read the title of the cover story, bold and black on the front page:

THIRD UNEXPLAINED FEMALE DISAPPEARANCE AT BELLINGHAM S WODENHOUSE MILL. GIRLS DISAPPEARING AS IF BY MAGIC!

"'May, 1889,'" August read. "'A third female disappearance has shocked Wodenhouse Mill, recently purchased by the Bellingham estate.'"

I frowned. "Bellingham estate. She bought a mill?"

"It appears so." He read on. "'The public is aware that two more women have vanished from the factory's floor in the past two months, and now there is a new name to add to that duet: Sylvia Todd. She was last seen on one of the mill's looms at half-past seven last Thursday evening.

"'There was nothing on the scene to indicate her presence except for blood and deep, scratch-like marks on the cement floor. They appear to have been made by some kind of large animal. The same marks were found when the previous girls disappeared, and as of now, there are no leads as to what could have made them. The police claim to have never seen anything like them before.'"

All at once, it was as if someone had poured ice water into my veins. Scratches made by a large animal?

"It can't be," I murmured. I shook my head, willing the numbing cold of a fright I knew so well away from me. "We vanquished it. It can't be the same creature. It's just a coincidence, like the fires."

"What fires?" August asked, his words sharp enough to cut.

"There was a fire at the theater, and at the Royal Café, about two months ago. On a Saturday. There were deaths. Tim couldn't remember the exact date, but I'm sure we can ask someone . . ."

I trailed off as I saw the scant amount of color in August's face seep out. His lips tightened to a thin line.

"She's taunting us."

I took a step closer to him. "Perhaps we're reading too much into it. It could have been an animal of some sort that left those marks." As I spoke, echoes of similar words I'd said to Ms. Simple circled me like carrion birds, looking for the slightest sign of weakness to swoop down on me.

"What could have possibly dragged a woman from a factory floor? I know London has rats, but I doubt any of them have quite reached that size. And to have gone through cement? You know as well as I do, Anne, that no simple animal could have done that. Throw the Bellingham name into this, as well as the fires at the restaurant and theater, and there is no real alternative. This is her doing. She wanted to gain our attention and has succeeded, leaving innocent people dead in her wake. And reminding me, always reminding me, that I am to blame."

I felt his energy change, roiling and churning in a way I hadn't felt from him since we'd left Rosewood Manor. It was like being swept back in time to when I'd first met him, when guilt at what he'd caused, at what he'd done to everyone around him, was as heavy and present in him as the cold that pervaded the manor itself.

I couldn't stand to watch despair consume him again.

I did it without thinking. I closed the gap between us with one step, pressing myself to his chest as my arms wrapped around him. He was tall enough that my head reached just to his heart. I closed my eyes and listened to it fighting like a caged bird, felt his warmth escalate through the layers of clothes to reach me, to meet the heat coming off the rose in my pocket. It was painful, like embracing a flame, but I didn't remove myself. Instead, I concentrated on doing what I'd been born to do.

The newspaper fluttered to the ground as August's arms slowly came around to encircle me. They were as light as petals at first, even as I felt his energy swiping at me, pushing me back, doing what it could to not be snuffed out.

"I'm sorry," he whispered. "I can't control it."

"I know."

Finally, my power fell over his like a blanket. August's pounding heart slowed to match my own and his muscles, knotted with untamed energy, relaxed under my hands.

He breathed in deeply, and his arms closed around me with more firmness. Every patch of my skin was alive with the heat of our dueling powers, but not even the discomfort could pull me away.

We were burning together in the middle of London, and neither of us cared.

It felt so natural to stand like this with him, as if we had never ended that first embrace at Rosewood Manor. The peculiar gap that had grown between us since then was bridged in an instant.

"Thank you," he murmured. His voice echoed through his chest. "I lost my way for an instant there."

I nodded and lifted my head away enough to look up at him. "You have to stop blaming yourself, August. If this is really her doing, the consequences are on her head, not yours."

He brushed a strand of hair from my face with his hand and let his fingertips trail my cheek. The skin on the back of my neck rose.

"It is not always so simple to remember," he said.

"That's why I'm here," I said.

He lifted an eyebrow. "Well, it's certainly not for your demureness. Embracing a man in view of all of London. What will the neighbors think?"

I pulled away with a smile and hit him lightly on the arm. "You won't see me doing this again, then, even if you're raving mad."

He released me from his embrace, but held on to my hand. "Fair warning, I suppose. So, what do you think? Does the Wodenhouse Mill warrant investigation?"

I was about to agree, but something in me hesitated. Why? We needed to find Lily, and the only real lead we had was this mill owned by her estate and its disappearing women. There was no reason to waver, but my mind fluttered about of its own accord, trying to find a reason, any reason, to postpone the visit. Was it just fear that we would encounter something similar to what we'd vanquished two months ago? We had done it once, and in more desperate circumstances; we could surely do it again if necessary.

August frowned. "Anne?"

"Sorry," I said, and shook my head. "My mind wandered off."

"Ah, well, perhaps it would be better to leash it, then."

"Amusing." I sighed. There was no excuse to give him, so I shoved the sudden worry as far back in my mind as possible. "Fine, yes, let us go explore the Wodenhouse Mill. We'll be able to see the scratches up close and hear from some of the other women about what's been happening. Besides, I've never seen a textile mill."

"Neither have I, though I admit that it has not been on my inventory of things to see while in the city."

"You have an inventory?"

"It's a figure of speech, Anne."

A cab appeared around the corner, its wheels splashing mud every which way. "There's our ride, I suppose," I said, lifting my hand. "Shall we?"

"Of course. May I offer you my arm, Lady Grey?"

"Why, thank you very much, Lord Grey."

I smiled, placed my arm in August's, and tried not to trip over my muddied hems or anxious thoughts as we boarded the cab.

FOUR

THE WODENHOUSE MILL WAS MONSTROUS.

It rose out of the Thames's southern bank like a great, smoke-colored beast, cutting into the London sky. It had no more shape than a box of matches, and rows of small windows covered in coal dust puckered its façade. I couldn't imagine that they allowed much light in.

"Are we really going in there?" I asked as I gazed out the carriage window.

"The mighty Anne Tinning, afraid? I never thought I'd see the day."

"I'm not afraid," I said. "I just . . . I don't fancy going into a place owned by any of the Bellinghams. It cannot be conducive to good health or mental stability."

August snorted. "You are probably right about that. Nevertheless, the foreman is expecting us."

Taking a deep breath, I opened the carriage door and stepped out. It had taken me all of yesterday to realize that it was better to exit a coach or other vehicle on my own, without having to rely on any gentleman's hand. It allowed me to take my own speed and have both hands free to pick up my voluminous skirts. I abstained from this strategy at the Salisbury, because it would have been unseemly to do so in the gaze of society's elite, but when it was just August and I, I could at least fling away this small slice of confining convention.

"Lord Grey!" a man called out from somewhere in front of the carriage.

His voice, coarse as bare rope, boomed out to us much as it probably did to the mill's factory floor. I winced. It would not be pleasant to have that sound greet you each morning, and it put Lady Caldwell's presence in very favorable comparison.

"I would like to welcome you to Wodenhouse Mill." The man continued at the same volume, though he drew near. "I am so pleased that you are considering making a donation to our production!"

"That's what you told him?" I whispered to August.

"What was I supposed to tell him? 'We're looking for a homicidal woman with magical powers who might be sending a wraith to kill your factory women'? There would have been a carriage from Bethlem Hospital waiting for us when we arrived."

The factory's foreman had finally reached us, so I smiled as demurely as a lady would and tried not to get my eyes tangled up in the colliding patterns of the man's jacket and vest. I knew very little about men's fashion, but I was fairly certain pinstripes and paisley were not the wisest of combinations.

He was probably wearing his best clothes to meet us, however, which had to count for something.

August offered a hand, which the man took with just an eyebrow's lift of surprise.

"It is a pleasure to meet you, Mr. Lovett."

"Oh, likewise, sir. And madam, it is an honor to be in the presence of such beauty."

Lord in Heaven. Would the fawning ever stop? I would have to ask August about it later. As it was, I still didn't know what to do with myself after hearing a compliment like such. It wasn't like I'd had much practice. So I merely inclined my head and did my best to appear simpering.

"I have heard quite a bit about the mill," August continued, "and since I've been searching for a worthy investment, I wanted to come see it for myself."

"Well, sir, I can assure you that you will not be disappointed. Wodenhouse Mill is the most productive textile mill in all of London, and our ladies are the hardest working you will find. Allow me to give you a tour of the place. We have a beautiful and comfortable sitting room where Lady Grey can wait." He didn't even look my way when he spoke about me.

To *that*, I was accustomed, though there was no chance I would wait around, twiddling my thumbs like the accessory he clearly thought I was. Was this really what it was like to be a lady? Once again, I decided that I had been fortuitous with my lot in life. At least as a maid, I was offered the opportunity to be both invisible and productive.

"I never make business decisions without my wife, Mr. Lovett," August said, just as I was considering speaking out of turn.

The foreman's face reddened. "Of course not, sir. My apologies, madam. It is a rare treat to see a woman with a head for business."

He made a small bow and stepped to one side to allow us entrance to the mill.

"I have heard it is now owned by the Bellingham estate," August said when we reached the front doors.

"Yes, sir. It is by their generosity that we were able to continue production after the previous owner passed so suddenly."

August and I exchanged a look. "The passing took you by surprise, then?" I asked.

Mr. Lovett opened the door. "Oh, yes, madam. It was very sudden. An apoplexy, we were told. We were sure the factory would have to close, but the following day, we received a note from the Bellingham estate's solicitor offering a sizeable amount to keep production going."

"Fortunate," I said.

"Indeed, madam. But we are always looking for investors to make it possible for us to afford the latest machinery and the like. Though the estate keeps our doors open and our looms running, we still need the help of benefactors like yourselves. Please," he said, nodding us into the building.

The mill was as dark as it had looked from the outside. The windows did nothing to dispel the shadows that clung like cobwebs to everything in the foyer. Although the front room was quiet and empty, the constant hum of machinery came from behind its walls. The scream of metal against metal, of continuous movement and shifting gears, created a discordant sort of symphony that grated on my nerves.

Mr. Lovett walked to another set of doors. "The main production floor is through here, unless Your Lord and Lady-ship would prefer to see the accounts first?"

"The production floor will be just the thing," August said.

The foreman nodded and flung open the doors, allowing a wave of sounds and smells to crash over us.

Every which way I looked, there was movement. Women stood in front of the largest pieces of machinery I'd ever seen, pushing levers and panels of wood. Cones of thread spun at dizzying speeds, buzzing like insects as they filled smaller cones with a kaleidoscope of colors. Children no older than six or seven crawled under and out of the machines as if they were part of them.

"Those are the newest looms," Mr. Lovett said, waving to one side of the room. "They were provided by the Belling-hams just two weeks ago. If you do decide to invest in our endeavor, your generosity would allow us to furnish the entire floor with these efficient machines."

I couldn't imagine that there were ever any issues with efficiency. It was all a bit overwhelming, actually, a sensation which only increased the more I looked at the women and children working.

"Please," Mr. Lovett said, "let me show you some of our most productive workers."

I felt something shift in the air as soon as I stepped prop-erly onto the factory floor. It was as if I'd just walked through a veil of air warm enough to be muggy; it made breathing a challenge, but only for an instant.

August sucked in a breath and flinched as if he had been slapped. Everything in me rose to attention as I watched his eyes lose their focus for the length of a heartbeat, and felt the arm I held stiffen into an impressive imitation of stone.

It passed with such speed that Mr. Lovett didn't notice our faltering. He continued walking down the long factory floor.

"Did you feel it?" August murmured, lightly shaking his head to dispel the remnants of whatever it was he'd experienced.

"Something, yes. Though I don't think I felt as much of it as you did."

"No, you probably grounded it without realizing."

"Are you all right?" I asked, searching his face for signs of pain or excess pallor. Not a simple task with someone as naturally pale as August.

"I'm fine." He nodded forward, and we began walking after the foreman again. "Though I am not hesitant to tell you that this is not the first time I have envied you your ability. That was quite an unpleasant sensation."

I was about to ask him more when the foreman spoke again.

"You can see the speed with which these women work." He pointed to two figures standing by some of the newer looms. One of them was perhaps a year older than I, though her body was hunched as if her shoulders held decades more. The older woman, who had to have been well past middle age, bent over her work in a way that pained me just by looking at her.

Their hands were extraordinary to watch, though. I'd once seen a street magician at Covent Garden while buying something or other for Lady Caldwell; his hands had moved like these women's. Nimble, appearing and disappearing, bringing thread forward and back, pushing wooden shuttles so quickly it was dizzying to observe.

"They work at this speed for twelve hours, with a small pause for a midday meal," Mr. Lovett said, pride staining his voice, as if managing people who were close to slaves was an achievement, something to applaud.

"Hmm," August said, and did his best to look impressed.

We moved down the row of looms at Mr. Lovett's behest. My stomach clenched every time I saw a child sliding out from under the machines, covered in dust, without shoes and clothes ragged enough to make working around steel mechanisms even more dangerous.

The sound of production was overwhelming. I thought I would get used to it as the minutes passed, but the grinding of gears, like ceramic plates scratching together, put me more on edge with every second. I found myself gripping August's arm tighter than was necessary, but he made no comment. His forehead was creased, as if he listened to something beyond the factory noise.

Mr. Lovett was still talking, motioning to this or that, to the row of women standing by large cones of thread, to the ones taking raw sheep's wool and spinning it into something workable, to countless and countless lives spent and used up within these walls.

It was too much, and since August was as struck as I was by the conditions the women worked in, I knew I had to do something, or we'd be stuck here for hours listening to the foreman gush.

"Excuse me, Mr. Lovett," I said as we neared another clump of working women, "can you tell me about the disappearances that have occurred on the factory floor?"

It was if I'd said some of August's magical words. Mr. Lovett halted, and the hands of the women at the nearest looms came to a stop.

"The disappearances?"

"Yes. We read about the latest one yesterday morning," I said.

"And there were two more, I think I recall reading," August added, finally pulling himself away from whatever had held his attention with a blink.

The foreman straightened and smoothed out his paisley vest. "It is utter rubbish. There have been no disappearances."

I frowned. "I'm sorry, sir, I might have misread, but the paper clearly stated that three women had disappeared, dragged away by some large creature that had left deep marks on the floor. Is that not correct?"

"Lady Grey, not everything you read in the papers is accurate."

"No women have gone missing, then?" August's voice had narrowed down to its coldest tone, a winter breeze of sound.

"They 'ave, sir."

It was a woman's voice and it came from behind us, thin but vibrant enough to carry her words clearly.

August and I turned to face the only woman who dared to look our way.

"Three of them 'ave disappeared, right from this floor." She pointed to a spot farther down the row of looms. "There is where it 'appened."

"Enough!" Mr. Lovett said. "How dare you speak out of turn? I am not paying you to run your mouth."

The woman held his gaze for an instant longer than the foreman found acceptable. He walked forward, heading for the woman, his face darkening with the anger pooling under his skin.

August stepped into his path. There was no outward violence in his movement, but the air around us changed in a way

I knew all too well. I'd felt it for the first time when he was still just Lord Grey to me and had stood against the wraith after yanking me out of the cursed fountain on Rosewood Manor's grounds. Even as I'd attempted to catch my breath and swipe at the horror that had enveloped me as I drowned, I had felt the anger in August's body. I hadn't known what that energy was yet, but I had felt it, nonetheless.

It was there now, as well, and Mr. Lovett sensed it. He stopped right where he was and stared at August.

"Mr. Lovett, I would appreciate it if I could hear what this woman has to say."

The foreman lowered his eyes under the barrage of August's stare. I could feel the edges of his power rippling up and down my arms like silk.

"Sir, she is no lady. You cannot trust the word of the likes of her."

"I think we would like to see that for ourselves," I said, coming to stand next to August. "It will only take a moment."

With another miniscule push of energy, so slight it must have taken quite a bit of restraint on his part to achieve, August turned away from Mr. Lovett and toward the woman who still stared directly at us.

"Can you show us where you say it happened?" he asked.

She held his eyes for a moment, and then nodded once. "Yes, sir." She released the lever she had been about to lower on the loom and stepped away from the machine. "It's this way."

She walked quickly past Mr. Lovett and down the row of looms, her movements like the scurrying of a hungry squirrel.

We followed close behind her, but came to a stop as we neared a deserted machine. It was the only one in the room that was completely still and silent. Right beneath a window, it looked like it rested in its own pool of shadows.

"This is where all three women disappeared." She pointed to the floor to the right of the loom. "That, and some blood, was all that was left of them."

I held my breath and felt August's arm tense under my hand.

The scratches were not the same as the ones I'd seen on one of the sitting chairs in Rosewood Manor. These were much larger. They had dug themselves into the cement so deeply that a falling nail or pair of scissors would have been lodged inside them. Each scratch was spread apart from the rest by a hand's width of distance, and continued for the full length of the loom, narrowing and becoming shallower toward one end, where whatever had created the marks had obviously lightened its pressure.

They might not have looked the same, but the sensation, like a blade of cold sliding up and down my spine, was identical to what I'd felt the first time I'd stepped foot inside Rosewood's doors.

This could not be happening. Not again.

August slipped away from my grip and lowered himself close enough to touch the deep grooves on the cement.

"These are peculiar, wouldn't you say, Mr. Lovett?" he said as he brushed a thin hand across the surface of one of the indentations.

To anyone else's eyes, there was no change in his expression, but I had spent months with August, months learning to identify every shift in mood because he was infuriatingly prone to keeping everything to himself. That was why I was able to see the slight contraction of fear on his face.

"They are just animal scratches," Mr. Lovett said.

August's lips twisted into a smile. "I am no expert in these matters, but I dare say I do not recall ever hearing of an animal of the size and strength required to make these kinds of marks, especially not loose in London. Has anyone seen such a creature?"

"No, sir. But if not an animal, then what else could it be?"

August stood and walked back to my side. "I couldn't possibly say, Mr. Lovett."

"People 'ave been talking, sir," said the woman who had led us here. I had entirely forgotten her.

Mr. Lovett's face darkened again. "You will be quiet."

I raised a hand to stop him. "I would like to hear what she has to say. If we are to make a sizeable donation to this factory, it is only fair that we know exactly what is happening within its walls."

The woman's eyes flicked from the foreman's to my own, and I could have sworn for a moment that there was something disagreeable in the weight of her stare. It was gone as quickly as it had appeared, though, and I chalked it up to the general unpleasantness of the entire situation.

"Madam, there's been a lot of strange 'appenings in the mill. Most of them right foul, if you ask me. The three women disappearing 'as gotten attention from the papers, but all the women 'ere . . . we're scared, madam."

"This is nonsense," Mr. Lovett said. "You are all perfectly safe."

"With all respect, sir, that is what you said when the second girl disappeared. We still ended with another girl gone and these marks from the Devil 'imself."

The foreman shook his head in obvious disgust.

"What other occurrences have there been, then?" August asked.

The woman did not hesitate. She had been waiting for someone to pay even the slightest bit of attention to what they had all been experiencing.

"All kinds of things, sir. Tools gone missing from one moment to the next. Work slashed to strips in the blink of an eye. One morning, we came in to find every spinning machine on, with no one manning them."

As she spoke, I expected to see her head thrown back in an unseen slap, as I had watched happen to Ms. Simple, or anything else that would keep her quiet. But she spoke freely, not even worrying about her employer, whose face was turning redder and redder with each of her words.

"Some of the girls 'ave felt someone breathing on their necks, 'ot breath like an animal's. But when they turn around, there ain't nothing behind them. If it weren't because we need the job, some of us would 'ave left already." She shook her head. "It ain't right, what's 'appening 'ere."

As she spoke, the looms had come to a halt, submerging the room in silence. I looked around at all the different faces, some as young as eight or nine, others so wrinkled and worn I could not even begin to guess at their age. All of them scared.

"It seems that you have a morale issue here, Mr. Lovett," I said. "People should not have to work under this kind of fear." I might not have been knowledgeable in the areas of whalebone stays and satin gowns, but I did know *that* much. Just the thought of the fear I'd felt at Rosewood Manor those first few weeks turned my stomach.

"Get back to work, all of you," the foreman said, his voice slamming through the silence in the large room. "I'm not paying you to stand around doing nothing."

With obvious reluctance, the women lowered their heads back to their spinning and weaving.

"That goes for you, as well," he said.

For a bone-chilling moment, I thought he was speaking to me, that I'd been found out as an impostor, but no, he meant the woman next to us.

She hesitated, but the fear of losing her position weighed more than the fear of death. It was peculiar, the way our priorities established themselves.

"I think, Mr. Lovett, that we can be of help," August said with a glance at me. I nodded.

The foreman's relief was evident in every part of his face. "That is wonderful to hear, sir. Your contribution will be gratefully received."

"That is not quite what I meant."

"Sir?"

"We have recently had a similar experience to the one you are struggling with. Not identical, but with enough similarities to have caught our attention."

Mr. Lovett frowned. "I don't understand."

Good Lord, he was thick. "We can help you get rid of whatever creature is making your workers disappear," I said.

The foreman looked from me to August. "You can?"

"Yes. My wife and I have . . . unique talents, let us say, that allow us to take care of matters such as these."

"So, you are not here to invest in the mill?"

August sighed with obvious impatience. He lacked as much of that particular virtue as I did. "No, we are not. I would have thought that was obvious by now."

"And you are not Lord and Lady Grey?"

"Oh, that we certainly are," August said.

I smiled. "And we are at your disposal."

The foreman's whole demeanor collapsed, deflating like my first attempt at a soufflé in my scullery maid days. His shoulders sagged, his obsequious smile disappearing. He suddenly looked like he hadn't managed a moment's rest in days.

"Oh, thank God. Thank God," Mr. Lovett said. "Please help us. There is something unnatural occurring in this factory."

August and I looked at each other, eyebrows lifted in mirrored expressions of trepidation. Whatever had we walked ourselves into?

Once Mr. Lovett was sure we were not going to donate a large sum of money to the Wodenhouse Mill, he was much more willing to share what he knew. Which wasn't much, as it happened. Just variations on the same themes: disappearing items escalating to disappearing women, strange noises, the feeling of being watched even when alone, the impossibly deep scratches on the floor, and a number of other familiar disturbances.

"I wanted the extra money to hire men who would guard the factory at night," he told us, passing a hand over his shining forehead. "The Bellingham estate is generous, but they denied this particular request."

If we'd had any remaining doubts as to whether or not Lily was behind all of this, they were snuffed out with those words.

August and I decided to return the following morning to ask some of the workers if they knew anything else that might help us learn whatever horror this new creature was and how we might be able to stop it.

"Any ideas?" I asked August as we stepped into our chambers at the Salisbury, an hour after we'd taken our leave of the mill.

"It's not a wraith, I know that much. It's too large and physically too strong."

I frowned and pointed at his walking stick. "I recall a certain wraith being strong enough to fling you across the room and do quite a bit of damage to your leg."

He waved my words away. "Yes, yes, but those marks at the mill felt different. You weren't too preoccupied with your skirts, I trust, to notice that it was warm in that factory, almost too warm. Would that be how you would have described Rosewood?"

He really could be infuriating sometimes. "Of course not. I still don't understand how none of us died frozen in our beds."

He shrugged off his coat and tossed it onto the nearest sofa. "Right, which means that whatever is haunting the mill must be something else."

"And you have no idea what that something else could be?"

"Not in the least."

"Or how to vanquish it."

"No."

"Oh, August, just as lighthearted and comforting as always."

I walked over to the sofa and took his coat, holding it up to see if there were any stains or serious wrinkles that needed laundering. The scent that was wholly him, like warm candles and the softest of roses, reached me, and I had to keep myself from bringing the coat up to my face. Instead, I crossed the room and hung it from a golden peg beside the door.

"You're doing it again," he said.

I nodded and turned to him. "I know. Tidying up calms me. If I had a feather duster or a rag or, God help me, some silver to polish, there would be no stopping me."

He smiled.

I saw something pass through his eyes, then, that gave me pause. It was no more than a shadow, like the tail of something slithering across his irises, but it dimmed both his smile and mine. He blinked as if he had dust in his eyes.

"What—?"

The knock on the door cut off the rest of my question.

August sighed. "Enter," he said.

Eustace stepped into the room like a fluttering bird, apologies leading the way. "Lord Grey, Lady Grey, please forgive my disturbing you. I know you asked for some privacy."

She was so pale I was afraid she would be ill, and the silver tray in her hands shook just a little.

"Just speak," August said.

"Please," I added with a sideways glance at him. Eustace was just doing her job, after all.

"I was asked to give you this. The lady who delivered it said that it was urgent." She held up the silver tray, and I noticed then that there was, indeed, a letter perched upon it. I couldn't help noticing that Eustace was careful to touch the silver with only the tips of her fingers to avoid leaving a mark. She had been well taught.

I took the letter, being just as cautious with the tray, and looked down to find "Lord Grey" written on the front in an ornate and obviously female hand.

"It's addressed to you," I said.

August walked over to me and glanced at the paper. "It was delivered by hand, then?"

"Yes, sir," said Eustace.

He glanced at me and frowned before opening the envelope and pulling out a wide rectangle of creamy paper embossed with golden letters.

"It's an invitation to a ball," he said. "Tomorrow night. A celebration for the reopening of the Lyceum."

My eyes widened.

August turned to Eustace, who had kept her gaze on her shoes until now. "The woman who delivered this, did she tell you who it was from?"

"No, sir. She said that you would know."

"Can you recall what she looked like?"

"Sorry, sir. She had a veil over her face. I do remember that her voice was quite low for a woman."

It had to be Lily. August had no other serious acquaintances in London, not after the Brothers and the Master died. But would she be so blatant as to come to the hotel and invite us to a ball?

"Would His Lordship like to send a response?"

"No." He waved her away. "That's all."

"Thank you, Eustace," I said with a smile.

"Madam. Sir." She curtsied and walked out of the room.

August did not wait until the door clicked shut. He began pacing the room, the invitation clutched in one fist, his whole body vibrating with the energy coursing through him.

"It's her, isn't it?" I asked.

"Yes, I am sure of it."

"She is being very bold." I walked closer to him and sat down on the sofa.

"You are invited, as well. She has your name written as 'Lady Anne Grey,' which means she has been watching us since we got to London. Perhaps even earlier. She knows that we are pretending and says nothing to discredit you, choosing to play along, instead. That does not bode well."

"That invitation is a trap," I said, my voice no louder than a whisper.

"Yes."

"But we are going to the ball anyway, I presume."

August stopped pacing and fixed his eyes on me. He looked tired, and older than his twenty-one years. Too much still weighed him down.

"Only if you agree," he said. "I won't force you to do anything you do not want. I've done enough of that in the past few months."

I sighed and looked away from him. "I don't want to do it. But I know we must."

"You don't have to do anything, Anne. You are free. This is my nightmare, and I have to see it through, but it doesn't have to be yours. Not anymore. I will repeat what I told you two months ago: you are free to leave whenever you like."

I could have slapped him then and there. "How can someone so bright and clever be so exceedingly dense?" I said. "First of all, this is my nightmare now, too, because I don't think Lily will just let me run off to live a normal, happy life. But more importantly, I am here helping you because I want to be. Because I—"

I took a deep breath, the words catching in my throat as I kept my face turned away. I couldn't bring myself to look up, afraid that I might see distaste at my flagrant honesty reflected on his face, or at the very least, eyebrows raised in familiar, taunting amusement. Which is why I didn't realize that August had slipped to my side until I felt the sofa shift under his scant weight. Gingerly, he placed his bare hand on my own, the missing layers of protective clothing making the touch nearly unbearable.

I gathered up my courage and turned to look at him. There was none of the amusement or biting sarcasm I'd expected, just his thin yet striking face, as open as I'd ever seen it.

"I suppose," he murmured, "I just don't understand why you would."

"You really are dense."

He smiled. "I must be." He leaned his forehead against mine. The burn of his skin made my breath ragged.

"That is quite painful," I said, closing my eyes.

"Yes."

Neither of us moved, however, letting the pain grow with each second we held on to each other. The words I had almost said faded from my lips, burned away by the pain. For now, it was enough that, like everything else we had to confront, we would face this together.

FIVE

WE HAD QUESTIONED TEN FACTORY WORKERS already, and the only thing we had learned was that these women were frightened. Awfully so.

"You do not remember seeing anything?" August asked the small woman in her forties, sitting across from us in a room the size of a cupboard, her body hunched in upon itself as if she could shrink into oblivion.

"No, sir." Her voice was barely audible, even in such a small space.

"Can you tell us what you heard?"

The woman looked around the room like a bird searching for an open window. I leaned forward and placed a hand on hers.

"What's your name?" I asked.

"Ingrid, ma'am."

I smiled. "Ingrid, then, if you remember anything, anything at all, it would really help us."

Whether it was because of my special powers or my kind tone, the woman's entire body relaxed a bit. She lowered her shoulders and sat up a little straighter, which made her appear younger than I'd originally thought.

"It was just so dark, ma'am."

"Just try your best to remember. Were there any sounds when you found Sylvia? Any odors that were unusual?"

Ingrid pressed her lips together, her eyes lowering as she tried to recall last Friday morning, when she'd walked into the factory floor earlier than usual to find the deep marks on the concrete and the blood.

"I came in early. I'd forgotten to wind some of the loom's bobbins the previous night and I was mighty scared to 'ave Mr. Lovett realize that."

"How did you get in? Was the door open? I doubt you had a key," August said.

Her eyes flitted from me to him before lowering to her lap.

I threw him a look that was less than cordial. *Let me handle this*, I mouthed. He lifted his hands up in surrender.

"You won't get in any kind of trouble, Ingrid. I promise you. It's admirable that you wanted to get in early to finish your work, truly."

I squeezed her hand and concentrated on extending my energy to her, letting it trail through my hand and into hers like a root.

"I need this position, ma'am," she said after a moment. "Please don't tell Mr. Lovett."

"I won't." I motioned to August. "We won't."

She swallowed and brought her eyes up to mine. "Some of us girls know there's a window pane in the back of the building that's loose. It's easy to remove it and crawl through into the factory floor. I ain't never stolen anything," she added quickly. "It was the first time I did this, ma'am."

"I believe you, Ingrid."

"I 'ad to tell the inspector that I came in later or 'e would 'ave called all of Scotland Yard on me."

"I understand." I nodded, attempting to be as encouraging as possible. August at least managed to keep quiet, with only a soft sigh of impatience announcing that coaxing the truth from a factory worker was not how he would have preferred to spend his morning.

"Well, ma'am, I came into the factory early. It was still dark—I could only see my own feet as I walked—but I know the factory blind after fifteen years."

Fifteen years of working here? The thought alone made me want to run out into the street, which, while not the best smelling in all of London, was still a better choice than being enveloped in the smells of the factory for fifteen years.

"I didn't know something was wrong until my foot slipped as I walked to the spinning area. I almost went face first into all that blood."

The horror of that morning was as fresh on her face as that blood must have been under her feet.

"I knew what it was at once. You won't believe me, ma'am, but sometimes I get these thoughts. They come out of nowhere, telling me things I don't want to know. Sometimes, I know what will 'appen before it 'appens. It's no lie, ma'am, and it frightens me something awful."

"Oh, I believe you," I said.

August cleared his throat.

"I clapped my 'ands to my face to keep from screaming and turned on one of the gas lamps we use when the electricity goes out. Ma'am, there was blood everywhere. A puddle of it right in front of the loom, and streaks of it heading in every direction. There was so much of it I didn't even notice the marks on the floor until after it was all cleaned up."

I frowned. "Was there a blood trail?"

Ingrid swallowed and shook her head. "Just the streaks, ma'am, and then a few drops of blood."

"It must have picked the body up," August murmured, leaning forward. "Do you remember if—?"

A sudden shriek shook the room. It was a thick sound, with an edge of silver to it, like the sound of the Indian tigers at the London zoo.

Ingrid screamed as it continued, making the walls around us vibrate with its echo.

It was like nothing I'd ever heard before, not even at Rosewood Manor. The force behind that sound reached into my skin, into my chest, painful enough that I pressed a hand to my heart to stop it from reaching that most important of organs.

August was frozen in place for as long as the shriek lasted, but leapt off his chair when it petered out. I saw him wince as his injured leg reminded him of his infirmity.

"Stay here, Anne."

"No, I want to go with you!"

Mr. Lovett rushed into the room, his face pale enough to belong on a corpse. "Did you hear it? Did you hear that ungodly sound?"

"We did," I said.

"What is it? Lord Almighty, what is it?"

Ingrid had begun crying, her face buried in her hands as her entire body shook with fear.

August turned to me. "I need to see where that sound came from, and I need you to stay here." He nodded to Ingrid. "You know how to help her."

"But what about you? What if you need me?"

He lifted an eyebrow. "Then I'll scream. Loudly."

"That is not exactly reassuring," I said, but it was already too late. August was already out the door with Mr. Lovett at his heels.

I bit my lips and turned to the still sobbing Ingrid. As much as I wanted to help her, I also wanted to be searching for the unknown creature that had made such a horrifying sound. To allay my own fear and nerves by confronting the thing, strip it of its power.

"Ingrid, you're safe in here," I said, walking to her side and placing a hand on her arm.

She trembled like a stalk of grass in the rain. "The sound . . . I can't bear it."

I could hardly hear her beneath the layers of fear in her voice. I closed my eyes and allowed my powers to spread out, up her arms, down her legs, blooming through her chest until I could feel the fluttering panic myself. I could taste it, bitter as black tea on my tongue. I allowed my powers to surge forward unchecked, pushing that fear down.

The trembling ebbed, and then stopped.

Ingrid lowered her hands from her face, her eyes wide. "What did you do?" she whispered.

"Nothing."

"It was something. You did something. I felt it."

"Well, it's a bit like what you were saying about knowing things before they happen. It's just something I can do."

Ingrid flinched away from me. "It's unnatural."

"It's not. I can simply calm people if I try, that's all."

She stood, slowly, avoiding any sudden movement, as if she were in the presence of a snarling animal. "I don't want to talk no more."

"Are you all right?"

Without another word, she turned and fled from the room.

All I could do was stand there, blinking. I'd never caused fear in someone else before, so I had not the faintest idea of what to do. She would probably be more frightened if I went after her to better explain, but I didn't want her thinking I'd harmed her in any way.

My own hands shook now with the rush of nerves and consternation. Why had she reacted like that?

A thump from above made me gasp, pushing away the thoughts of Ingrid.

I held my breath and listened as something large—larger than seemed possible—made the floorboards above me buckle with its weight. Scraping filtered down through the roof and walls, as if there were indeed tigers running their claws through the wood above my head.

No human could have placed that kind of pressure on the ceiling, and besides, Mr. Lovett had ensured us that everyone was on the ground floor today, so that we could question them. So what, then, was roaming the second story?

Another sound trickled down to me; a swishing, whispering noise that took me an instant to recognize.

Whatever was up there was dragging something behind it, pulling it across the second-story floor like a sack of flour too heavy to lift. But that was no sack of flour. I could have wagered my life on it.

Fear like I hadn't felt since leaving Rosewood Manor overtook me. My mind filled with the worst images it could conjure.

August unconscious, his limbs limp as a horrifying creature dragged him across the floor. Or worse, an unrecognizable body covered in blood that just barely retained the spiced rose scent of the man I loved.

"You had to go alone, didn't you?" I muttered under my breath as I hiked up my skirts in a way that would have earned me quite a reputation if anyone were looking. "Damn it, August."

I hurried out of the room and into a factory floor alive with panic. Women clutched at one another with hands cracked by endless labor, the children I'd seen ducking in and out from under the looms pressing their dirt-streaked faces against their skirts.

"The stairs," I called out, my heart thumping so loudly I could hardly hear the words. "I need the stairs to the second floor!"

As I spoke, another creak from above sent a bolt of cold into my spine.

"Don't go up there, ma'am," one woman said, launching the rest of them into enumerating the reasons why going upstairs was courting certain death. Their voices cut into me, each of them a blade that I wanted—no, *needed*, to stop. I couldn't think with all this noise.

My hands warmed, that peculiar tingling sensation running down from my very center to my fingertips. A burning knot, like I'd swallowed a miniature sun, formed right beneath my ribs as something within me shifted. Opened.

"Enough!" I yelled.

My voice rang out through the factory, much louder than I had ever heard it, much louder than I had meant it to be, and behind it, on its heels, came something else: sudden silence.

Every machine, every voice, every noise in the factory had been smothered by my command.

Like I was watching it all from a long distance away, I saw the women open and close their mouths as they attempted to finish their sentences, their hands flying up to clutch at their throats when they realized they couldn't crack the silence. Their eyes widened, glittering in horror. They turned to each other for help, gestures becoming more and more frantic, before all of them, almost as one, looked at me.

I wanted to reach out and soothe them, tell them there was nothing to fear, but I found I couldn't move, not even so much as a finger. I couldn't blink. Was I even breathing? All of my energy lay scattered across the factory floor.

But my head! Oh, my head!

It throbbed with what felt like dozens of different heartbeats. Each tangled over the others until they became one unending pulse that wanted to break me open.

I had to stop this, whatever I was doing. I couldn't sustain it.

My knees shook, threatening to buckle under the weight of all the sound I'd stifled, all the sound I was still stifling.

But no, I couldn't allow myself to collapse. I had to get to August. Now.

With a groan that all of London must have heard, I tore my powers away from the women and the entire factory. Snapped it all back into me.

I staggered back with the force of it, willing myself to stay upright despite every urge to do the opposite. I had no time to recover. I couldn't wait anymore.

Doing my best to ignore the way the women recoiled the instant that I moved, I ran across the factory floor, to one of the three doors located at the far end. Deep exhaustion tugged at me, demanding that I rest, blackening my vision like my eyes themselves were covered in soot.

Shaking my head fiercely to clear it, I yanked the door open. I would find August first, then I could swoon if I needed to.

"Damn it," I said, when I saw the room was just another office.

I ran to the next one and pulled the door open, my heart fluttering in my throat.

"Oh, thank God," I said.

I hadn't expected a normal staircase, but I was certainly not prepared for the one that faced me now. It was made of metal, with gaps between each step that looked as if my feet would slip through them to dangle on the opposite side. More alarming, however, was the fact it shifted when I placed my foot on the first step.

Glancing up, I saw that the stairs were connected by steel cords to a walkway that led to the second floor. That's why it shook, I suppose, though seeing the mechanics behind it did nothing to assuage my anxiety over climbing it.

A monstrous screech from above made the decision for me.

All of those women behind me probably went up and down these rickety stairs every day. If they could do it, so could I.

Allowing myself no further hesitation, I launched up the steps, figuring that if the stairs were going to fall, they would do so whether I walked or ran.

Everything shook beneath me, but I made it to the walk-way that led to the door.

"Please don't let it be locked," I said as I went to grab the doorknob.

Another growl sent the walkway shaking enough that I had to hold on to the railing. Not that the railings would do me much good if the entire contraption collapsed.

I waited until the last traces of sound had disappeared before taking hold of the doorknob and twisting it open.

The second floor welcomed me in with cobweb-like light from the small, filthy windows on the opposite side. Unlike the first story, with its doors leading to Mr. Lovett's office, to cupboards, to other small work rooms, this floor was just a wide-open space. A few machines loomed like paralyzed exotic animals over the wooden floorboards, but not nearly as many as there were downstairs. Above me, a number of metal walkways gave access to a few rooms on the third story.

There was a peculiar scent to this floor as well, like overturned gas lamps, and something else I couldn't place. Though it wasn't wholly unpleasant, the odor was most assur-edly strong.

"August?" I called out as I stepped into the large room. If he had followed the growl, he had to be up here somewhere.

I tried to picture a diagram of the floor below. Directly beneath me should be the factory floor and all the looms, which meant that the cramped room where we had ques-tioned Ingrid had to be . . .

I followed my internal diagram and sighed. There, in the darkest part of this floor. Of course. These inventions of Lily's might have been frightening, but they were somewhat pre-dictable, as well.

Clasping my skirts a bit higher now that there was no one around, I crossed the floor toward the dark patch from where the first shriek had come.

It was unnaturally silent. Even the floorboards appeared to be holding their breath as I took step after step. It was somewhat disconcerting to hear nothing more than my own footsteps, but it would at least allow me to hear the creature if it moved. Or August, for that matter.

I was also becoming accustomed to the smell, it seemed, because it no longer bothered me. On the contrary, it was now almost pleasant, reminding me a bit of the brand of pipe tobacco my father preferred. It was difficult to imagine anything that smelled so pleasant being a danger.

My feet stopped of their own accord. With surprise, I found that the tips of my fingers had begun to tingle, as if I'd just come inside from a winter's day. That meant something, didn't it? Yes, I knew it did, but it my head now that felt like it had cobwebs, and I couldn't recall what it signified. There was a sudden pain right below my rib cage, as if something there were trying to get out, and I could almost, almost remember what that meant. It was such a familiar sensation . . .

I blinked and looked around me. What had I come up here for? To find something, perhaps. I hadn't realized how beautiful this floor was, how welcoming, with all that warm sunlight and that sweet tobacco scent. The warmth had made me somewhat drowsy. More than somewhat, since I could hardly keep my eyes open.

Something as hard as cement slammed against me and flung me backward into the nearest wall. Pain rushed in across my stomach and my back. I heard the scream of shattering glass.

The cobwebs I'd begun to feel had been torn right out of my head in an instant, taking with them the confusion, the drowsiness, the warmth in the room, the comforting silence, the smell of tobacco, and everything else that had invaded my mind.

"Anne!"

I turned toward August's voice, my heart attempting a daring escape through my mouth.

"Didn't you hear me calling you?" He was running toward me, his walking stick completely forgotten. "I kept screaming your name."

I couldn't catch my breath. It felt as if my entire body had slowed down and was now trying to make up for lost time.

"Are you all right? Are you hurt? I didn't mean to use so much force, but you didn't hear me." His hands were on my arms, his face searching mine.

"Force?" I managed to squeeze out.

He frowned. "I had to use my powers to get you out of the way. I wouldn't have reached you in time, otherwise."

He pointed to where I had been standing just a few seconds before, the area now showered with a storm of jagged glass. If I had still been standing there when that fell, I would have been bled dry. Even here, and at least a whole body's length away from the glass, I felt slivers of it in my hands and even in my face.

My knees buckled.

"Oh!" August said as his hands tightened around my waist, keeping me upright. "Take a breath, Anne."

I did. A few of them, actually, because it took more than one to slow my heart's frantic beating. I concentrated on August's burning touch, which I hadn't been truly able to feel until now, allowing the pain to chase away the last vestiges of numbness left on my skin.

"I don't understand what happened," I said once I could trust my voice.

August shook his head. "Nor do I. You were just standing there, unresponsive, even when I yelled your name."

"And the glass?"

"It fell from one of those walkways. I think it is one of the factory's window panes." His hands tightened. "You do realize it would have killed you."

I closed my eyes and nodded.

"We should go back downstairs. Can you manage?" he asked.

"Yes," I said, with more confidence than I truly felt. My legs still seemed as insubstantial as pudding under my skirts, but I wanted to get out of this place as much as he did.

I straightened my back, feeling August's grip on my waist loosen with tentative caution.

"I'm all right," I said.

"You'd better be sure, because we do not need two of us with unseemly limps."

With a smile, I took a few steps away from him. "See? I'm fine."

We made it downstairs in a couple of minutes. Somehow, the second story had felt larger when I'd walked to that dark corner on my own, as if I'd spent at least half an hour trailing its length.

"Tell me what you felt," August asked when we were at the bottom of the metal stairs. "Did you see anything when you went up?"

"No, I didn't see anything. But I did feel a peculiar sensation." The more I thought about it, the more I realized that something had been wrong about the second story as soon as I had stepped into it.

"What?"

I shook my head. "I can't say, really. It was a sensation of . . . of being overwhelmed, more than anything else."

I told August everything, from the moment I'd walked onto the second floor to the moment his magic shoved me out of the way of the falling glass. Everything I could recall, at least, because I found holes in my memory of those few minutes, lace patterns of missing seconds that widened the more I picked at them.

He watched me as I spoke, his peculiar eyes darkening with thoughts I had no inkling of.

"Before you intervened, I knew that I had to do something to stop whatever it was I was experiencing, but I couldn't remember what."

He frowned. "You couldn't access your abilities?"

"I didn't even recall I *had* abilities."

August's frown deepened. "That is disconcerting."

"Bloody right, it's disconcerting," I said, loudly enough to echo up the stairs. I lowered my voice. "Any idea what it is we're facing?"

He looked away from me, which was not immediately comforting, either. "I'm afraid not," he said. "But it is something that means you harm, Anne. I hope you understand that the falling pane of glass was no accident."

"I never thought otherwise, not when dealing with one of Lily's creatures. And speaking of glass," I said with a wince. "I think I have slivers of it in my cheek." I touched my face lightly, brushing two or three areas were the skin felt like miniscule blades were separating them from the rest.

August smiled. "As do I, unfortunately. Would you happen to know how to remove them?"

"Of course. I've had my fair share of them in domestic service."

"Ah, yes. Well, I defer to your greater expertise in these matters, then." He looked up at the door leading into the second floor. "I think I've had enough of this place for today. Would you agree?"

I nodded and sighed. "We are never going to have a normal day together, are we?"

August offered me his arm, which I took gratefully.

"I'm afraid that ship set sail a long time ago, Anne."

He was right, of course, but that made it no less frustrating to accept.

SIX

AS I PEERED INTO THE MIRROR, EVEN I HAD TO admit that the gown suited me.

Eustace had left moments before, after finishing with my hair, and I had not known what to expect when I stepped in front of the mirror, which was why the image that met me was such a pleasant surprise.

August had insisted that I purchase an evening gown along with the rest of my new wardrobe, and for perhaps the first and only time, I was glad he had been his usual stubborn self and not budged from this point. I had drawn the line at having it especially made, however, and had instead chosen one that was pleasant to look at and had a manageable length of train.

It was made of heavy silk and brocade, in tones of creams and coppers. The bodice had frills of simple lace that accentuated the neckline, along with perfectly placed lines of caramel beading. The most beautiful part, however, the part that had caught my eye when I first saw it, was the gown's skirt and train.

The skirt was covered in large embroidered leaves in yellows and browns, and the train was a forest floor of wine-red flowers resting on pale gold silk.

I turned to the side in front of the mirror, admiring the way the light caught the silk, making the flowers ripple with movement. Never in my life had I ever dared to imagine doing more than helping someone else into a gown like this one. But here I was, and it didn't look as ridiculous on me as I feared it might. On the contrary, the dress looked like it had always been meant for me.

I turned away from the mirror, frustration at my thoughts sweeping through me. Whatever I was pretending to be, I had to know the truth. And the truth, as difficult as it was to acknowledge, was that this dress had not been meant for me. It had been created with a lady, a *real* lady, in mind. That I now owned it was just a matter of circumstance, not fate. I could not allow myself to grow used to something that might not last. Neither August nor I could possibly know what would happen to the two of us in the future.

Tucking my emotions away as best I could, I walked to the dressing table and picked up August's rose. I hadn't sewn any pockets into this because I hadn't really been sure I would need it, so the flower could not come with me. It would be the first time since he gave it to me that I would not be carrying it. The thought was less than pleasant.

Actually, the entire evening looming over me was less than pleasant. I would have much preferred to stay here, trying to find any bits of information we could about the factory and the women who had disappeared, rather than spend hours trying not to fall or drop anything. At least August would be with me, and I knew he disliked these things as much as I. Perhaps more, for reasons that I still couldn't grasp.

Speaking of whom, I'd better ensure that he hadn't completely forgotten about this evening in the hour since I'd last reminded him about it. With him, it was not beyond the realm of possibility, sadly.

I bent as much as I could at the waist and gathered an armful of heavy silk train before heading for my bedroom door.

The sitting room was empty, and there was no noise from August's room. I walked to his door and hesitated only an instant before knocking on it.

August opened the door, his eyes locked on his right wrist.

"I have been battling with this cufflink for the better part of ten minutes," he said, "and I am no closer to getting it settled where it belongs. Could I request your assistance?"

I smiled. "Give it here, then."

He handed me a small golden cufflink with a black stone, like a pupil, in the center of it. It was heavier than I expected, which meant it was probably made of solid gold. To think that just one of these cufflinks was worth more than what I'd earned for an entire year at Caldwell House!

I slipped the cufflink into the hole on August's sleeve, being careful not to touch his skin with my bare hands, and then turned the end of the cufflink so that it wouldn't slip out during the evening.

"There," I said.

"Ah, perfection. Thank you, madam."

"You are very welcome, sir."

He finally looked up from his sleeve and seemed to take me in. The dress, the curls tumbling down around my neck, the bit of rouge Eustace had so carefully applied.

I took August in, as well.

Men in evening wear were an almost everyday occurrence at Caldwell House, since Her Ladyship had loved to entertain and her husband did not dare refuse her. They always looked quite handsome, the waistcoats enhancing their torsos, their perfectly pressed trousers elongating their figure, but I'd never seen a man I loved wearing evening attire until now.

In his coal-black tail coat and winter-white waistcoat and shirt, August was striking.

My face warmed when I noticed I was still staring. I looked away.

"Anne," he began softly, then paused. I waited for him to continue, but his body tensed in front of me, as if he were suddenly holding his breath.

I glanced up at him and found his face cocked to the side, his brow creased, his eyes locked upon a spot on the wall on the other side of the room.

"What is it?" I asked.

"That sound, it's so strange."

Sound? I frowned and concentrated on the noises around us, but I could pick out nothing that wasn't part of the hotel's everyday machinations: low voices from the floor below us, the muffled clatter of teacups and crystal as the tea trays were cleared away . . . not even the ascending room's gears stood out of the normal din.

"I don't hear anything unusual," I said.

"But it's like bells ringing, Anne. It sounds so familiar."

"Bells?" I walked to one of the room's windows and listened, but there weren't even church bells ringing now.

"No, the sound is not coming from outside," August said. "It's on this floor, somewhere." He walked to the room's double doors and opened them. I joined him, and we both listened at the threshold.

There was nothing but silence.

"It's beautiful," he said, and his voice was hushed, like someone speaking in church. It made the fine hairs on the back of my neck rise.

I placed a hand on his arm. "August, there are no bells. There's no sound at all on this floor except for our own voices."

As soon as the burning energy created by our touch reached him, August blinked as if he had just been yanked out of a complicated chain of thought in his head.

"They're gone now. The bells," he said.

"I don't like this, August. There were no bells."

He turned to me, and his eyes widened slightly, as if he were seeing me for the first time this evening. "You look beautiful."

Even though my mind still struggled to find a way to make the last minute or two appear normal, I couldn't help reacting to the compliment. A current of warmth enveloped me, bringing—I was sure—more color to my cheeks than any amount of rouge could create.

"Thank you," I said. "You look rather dashing yourself. But," I said, lifting a hand to stop him from speaking, "I want to know what just happened."

He shrugged. "I don't know, Anne. I was standing with you one second, and began to hear bells the next. Not melodious and thick like church bells, but the kind horses sometimes wear on holidays. There was just one at first, then a few."

His words chilled me. "You looked like you were somewhere else entirely, and you said the bells sounded familiar."

I saw a shadow of fear sweep through his face, like a cloud crossing the sun's path.

"Did I? Strange."

"Something is not right, August."

He forced a smile that did not quite reach his eyes. "I'm fine. I must just be tired from this morning. Rescuing damsels from unseen forces that early in the day can leave a man rather worn."

"I don't think that's all, August. I could fetch a doctor if you're feeling ill."

"I said I am fine." His voice was suddenly icy, as cold and distant as the first time I'd spoken to him. He turned away from me. "I think it's best we head out, otherwise we'll be more than fashionably late."

I hated that he could do that to me, erase the months of familiarity, of closeness, that we had acquired and leave me feeling as if I were a stranger. I knew he had lived for too long on his own, first in London and then at the manor, and was so unaccustomed to anyone truly caring about him that he couldn't fathom how to handle someone else's worry, but it still hurt. I wasn't a stranger. I would never again be a stranger to August Grey.

After what I had just seen, however, the last thing I wanted was an argument that would only serve to push him further from me. What had happened was not normal, and I needed to speak to him about it, but now was not the time.

With worry tumbling through my mind, I once again picked up my dress's train and turned to the door.

"I'm ready," I said.

August nodded once. "Very well." He walked toward me without meeting my eyes.

Suddenly, I suspected that this would be a very long evening, indeed.

It was difficult for worry to maintain its fevered level of panic when faced with a room that sparkled like a gigantic jewel.

"Your eyes look like they're about to roll out of your head, Anne," August said in a murmur. His voice was no longer the cold husk it had been in the hotel room, but instead held his usual mockery.

"How can a place like this exist?" I said.

I didn't know where to look. In any spot my eyes landed there was something gleaming and glittering, asking for attention. It was like being inside a precious stone held up to a flame. I couldn't begin to imagine the work it took to keep a place like this spotless.

"Is this a private home?" I asked as the two of us walked toward the golden double doors that led to the ball's main floor.

August nodded. "According to the invitation, it is. It is the home of a Sir Blackwell. Never heard of him, but then again, I never kept up with London society, even when I lived here. Apparently, he is one of the people responsible for the rebuilding of the Lyceum."

The movement and colors around us were dizzying. Women in dresses of all hues, like a multitude of rare birds, swayed fans or bowed heads to one another in an intricate ritual I was not privy to, while men in dark suits and cream-white shirts strutted and laughed in surprisingly booming voices.

I remembered evenings like this at Caldwell House, the flurry of activity in the kitchen competing with the drawing room as Mary barked out orders and women and men in perfectly starched uniforms carried dishes in and out of the room. Elsie and I used to press ourselves against the door that separated the servant's part of the house from that of the master and mistress, listening to the chatter and clink of crystal, imagining the gowns the women wore and thinking about what colors we would wear if we had been guests instead of servants. I remembered it all, sketched so vividly in my mind, as I crossed the room with August.

Never had I imagined I would truly be on this side of the door, and none of my most fanciful of dress creations had ever equaled the one I now wore. Never had I ever felt more out of my depth.

We were almost at the entrance to the ballroom. A man standing as still as stone opened his mouth and called out a series of names into the room, where there was a lull in the chatter for the length of a breath.

"What is he doing?" I asked as softly as I could.

"Introducing the guests. It's a pretty common practice in a ball as well-attended as this one." August nodded to a man with a set of medals on his broad chest and continued, "Most of these people know each other by name, but this ritual allows them the opportunity to inspect gowns and coats with impunity."

I stopped walking, bringing both of us to a halt in the center of the room. "Will we be announced into the room, as well?"

"Of course."

"I don't think this is a good idea. No one knows me. No one has even heard that you have supposedly married. Won't that be suspicious?"

August's eyes widened in false horror. "Are you frightened, Anne?"

I nodded. "Yes."

He wasn't expecting the blunt truth, because all mockery left his face at once. He gestured at the room. "Anne, these people would rather lose their fortunes than honestly reveal ignorance about the identity of someone in their midst. They are the epitome of predictability. They will pretend to have known you for years, to have heard of your name and beauty in drawing rooms, and to have been in the same room when you were introduced to society. They will claim to have met your illustrious father while fox hunting and your beautiful mother at the opera. The word about the size of your fortune will spread through the room like a fire, and before the evening is over, most of them will come to believe they really did know about you before tonight. There is no one here, except Lily—if she is indeed behind all of this, as we suspect—who poses any danger whatsoever. Not to us." He shrugged. "Besides, they do know me, or they know of me through my father's reputation and fortune, and if I chose you to walk on my arm, then you are certainly the caliber of woman they want in their ballroom. That said, if you would like to leave, we can. We will find Lily some other way."

I took a deep breath and looked around the room. Would it really be that easy to just join this crowd? To just walk through it on a path cleared by the Grey family name?

"We're here, already," I said, more for my benefit than August's. "And I do have a pretty gown."

August smiled. "The loveliest one I've seen so far."

"And I suppose it would look even stranger if we left right now."

"Oh, it would be a scandal. Our lack of decorum would offend the other guests and our hosts, but I've never cared about that, and I won't begin tonight. If you want to leave, I'll gladly help you make a daring escape."

It was my turn to smile. "I would prefer to keep scandal away from our door just a bit longer."

"As you wish." He nodded to the man still calling out names. "Let us proceed, then."

"Yes."

The walk to the ballroom's entrance was both the shortest and the longest of my life. I wanted to simultaneously get through this as quickly as possible and avoid it altogether. There was just one other couple in front of us being announced, the names still ringing as the two of them walked down the handful of marble steps and into the room below.

August stepped forward, and I had no option but to follow.

"Lord August Grey and Lady Anne Grey," he said to the man, who gave us both a bow and announced our names into the room.

If I had expected gasps or an overly dramatic pause, I would have been sorely disappointed. Yes, a few heads turned our way, mainly women who swept their eyes from the crown of my head to the last folds of my train, but they soon returned to whatever intricate conversations they had been weaving.

I sighed with relief.

"See?" August murmured. "Nothing to it."

By some miracle, I was able to maneuver the marble steps without tumbling head over heels, taking August with me, and we both reached the main ballroom floor intact.

The voices were louder here as guests joined one another and created dozens of different conversations. I had always imagined men and women of the higher classes to be softer-spoken, but it appeared I had been incorrect in that assumption. They spoke with confidence, as if everything they said deserved to be said with conviction.

Or perhaps the trays of champagne gracefully making their way through the room were the real culprits.

One such tray, in the gloved hands of a man who had his eyes carefully averted from everyone in the room, was soon before us. He bowed his head to us, lifted the tray, and waited as August passed me a glass flute half full of sparkling liquid before taking up his own.

I'd never had champagne before. Mary had occasionally allowed Elsie and me a sip of wine on special days, taken directly from whatever the Caldwell's guests had left in their crystals. But there was never so much champagne left over that a few sips wouldn't be noticed.

I knew it had bubbles, but I wasn't prepared for the way my nose tickled just from bringing the flute closer to my mouth.

August watched, his drink untouched, as I took my first taste of champagne.

It was like drinking laughter. Like someone had bottled up a cascading giggle.

It was sweet, but there was an edge to it that kept it from becoming cloying, and I felt the alcohol's effect almost immediately. *Sip it slowly*, I told myself, as the urge to taste it again tempted me.

"It is an interesting flavor, isn't it?" August said, and brought his glass to his lips. "My father didn't favor it, so we never had much of it at Rosewood, but it is served copiously throughout all of London's society events. It is stronger than it tastes," he said. "Best not to drink too much of it on an empty stomach."

"Lord Grey!"

Both of us turned toward the man who had called out. He was of stocky build, much shorter than August and many times wider, and by the flush that stained his face and neck, he had already left a number of empty champagne glasses in his wake.

August groaned softly beside me, but forced a smile to his face as the man drew near. "My lord, what a pleasure. May I introduce my wife, Lady Anne Grey?" He turned to me. "This is the Right Honorable Earl of Falmouth, an acquaintance of my father's."

My heart gave a lurch. What was I supposed to call him? I'd never met an earl before, and I had not the slightest idea what his proper title required me to address him as. Should I use my lord, as August had?

Thankfully, the earl did not wait to hear what I had to say. "I heard you had married, you scoundrel, and to this lovely lady, no less." He nodded. "Your father would have been proud."

"I hope so, my lord." August placed a hand on my arm. "We would have loved to see Your Lordship at our wedding, but it was a small affair in the continent, and I'm afraid the invitations were sent out rather late. I'm sure there were more important things Your Lordship had to attend to."

I swallowed and tried not to appear as if I wanted to throttle August. It was one thing to get through the night hoping that no one paid us much attention, but quite another to flaunt our false marriage in their faces.

The earl did not even blink. "Yes, we had already planned a visit to Bath when we received your invitation. A shame, of course. It promised to be a lovely event, I'm sure. Especially in . . ."

"Marseilles," August said.

"Ah, yes. I recall speaking with Lady Grace about how much we would have enjoyed attending."

"It was a beautiful day. Perhaps we can have you over to our summer house when London's season is over."

The earl nodded and took a gulp from his champagne glass. "That would be lovely. I am sure Lady Grace will be ecstatic. Now, if you'll excuse me, I think I see the Viscount Murchison and must pay my respects."

"Of course," August said.

"It was a pleasure to see you, dear boy, and madam, it was an absolute honor." He bowed his head and disappeared with an agility that I would not have expected from a man of his girth.

For the first time in what felt like hours, I was able to breathe. "Were you trying to see how long I would last before requiring smelling salts?" I said.

August chuckled. "Merely proving my point. I could have told him we got married in Timbuktu and he would have nodded and claimed he'd been there the summer before." He shrugged. "No one here really worries about anything but appearances. It has been this way since before I was born, and I doubt it will ever change." He sipped from his glass and smiled. "I also rather enjoyed watching your face slowly lose all its color."

I shook my head. "You are infuriating."

"So you have told me, numerous times."

A woman in a dress the color of mustard seeds swept past us, her eyes taking in my gown before reaching my face and nodding. She did not even glance at August before continuing on.

"It's not considered rude to stare in that fashion?" I asked.

"Not in a ballroom." August was watching the room, searching, I supposed, for a crown of auburn hair framing the most beautiful face I had ever seen. His height gave him a considerably better vantage point than I had.

"Do you think Lily will be here, out in the open?" I asked.

"She wouldn't make it so simple for us, but it won't hurt to be sure."

We watched the room in silence, the noise of the crowd growing as we listened, the man by the door's voice rising above it all, announcing lords, earls, and dukes. All names I had never heard before.

Until I heard Lord Exter's name.

I gasped.

August turned to me. "What is it? Did you see her?"

"No. Just . . . they announced Lord Exter."

He blinked. "And?"

"My father is his manservant. Has been for years. The last time I heard, he was carrying Lord Exter's pomades and brushes throughout all of India."

"I see," August said. "Your father won't be here, of course."

"No, but it's comforting to know he is back in London." I knew seeing him would be impossible, even more so now that I was pretending to be someone I wasn't, but the knowledge that we shared the same city once again made this evening and all of its anxieties worthwhile.

Would he have heard about Rosewood Manor burning to the ground? I could at least send him a brief note letting him know that I was all right.

"Come on," August said, placing his hand lightly on my arm. "Let's become acquainted with this Lord Exter."

He started off across the room before I could say anything to deter him. It was risking too much to speak with someone who saw my father day after day. What if he saw a resemblance? According to Mary, I did look more like my mother than my father, but there still had to be vestiges of his features within mine. Heritage was not so easily concealed.

"We can't just walk up to him without being introduced," I said as I caught up with August.

"I have met him before. Years and years ago, when my mother still lived. It's very likely that he will not remember me, but he certainly won't admit it."

He took my arm and wove it through his as we reached Lord Exter and his wife.

I'd seen my father's employer only once before, and my memory of him did not match the man in front of me. He was older, much older, with folds of skin drooping over one another as if they had once encased a much more corpulent figure. He had also lost the head of almost black hair, leaving his pale skin uncovered, with only a bit of white, like a wreath, along the back of his head. It couldn't have been more than ten or eleven years since I'd first seen him, yet in that time, he had lost all signs of youth.

"Lord Exter, what a pleasure to see you," August said in his most honeyed voice.

The older man turned to us, blinking as if a bright light had been placed directly before his eyes. There was no recognition in his face.

"Thank you . . ." Lord Exter began, but his voice lost its strength after just those two words.

The woman next to him, Lady Exter, took his arm and smiled at us. "You'll have to forgive my husband. His memory is not what it once was—"

"Nonsense, Laura," Lord Exter said. "There is nothing wrong with my memory. I know exactly who these young people are."

Lady Exter slowly fanned herself, more out of nerves, I thought, than actual overheating. "Forgive me, dear, of course you do."

August glanced at me, and I had to bite back a smile.

"As I was saying," Lord Exter began, "I am very glad to see both of you, as well. Yes." He smiled, but there was a vagueness on his face that reminded me, with a shock, of Mr. Keery when the wraith had begun wrapping itself around his life-force.

This man, I realized with a jolt, was ill. He looked like he had trouble even recognizing where he was; there was certainly no danger of him recognizing me.

Lady Exter's smile was tight as she pressed away a wrinkle on her husband's sleeve. "That new manservant of yours is not up to par," she said. "He should have noticed the coat needed more pressing. This is not acceptable."

The words dug into my suddenly cold skin. They had a new manservant. Why? Where was my father? Had they dismissed him from service after all the years he'd served in their household?

A multitude of questions crowded me out of my own head. I wanted to demand to know where my only parent was, but I couldn't. That was not how these things were dealt with in a glittering ballroom.

I swallowed back my avalanche of questions and tried to steady my voice. "I am sorry to hear that you are having difficulties with your new manservant."

"Yes," August added. "It is always a trial training new servants to the way a household works. I recently had a maid come in who did nothing but overstep her bounds. I hadn't the slightest as how to deal with that. Tell me, since I am on the search for a manservant of my own, what made Your Lordship let yours go?"

I held my breath as Lord Exter searched for the words. His eyes were as vacant as rooms closed up for the season, though. His wife patted his arm kindly, and did her best to smile away her husband's confusion.

"We would never have let Henry go. He was the best servant we have ever had in our household, and we have had quite a lot of them."

Was. My mind stuttered at the past tense.

"No, unfortunately, he passed away a month ago. It was very sudden, from one week to the next, he was gone, so we didn't even have the opportunity to have him train someone new."

I felt as if someone had dropped me in a bath of ice water. The room pulsed around me, dimming and brightening with each surge of blood from my pounding heart.

August placed his arm around my waist, and I had never been more grateful for the burning his touch created. I latched on to the pain to keep from racing out of the room.

"Most unfortunate," August said softly.

I could only nod.

"Yes, it was quite a disappointment. Henry knew exactly how everything needed to be done, and now, with, well . . ." She nodded toward Lord Exter, who was glancing around the room with no flicker of recognition. "It would have been better to have him with us, still."

I should have been used to this kind of talk after working in domestic service for so long, but the words stung me like hornets. She was speaking of a man's life extinguished, my *father's* life, and all that mattered to her was how it complicated her own.

I realized suddenly that I had to find a way out of this room, or I would end up behaving in an inexcusable manner. With a glance, I found the door leading out to what I imagined was the garden.

"If you'll pardon me, Lord and Lady Exter, I'm feeling a bit indisposed," I said.

"Oh, dear," Lady Exter said with a frown. "I hope it's nothing serious."

I was finding it almost impossible to stop the tears from spilling out. "Not at all. Just feeling a bit flushed, that's all. Nothing a bit of fresh air can't cure." My lips quivered as I tried to smile.

Without waiting for another word, I handed the champagne glass to August and walked away from the group. The room threatened to tilt on its side with each step I took, and I had to force myself to breathe in a measured manner and not at the speed my body demanded.

Faces turned to me as I crossed the room, but I didn't mind them. My only goal was reaching the door, which was thankfully open to allow fresh spring night air into the ballroom. I didn't know if August had followed me, or if he was still apologizing for my behavior, and I didn't care.

A sob shook me as soon as I stepped out into the night, seeming to tear me apart like lightning splitting open a tree. I hurried away from the golden light and noise spilling from inside and toward the darkness of the perfectly mani-cured garden.

My knees trembled. I reached for the nearest tree and dug my fingernails into its bark.

He was dead. He had died without my having said any-thing to him, without my having told him I loved him for the last time, without my seeing his face. I couldn't recall the last time I had spoken with him. What had we talked about? Had I told him I loved him, then?

My mind scrambled for the image of my father's face and couldn't find it. My breath knotted. I had nothing to re-member him by, not even the Bible he had given to me. Not a single drawing or daguerreotype of him, not a piece of cloth-ing, nothing at all. He had disappeared from my life like dust swept away on a breeze, as if he had never been there.

I'd felt a bit like an orphan since my mother died, but now the feeling was multiplied hundreds of times over.

I clutched the tree and allowed the tears to flow.

"Poor little Anne," a murmuring voice said.

My head jerked up at the sound. I knew that voice.

"It is a pity that your father had to die, but you left me no choice."

I pulled away from the tree and caught a glimmer of movement ahead of me.

"Lily," I said.

A chuckle as soft as velvet wrapped around me as an egg-white beam of moonlight revealed a bit of her dress, which was scattered with crystals that grabbed on to the light with icy claws. With the agility and grace that belonged to a deer, she launched into a run, racing across the garden toward an even darker section at the edge of the property.

Anger rose like bile. I didn't think twice about it; I ran after her. It was probably a trap, and August was not behind me to help if I needed it, but I didn't care.

I couldn't see anything but the glitter of her dress as I ran. Each breath was painful in the corseted bodice of my own gown, and I had half a mind to rip it open, but there was no time for that. I couldn't lose sight of her.

She took us both to the very edge of the property, and then past it, into the untrimmed greenery behind the Blackwell manor.

Lily made no sound as she slipped into the woods, melting into them, but my gown caught in the roots and branches that sprang out like skeletal fingers all around me. I stopped running.

The woods were silent. Unnaturally so. This was probably where the Blackwells hunted for foxes and pheasants, where they brought their baying dogs and their horses. There should have been the noise of small animals scurrying away from me, and yet the only sounds were my own clumsy steps and the hiss of my breath.

Darkness pressed against me as the moonlight barely slid through the lattice of branches. This was a mistake.

Laughter erupted from somewhere to my left. I turned in that direction with a gasp, catching one of my sleeves against a tree.

"You look quite silly, Anne," Lily said, her voice full of dark laughter. "A rat in a trap. But then, that is a bit what you are, isn't it? Insinuating yourself into August' life, getting your sticky little paws on things that are not for the likes of you." She shifted, and I caught the glitter of her dress in the darkness. "That's why I had to do what I did to your father, you know. To punish you."

A rush of heat raced to my head, and I was sure it would split it right open. I grabbed on to the branch that held my arm captive and squeezed it. "What did you do to him?"

"Nothing that your precious August didn't do to mine." Her voice vibrated through the woods, filling the trees with sound.

Tears trailed down my cheeks, and I swiped at them with a shaking hand. "He was innocent. He had nothing to do with this, Lily."

She sighed. "I'm getting quite tired of hearing you use my given name. You are nothing more than a glorified parlor maid, born to another maid and a manservant who, themselves, came from a long line of servants. I don't care what August allows you to do, or what privileges he's buying by doing so, but when you speak to me, you will address me as Miss Bellingham."

A rush of cold air brushed me as a shimmer from her dress suddenly appeared close by. I tried to take a step back, but couldn't release my dress from the branches. Panic overtook me.

Lily wouldn't even need magic to destroy me now. A knife in the right place would do just fine. I wouldn't even be able to see it coming. I expected sudden pain, which is why I gasped when she touched my face. Before I could move my head away, her hand clasped around my chin in an unshakeable grip.

Her touch seared my skin, filling it with burning needles that dug deeper with each passing second as I tried to pull away from her. Everything in me rejected what she was.

"So this is what touching a Grounder is like," she said into my left ear. "Fascinating."

I whimpered as the pain intensified. Did she not feel it, as well?

"It must make for some interesting sensations between two lovers, or, forgive me, between a married couple," she said, and laughed again.

She released me with such force I lost my balance. Not even the branches that still clutched at me managed to hold back my fall. All air was knocked out of me by the root-strewn ground.

"Now, you've both been rather dull, taking much too long to come looking for me," Lily said, moving away from me. "Two entire months of boredom. I had to fill my time with something, and that something was your father."

The moonlight caught the glint of an earring as she paced.

"It was so simple, Anne. Just a small curse, nothing more, but unfortunately, your father did not possess any of the unique talents you do. It destroyed him in two weeks. Imagine that. While you and August were recovering from your ordeal, your darling father was in the throes of imminent death. If you had set out to find me sooner, he would still be alive."

I clenched my hands into fists and shook my head. "Please stop. Please, L—Miss Bellingham, please stop."

"Oh, it's painful, isn't it? You have some idea, then, of what it means to lose your only parent. But you may be right, dear Anne, perhaps I should stop. After all, my fight is not truly with you." The tinkle of crystal against crystal revealed her presence just an arm's length away.

I pressed a hand to my pounding heart, to stop it, to make it behave, to allow me to think.

"No, it's August who has yet to pay."

"But you killed his father, too. You held him prisoner for years. Isn't that enough?"

"No!" she said, with a laugh whose edge could have torn through skin. "He could not stand his father, therefore his death was nothing more than an inconvenience. If that."

I shook my head. "That's not true."

"Of course it is, dear girl. August used his father, as he used me, as he is now using you."

I flinched at her words. I'd heard them before, trapped in the burning conflagration that was Rosewood Manor. They didn't sting any less now than they had then.

"Oh, you don't really think he cares for you, do you? For a maid? No, you can't possibly be that naïve." She sighed. "Though, of course, he does put on a rather convincing performance. One that even I believed, so I suppose I can't fault you too much for that. He's probably doing his best work yet with you. Heavy glances, touches that last just a bit too long, the casually tossed mentions of a life together."

Her words seemed to crystallize the blood in my veins.

"The false marriage is cleverer than I expected, even from him. It helps him keep you all to himself, as isolated as you were at the manor, so that all you can see and hear and feel is August Grey. The plan was his, wasn't it? To avoid those pesky chaperones?"

"Stop it." My voice wavered as I said it, and I hated myself for that. She was lying. Of course she was. It was all she did.

"Poor Anne. I'm trying to help you, you know. I don't want another young woman to suffer at his hands. Even if you do belong to the serving class."

I shook my head. "You're wrong about him."

"Am I? Just think, would someone like August ever have looked twice at you if you hadn't had the abilities you do? Be honest with yourself. There's a pattern here which your affection for him is not allowing you to see."

"Enough, Lily."

I felt her powers froth up. The hairs on the back of my neck rose, as if sensing imminent lightning, and my body reacted by pure instinct. My energy uncoiled and struck out, expanding like a shield that slammed against Lily's with an audible hiss. Water smothering fire.

Her power was muscular, much stronger than August's, stronger even than the wraith we had faced, and I had to strain to hold her back. All of my focus went to keeping that shield in place, but it was not enough.

With a laugh, Lily's magic surged forward like a whip and cracked through it. I gasped as it lifted me off my feet and flung me against a tree. Her powers held me suspended, only the train of my dress touching the earth beneath me.

"You are powerful. I will hand you that," Lily said.

It was as if her own powers had made her luminous, because I could suddenly see her, her dress alight with cold moon-glow, her perfect features carved out as if of ivory. A pair of dark eyes glittered like jewels close enough for me to see that there was nothing reflected inside them.

"Unfortunately, not powerful enough. You are of low birth, of course, so that is to be expected, and even excused. Which is why I will be generous and give you a choice. Listen carefully, dear Anne, because your life and the lives of a number of people depend upon it."

She walked forward until I could smell her perfume, the sweetness of jasmine blended with the sharpness of citrus.

"If you leave August, you are free. I will not search for you or harm you in any way," she said. "You will be able to live your life as you please without fear, but you must leave him tonight and never contact him again."

I struggled against the invisible hands that held me, but it was useless. She was too strong.

"He is the one who still has to earn his punishment for everything he's done to me." Lily smiled, and I shuddered. I had been inside her head. I knew the distortions that lurked there, and they were revealed in that smile. "Now, I know that it will take more than my words to convince you of the falsehoods our young man has told you, and you do have a rather dull penchant for self-sacrifice, so there is further incentive to help you make the right decision. If you do not leave August to his fate, more people will die at Wodenhouse Mill. One person's life for each day you refuse to cooperate. That should be fair enough."

My eyes widened in the dark. "You can't do that."

"Of course I can. Who is going to stop me? You?" She cocked her head, and her smile widened. "Based on tonight's little encounter, it doesn't appear so."

"The police. I'll go to the police."

"Oh, Anne, they still think it was a wild animal that dragged those women out. A wolf, perhaps." She chuckled. "Besides, I am supposed to be dead, remember? You would first have to convince them that I am still living. No easy task, I'm afraid. One of the beneficial outcomes of my father's aversion to parading me in public is that very few people know what Lily Bellingham looked like. And, since the only existing image of me burned to ash with Rosewood Manor, I am in no danger of being recognized. No, I'm afraid you have no way out of this except to do as I say."

I shook my head. "I won't abandon August."

"He has you quite in his thrall, doesn't he? It's unfortunate that you and I did not meet earlier. I think, despite the vast gap in our stations, we would have made a much better team. One that didn't rely on emotional manipulation to be effective."

She couldn't possibly believe that. She couldn't imagine I would ever have joined her in her revenge on August.

"You're mad."

"If I am, dear Anne, then think of the one who has made me so and consider if you won't be where I am when he tires of you."

She released me from her magical grip and I dropped to the twisted ground with a gasp.

"You have until dawn to make your decision," she said, stepping closer. "It would be wise of you to take my offer seriously. Will you be able to live with yourself knowing that you could have prevented all future deaths at the factory? This will be the only chance you get before things escalate. And believe me, I have a number of nightmares planned for August. Your brush with death this morning was just a warning."

"So that . . . thing roaming the factory is your creation."

"Of course it is, silly girl. And you still haven't seen just how special my little beast can be." She locked her dark eyes on mine. "Everything is about to get much worse, Anne. Is our lying boy really worth it?"

In an instant, the darkness enclosed Lily in its embrace.

"Wait!" I called out.

But Lily only smiled and took a step back, into the swarming darkness. Soon, the only trace of her left was the fading breath of jasmine.

I stood, as locked in place as if her magic still held me pressed against the tree. Her words beat inside my head like living creatures I could not shake off.

"Anne!"

I closed my eyes at his voice. What was I going to tell him? All I wanted was to stay still, right where I was, stop time from moving forward, stop the need to make an impossible decision.

"Blast it," August said as I heard him stumble over the tangled roots and branches. A sudden warm glow appeared through the trees, revealing his tall figure in silhouette. "Anne!" he called again.

"I'm here," I said and walked forward so that he could see me.

"Do you realize that this is the second time today that I have had to set out in search of you. Is this going to become a habit?" he asked as wove his way through the trees, a ball of ghostly light hovering over one of his hands.

"I'm sorry. I saw Lily and didn't have time to warn you."

The magical light flung shadows on his face, so I couldn't read his expression as he paused. "You saw her, and you chased after her on your own? Have you taken all leave of your senses?"

"I knew it was a risk, but I didn't want to lose sight of her."

"She could have killed you."

Does he worry for you, or for the loss of access to your powers? Lily's voice whispered through me. I couldn't tell if it was my own mind creating the words, or if she had insinuated herself into my thoughts.

I swallowed the dryness in my throat and started making my way over to where he stood. "I'm . . . I'm all right."

"This time."

"I'm sorry, August. I am. I won't do it again."

He moved the light up with a flick of his fingers as I came to stand in front of him, so that it illuminated my face. "I don't think you are all right even *this* time. You spoke with her, didn't you?"

I hesitated. My instinct was to tell him the truth, to share each of Lily's words and actions so that we could come up with a plan together. But my voice faltered. Nothing I said would truly help us, and if I told him of her offer to set me free and the promise of no more deaths in the factory, he would never hear any argument on the matter.

You could tell him and see how he reacts. See whether he'd try to find a way for you to stay. That would tell you a lot, wouldn't it?

No, enough. I couldn't allow Lily to do this. I would not doubt August on the words of someone so willing to take innocent lives.

I would tell him only as much as I could without revealing the proposition she'd made me and try to come up with a solution myself.

"Yes, I caught up with her," I said.

"And?"

"She killed my father."

The hovering warm light faltered as August closed his eyes. "I suspected as much. I'm sorry, Anne."

My throat tightened as the need to cry rose again. I shoved it back. What good would crying do now? "The creature in the factory is hers, and she said she had more surprises for us. She called them 'nightmares.'"

"More deaths," August said, clenching his free hand into a fist. "More suffering."

Yes, I was doing the right thing. Lily had made this my decision, and I would be the one to decide on it. No one else. If ignorance would prevent him from feeling the full weight of her madness, then I would keep him in the darkness until I couldn't anymore.

I lifted a hand and brushed a lock of hair out of his face, careful not to touch his skin with my bare hand. "We'll find a way. We've managed so far."

He met my eyes and held them. The glow from the light was reflected in the shifting greens and blues of his irises, so that it seemed they were on fire. "After everything we have lost, can you really say that? Have we truly managed, Anne, or are we just playing a game we cannot win?"

I opened my mouth, but the salted trace of choked tears erased any answer I might have given him.

We arrived back at the hotel encased in silence. Neither of us knew what to say, how to comfort each other, so we said nothing throughout the long ride back to the Salisbury.

I felt a pang of guilt at seeing Eustace's tired face when August opened the door to our chambers. I should have told her not to bother waiting up for us to help me undress. There had to be a way to get out of these fashionable contraptions without requiring a second pair of hands.

She curtsied when we entered and kept her eyes on the floor.

"Hello, Eustace," I said, removing my gloves and folding them carefully on a side table.

"Good evening, madam. Mr. Rushworth let me know that Your Ladyship and Lordship would be coming in later than usual."

I smiled, though it was the last thing I felt like doing. "It's all right."

"I can fetch tea if Your Ladyship likes, or run a bath. I brought up a fresh decanter of water for His Lordship, as well," she said.

August waved her words away with more annoyance than was necessary and walked over to one of the windows. He pulled aside the heavy curtain and looked out.

"It's late, Eustace. Help me undress and you can head off to bed."

"Of course, madam." She bowed her head and walked into my bedroom.

I waited until she had closed the door behind her to turn to August. "I think I'm going to turn in."

August didn't give any indication that he'd heard me, remaining instead as he was, staring out the window into the London night. I knew that he was troubled by everything that had occurred today, but I couldn't help him. I could barely help myself at the moment. It was taking every bit of my concentration to not splinter into thousands of tiny pieces.

He doesn't care about what you've lost. What is it to him, when he never cared for his own parents?

Wishing I could rip those words right out of my head, I walked into my bedroom and allowed Eustace to begin the process of undressing me. The time it took to undo buttons and laces felt interminable, and there was nothing to keep my thoughts away from my father and Lily's words, no distraction throughout the entire process.

When I sat down on the plush seat in front of the vanity so that Eustace could unpin my hair, something did catch my eye in the mirror, however. August's rose, which I had left inside the night table's drawer, was perched in a crystal vase full of water.

Eustace followed my eyes. "I hope Your Ladyship doesn't mind that I took the liberty of placing the flower in water. It'll keep it alive for perhaps another day. I can remove the vase, if it doesn't suit Her Ladyship's taste, of course."

I smiled despite the heaviness I felt. If she only knew the truth of that rose.

"Thank you," I said. "It looks beautiful."

She opened her mouth to say something, but stopped herself.

"What is it?"

"If . . . if I may be completely honest, Your Ladyship."

"Of course, Eustace."

"Well, madam, I was rather shocked to see the flower still alive. It has been a number of days since I first saw it, and it looks just as beautiful now as it did then." She met my eyes for an instant through the mirror, and I saw something familiar in them. Curiosity, yes, but also something else that I couldn't quite define.

I had to tread carefully here, or she'd react just as Ingrid and the rest of the factory women had this morning. With everything that had happened later in the day, I realized that I hadn't even mentioned their reactions to August. I would have to deal with it tomorrow. But for now . . .

"It's not the same flower," I said, looking down at my hands to avoid betraying myself. "I love roses, so Lord Grey gifts me with a new one most days. It's a tradition, of sorts."

"Oh, I knew it was silly of me to think that it was the same rose. I'm sorry to have intruded, madam."

She removed the last pin from my hair, and all of my curls tumbled down over my shoulders and back. I sighed with relief.

"Would Her Ladyship like anything else? A nightcap, perhaps?"

That brought to mind Lady Caldwell and her blasted peppermint tea, and with her came a flash of Elsie's face so vivid it made my breath catch. The need to see her, to speak to her, to tell her about my father and everything that had occurred since I left Caldwell House was overpowering. I needed a sibling's comfort now.

I tucked my hands into the folds of my dressing gown so that Eustace wouldn't see them trembling.

"No, thank you," I said. "You can go to bed. We'll say eight thirty, like this morning."

"Of course, madam."

As soon as she left the room, I stood. I couldn't pretend to be calm and composed for one more second. I glanced at the ornate clock on the night table. Only six or so hours until dawn, until Lily's ultimatum brought death to someone else.

But would it really be her, or me who would be blamed for the next missing woman? I knew what her mind was like, how her sanity had twisted into something dark and unrecognizable, which meant that she might not be wholly responsible for what she was doing. But I? I had not taken leave of my senses, yet I was still choosing the route that would end in someone's death. Not being able to share the truth with August and find a solution together made everything worse. But I wouldn't tell him until there was no other option.

The responsibility would be mine.

As was my father's death.

Each time I thought of it, it hurt anew, grief and guilt mixing into a dizzying tonic.

Pressing my lips together, I walked to the window and looked out at the night. Only the streetlamps were aglow, their light pale and wan in the darkness. London had never looked as dark and unfriendly as it did now.

I stood there, staring out and thinking myself into knots, long enough for exhaustion to overtake me. The decision was made, but I couldn't stop watching for the dawn, as if its arrival would bring an acceptable resolution to a predicament that held none.

There was a soft knock on my door.

"Anne?"

I wiped at my face. "Yes, come in."

August opened the door and stepped into the room. He looked as tired as I felt.

"I saw your light on," he said. "I wanted to know how you were. The first night is always the hardest, but it can help to have someone to talk to. I know I am not Elsie, but I can listen if—"

Another onslaught of tears rose with sudden violence, and I hid my face in my shaking hands. I didn't want to cry like this in front of August, but I couldn't stop it.

I was vaguely conscious of him moving across the room, but it still surprised me when he placed a hand lightly on my arm.

"Come," he said, and led me to the edge of the bed. "Sit."

I did, still trying to catch my breath in between each sob.

August took the ornate coverlet that had been perfectly smoothed out on the bed and draped it over my shoulders. He knelt in front of me, hesitating for a moment before wrapping his arms around me. The heat our energies generated was dulled just enough by the fabric between us to make the embrace bearable.

"My deepest condolences," he said.

Gripping him as tightly as I could, as if he were about to be ripped away from me and this was the last time I would ever see him, I brought my head to rest against his shoulder and cried until there were no more tears left.

SEVEN

I WAS NOT ABLE TO COAX SLEEP ANY CLOSER that night, which was probably why I didn't see the first stone coming the following morning.

August and I had arrived at Wodenhouse Mill a few minutes to ten, ready to search every inch of the place until we found something, anything, that would point us in the right direction of how we might prevent further deaths. I still clutched at my secret with both hands, though it weighed more and more by the second.

"If anything happens today," August said as we walked to the factory's entrance, "you have to promise me you will do as I say." The shadows under his eyes had grown, making his face look as gaunt as when I'd first met him.

"Yes, I promise," I said. I was too exhausted to argue.

He opened the factory door and allowed me to enter first. "You!"

I looked up and met Ingrid's angry gaze. The door that led to the factory floor was wide open, and she stood in the center of it, blocking our path.

"You're shameless, you are. 'ow dare you step foot in 'ere? You've done enough!"

"Ingrid—"

"Get out!" she shrieked at me.

Behind her, some of the other women had abandoned their looms and spinning machines, some of them unsure of what was happening, but others heading for the door with resolution.

"Another woman is dead, and it is your fault!"

I gasped at hearing her words echo my guilt. Did she know that I could have ended the danger they lived in and had chosen not to?

"Witch." Ingrid spat it at me.

I barely registered August's presence beside me. "What is this?"

"She's a witch!" Ingrid said. Some of the women behind her nodded.

"We all saw what you did," one of them said. "Ain't natural."

I blinked. This wasn't about Lily at all, then.

"She's behind all these disappearances and deaths," another woman said, the hate in her eyes like a slap.

How could they think that? Why would I volunteer my help if I were the culprit?

"Witch!" Ingrid said again. "Witch!"

"No, listen—" I began, and took a step toward them.

The first stone hit me on the left side of my face, right beneath my eye. The pain was sharp enough to know that the force of it had broken skin. I stopped moving.

But it was too late.

I watched in shock as most members of the makeshift barricade pulled stones from their apron pockets. They had been prepared for this. They had been waiting for me to step into the building.

An avalanche of stones rained down on me before I could even think of using my grounding powers. All I could do was bring my hands up to shield my face from the blows.

August stepped in front of me, blocking the strikes with his body.

"Stop!"

I looked up just in time to see him fling the women back with just a movement of his wrist. They yelped in chorus as they crashed to the floor.

"Have you all gone mad?" August said in a voice that bounced against the factory's walls. "This is outrageous!"

The first one to regain her feet was Ingrid. Anger and fear had transformed her from the timid, tear-drenched person I'd met yesterday into someone with so much violence in her eyes it was painful to meet them.

Could she really think I had done all of this?

"You all saw that," she said, pointing at August. "Evidence of un'oly powers from 'im, too. They are the ones 'unting us down like animals."

A murmur of voices began. This was going to get worse very quickly. A few more of Ingrid's words, and we would end up with a full-fledged mob on our hands. The best option would be a hasty retreat, but I wasn't even certain they would allow us to leave without further violence. August's tight lips revealed a similar train of thought.

"Where's Mr. Lovett?" I said. "We need to speak with him."

"Ain't no need to get 'im involved," Ingrid said.

"Go fetch him, please," I said to an older woman standing at the fringe of the group. "We need to speak with him and resolve this."

"We 'ave nothing to resolve. You're murderers. Fiends from the very bowels of 'ell. What we need is Scotland Yard—"

"Fetch him!" It came out louder than I'd intended, making some of the group flinch, but I'd had just about enough.

The older woman lowered her head to avoid Ingrid's stare and hurried off to find the foreman.

I could sense August's tension next to me as the woman's footsteps became softer and softer, and faded completely. He was poised to use his powers at the least show of violence, which would only make things worse. I reached out to him with my own energy, just a soft, feathery stroke of it against his arm. August turned to me slightly and gave me the smallest of nods before allowing his stance to relax.

I let that wave of grounding energy grow, extending it like a sheet and flinging it over the group of women as if I were getting ready to make a bed. It touched them for less than an instant before something tore it away.

I held my breath as the tension in the group grew once more.

Whatever was taking these women, whatever creature Lily had conjured up, it was in the factory right now, exerting its own immense power, propelling them toward violence. And there was nothing we could do about it without risking further attacks from the very people we were trying to protect. The more we tried to help them, the more fearful and mistrustful they would become and the less protection we could provide; the being roaming the factory would be granted free rein. Without meaning to, my lack of caution yesterday had given Lily exactly what she needed to keep her word. If we didn't continue investigating, the disappearances and deaths would continue for as long as she wanted.

For as long as I disobeyed her commands.

I tried to swallow back that thought, but it lodged in my throat.

Footsteps drew near and the older factory worker came into view, followed closely by Mr. Lovett.

"Lady Grey, Lord Grey," he said. "I was hoping you would not come in today."

His voice had none of the falseness from the first day we'd met him, and none of the enthusiastic willingness of yesterday. In fact, he looked as if he had gotten as little sleep as August and I had.

"We've heard there's been another disappearance," I said.

He shook his head. "Not a disappearance this time. A death. She was, forgive my crudeness Lady Grey, disemboweled. "

I felt as if all blood had left my head in a rush.

"The constables have already been here, and they've advised me not to allow the two of you in."

"Why?" August asked. "We will not disturb the location of the body, if that's a concern."

Mr. Lovett shook his head. "It's more complicated than that, I'm afraid. Some of the workers"—he motioned to the women behind him—"mentioned what they saw you do, Lady Grey. Of course, the constables thought it was all poppycock, as do I."

"It is the truth!" Ingrid called out. "And now we know that both of them are involved."

"Be quiet," Mr. Lovett said.

"We all saw it!"

He turned his head to face her. "You either shut that trap you call a mouth, or you will not step foot inside this factory again. This is your last warning, woman." He turned back to us, his face mottled with anger. "I apologize for all this nonsense. Uneducated folk will believe anything, and not one in ten of these women can read so much as her name. As I said, neither I nor the police take this ingrate's word as truth." He shrugged. "Still, Scotland Yard found it curious that you were both so interested in what is happening in the factory."

Next to me, August sighed. There was no surprise on his face or in his stance, just resignation. He had been dealing with these kinds of reactions his entire life, I realized. Not being believed, suspicion at everything he did swarming around him because he was different. Not even the Brothers had accepted him completely.

"They will want to speak with us, I gather," August said.

"Yes, sir, though I'm sure it is just routine questioning."

Questioning by Scotland Yard. Not the best way to begin the day.

"Did they mention when?" I asked.

"No, madam. But they did say I should not allow you into the building until all of this is resolved."

"Did they also say to throw stones at my wife?" August said, his voice as cutting as bare glass. I placed a hand on his arm, but he shook his head and continued. "Because that is what these workers of yours have done. She could have been severely injured."

Mr. Lovett's face grew even redder, his eyes widening until they were completely round. He opened his mouth, but no sound came out. He tried again as he glanced from me to August.

"I . . . that is . . . inexcusable. My humblest apologies, Lady Grey. There will be consequences for the culprits, never you fear."

Behind him, the women exchanged glances.

The last thing I wanted was to cause all of these workers to lose their livelihoods. "That is not necessary," I said. "They were confused, that is all."

"That is too generous of you, madam. They don't deserve that kind of benevolence, let me assure you. Do you require a doctor, Lady Grey?"

"No, not at all."

He bit his lip and sighed. "Then I'm afraid I will have to ask you both to leave. I just, well, I do not want trouble from Scotland Yard."

August snorted in obvious derision, but I did my best to offer Mr. Lovett a genuine smile. None of this was his fault, and he still had a business to maintain.

"Thank you, Mr. Lovett. And please, all of you," I said, casting my gaze across the room, "please stay away from the factory at night. During the day, do what you can to stick together, in groups. Don't go anywhere in this building alone."

"Like we'd listen to you when we know that this is all your doing," Ingrid said.

"I told you to keep your trap shut," Mr. Lovett said.

I opened my mouth to try again, to try to convince Ingrid, but I knew there were no words I could choose that would make a difference. Instead, I turned to Mr. Lovett again. "We still want to help you and your workers, so we will be seeing you again, as soon as we speak with the police."

He bowed his head. "Thank you, madam."

I looked at August and motioned toward the factory's front doors. We had been dismissed.

"If you're not going to eat anything, at least drink your tea," I said.

August waved my words away and sat back in the carved iron chair. He had his back to the passing traffic of carriages and people, apparently oblivious to the noise of a flower seller who called out the virtue and beauty of her perfumed wares every few minutes and just steps from where we sat.

After leaving the factory, I had managed to distract August from the truthfully minor scratch under my eye by suggesting that we stop for refreshments at a small café near St. Paul's. We hadn't had more than tea for breakfast and after the difficult night I'd put us through, we both needed the energy.

We also needed a plan.

"You should have told me what happened in the factory," he said.

"I know. With the ball, and Lily . . . it slipped my mind." I sighed. "Perhaps we should go to Scotland Yard ourselves. As a show of goodwill."

"Yes, perhaps," he said, his fingers fiddling with a teaspoon. "But that only resolves the smallest problem we are facing. If the workers do not trust us, they won't speak with us or help us in any way. On the contrary, they will do their best to impede our progress."

He was right. The already difficult and dangerous process of finding out what Lily had unleashed would be made much, much worse without their support. "Maybe Mr. Lovett can help with that."

"He has no real control over those workers. They neither fear him nor respect him; we saw that from the very first day."

"Well, we can't just let more women die every day."

He looked up at me, his brows drawing together. "What makes you think they will die every day? So far, there have been three disappearances and one death in two months."

Damn. I shrugged and glanced away from him. "I'm assuming that now Lily knows we're investigating the disappearances, she will give us enough of them to try to overwhelm us." I brought my cup to my lips and sipped at my tea, sure that the lie was clearly written on my face.

He was silent for long enough that my heart began thumping louder. He knew I wasn't telling him everything. If he confronted me about it and demanded the whole story, I wasn't sure I could keep quiet. The truth would come spilling out of me without reserve.

I gathered enough courage to look up and face his curled smile and hard eyes.

But he wasn't smiling in his cold, mocking manner. He wasn't even looking in my direction. He had his head half-turned, as if listening to something in the street behind him.

"What is it?"

His face had paled to a frightening level, the blood seeping even from his lips. He rose and almost toppled his chair in his hurry toward the street.

"August," I said, but he paid me no mind.

Two of the other people having a late breakfast a few tables over turned to glance after him, and then at me. I acknowledged them hurriedly with a nod as I stood.

By now, August had made it to the street. To my horror, he stood in the center of it, turning first one way, then another, as if something were flitting around him. A man on a bicycle swerved to avoid him and almost crashed into a woman carrying a basket full of vegetables.

What in God's name was he doing?

"August!"

I started after him as quickly as I could, but the blasted corset and layers of skirts were like anchors.

August looked up at the sky and stopped moving.

That's when I saw the two carriages, each one on the opposite side of the street, coming toward each other with the usual violent speed of London broughams. Heading directly for him.

I saw it all in the breadth of a heartbeat: the carriage on August's lane would not have enough time to stop the horses and avoid hitting him, so the driver would pull on the reins and swerve, crashing into the carriage heading in the opposite direction. At the speed they were going, they would topple over on impact, bringing both horses and carriages down, and at least one of them would slam into August's frozen body.

"August!" I screamed, but he did not even flinch at his name. "Goddamn it!"

I flung propriety to the Devil, picked my skirts up above my ankles, and ran toward the street.

It had seemed like such a short distance while we sat and drank tea, but now, it was interminable. My ribs pushed against the corset as I struggled to get the breath I needed, but it wouldn't budge. I was only halfway to the street, and the world was already starting to darken at the edges from lack of air.

The horses whinnied as the carriage drivers pulled at their reins, trying to slow them down, but there would not be enough time. If August didn't move, they would crash, either into him or into each other.

Everything was happening too quickly and too slowly at the same time. I saw each twitch of the horses' flanks, each flick of their manes as they rebelled against the sudden jerk on their bridles, the grimaces on the drivers' faces as they caught, just as clearly as I had, a sliver-thin view of the immediate future.

And then everything sped up. And I was still too far away.

For the first time, I wished I had August's powers. With just a swipe of my hand, I could push him clear, away from the danger, as he had done for me.

I screamed in frustration, because I knew I would be too late.

That's when a small figure darted out from the side of the street and ran into the coming crash. He grabbed one of August's sleeves and pulled him enough to get him out of the path of the carriages. Together, they tumbled to the stones of the pedestrian sidewalk. Safe from wheels and falling horses.

It all happened in less than a breath.

"Oh, thank God," I said as I ran toward them. "Thank God."

Timothy, his face bearing even more smudges of dirt than it had the first time we'd met him, swiped at his short trousers. "'ello again, ma'am."

I didn't even stop to think. I fell to my knees and embraced August with such force I almost pushed him from his half-sitting position back down onto the stones.

"Are you blooming mad? What were you doing?" I said in his ear.

He had neither time to respond or react before I'd released him and turned to the boy, embracing him as well.

"That was so brave. Thank you."

Timothy patted my back clumsily. "It's all right, ma'am. Nothin' to it, really."

I released him and smiled. "You saved his life."

"Ain't the best idea to stand like that in the middle of the street."

That was the most sensible thing I'd heard all morning. "Quite right. But my husband is not always one to follow the best ideas." I turned to August.

He was still half-sitting, blinking and frowning, as if someone had dragged him from a dream and thrust him into the bright day. He closed his eyes for an instant before looking up at me.

"The bells," he said. "I was trying to see where they were coming from."

My stomach dipped like it sometimes did when I fell asleep too suddenly. This again. "The bells?"

"They were incredibly loud. Couldn't you hear them?"

"There were no bells, August."

His eyes narrowed. "There were. The sound was coming from somewhere above the street."

"Could'a been birds, sir," Timothy said as he picked up the stack of newspapers he had tossed aside before rushing into the street.

A cough nearby brought August and I back to our circumstances. Curiosity had drawn the attention of people from all corners of the street; even the beggars perched on St. Paul's steps had stood to look in our direction. We had to move, or risk attracting even more attention.

August winced as he shifted his weight from his recuperating leg to his healthy one, and stood. He offered me a hand, which I was most grateful to accept because I wasn't sure I could untangle my feet from my skirts enough to stand without help.

"There really are lots of birds 'round 'ere, sir. Some can imitate most anything."

August avoided my eyes and nodded. "Yes, that must have been it." He reached into a pocket of his waistcoat and pulled out a few pound coins. He handed them over to the boy. "Thank you for your help once again, Timothy."

Timothy's eyes were as wide as the coins. "Anytime, sir. You know where I am." He tucked the coins into a pouch inside his shirt and walked away.

"Now," I said, "tell me what in Heaven's name is going on."

"The boy is probably right."

Violence had never been in my nature, but I could have slapped him at that moment. Instead, I closed my hands into fists and turned to look at him. "You want me to believe that what you heard were birds? Birds that *I* did not hear, and that held your concentration enough to almost get you run over. And were there birds in our chambers yesterday before the ball, as well?"

"It was nothing, Anne."

Anger bubbled up. "Don't you dare do that again," I said, lowering my voice instead of yelling the words at him as I wished to do. "Don't you dare keep me at a distance as if I were a stranger. Not after everything we have gone through together."

I was shaking. The shock of the last few minutes had been added to the grief of my father's death and Lily's words and threats, creating an internal storm that not even my own powers could defeat. I knew I was being a hypocrite. I was keeping a secret from him, too, but his lack of trust wounded me too much to think rationally.

He doesn't trust you, so, Anne, how can he love you?

With a sharp exhale, I looked around, at the people who had already lost interest in the two of us, at the colors and shapes of London, at the uncomfortable, lush dress I wore. "If you can't trust me, why am I—?"

August brought his hands up to halt my words. They trembled as much as mine did. "Of course I trust you, Anne." He shook his head, frowning. "I know I am being distant and tiresome, as well as a number of other things, but I don't know how you could ever question that."

He took a deep breath, closing his eyes for a moment. "The truth is that I don't know what is happening. It might be Lily, or it might be completely unrelated."

"How could it be unrelated?"

"Well, it could have something to do with my mother—oh, it doesn't matter. In all likelihood, it's Lily. I just . . . I have no inside knowledge this time, and it . . . it frightens me. At Rosewood, I knew what was occurring, even if I was powerless to stop it until you came, but this is different. I'm hearing these blasted things that no one else can, and though I don't know what any of it means, we're both intelligent enough to realize that it does not bode well."

I couldn't deny that truth, even as I so very badly wanted to.

If this was her work, then what was Lily doing?

August lowered his hands and touched my sleeves lightly. "I've been alone with my secrets for so long, I sometimes forget that I don't have to shoulder their weight wholly on my own anymore."

EIGHT

I met his eyes as he tried to smile. Everything had changed since the first time I'd seen him, yet here it was, that same haunted look, the same smothered fear and barely contained despair in his eyes.

Would that look ever disappear for good?

Oh, Anne, is that look even real?

WE NEEDED INFORMATION IF WE WERE TO come to even a semblance of an idea about what was happening, both to August and to the women at the factory, now that none of them would help us.

"If I'd had some of my books from the manor, I know I could have found something we could use," August said as he led us down a narrow side street. "As it is, there might be a few places left like this one, which used to have some serious tomes on the occult."

He pointed to an even narrower staircase that led down to a door marked "Books" in fading letters. The place had the air of a cellar more than a bookstore.

"Will you be all right out here?" he asked. "The owners are not too keen on having a woman in their shop, and even less so if that woman happens to be a Grounder who could wipe clean their entire stock of magical artifacts with a touch."

I glanced around. It was a pretty isolated location, but I was more worried about letting August out of my sight, in case he had another bout of confusion, than about being on my own.

"I wouldn't ask if there were any other way," he said.

I nodded. "Go on. I'm fine."

"I'll try to be as swift as possible." He grabbed the railing to aid his descent, which was the only sign he'd given so far that Timothy's rough rescue had left his leg aching. In a moment, he had disappeared into the store.

He was gone for long enough that I was starting to consider how I might insinuate myself inside without causing too much damage. And when he did finally leave the store, he had a thick, paper-wrapped parcel in his arms.

"Just one tome, and not even a great one." He shook his head. "Hopefully the next two stores have more to offer."

And so we walked down a labyrinth of streets, some cobbled, some so muddied my shoes sank in with unpleasant squelches. August's memory failed him a couple of times, and we had to retrace our steps to find the last shop. I watched him for signs of distraction and was ready to restrain him any way I could if he gave even the slightest indication of wanting to rush into the busy streets again. But he seemed his usual self, if a bit annoyed at his memory lapses.

At least, by the time we opened the door to our chambers at the Salisbury later that afternoon, we had six books to scrutinize.

August handed me one of the volumes. "This shouldn't burn you, but don't lay a finger on that one," he said, pointing to the largest parcel. "Not unless you want to sear your skin off."

"Duly noted." I took the offered book, which wasn't even warm in my hands, and sat down. It was an encyclopedia of sorts, enumerating some of the most ancient occult practices around the world. The writing was so small I had to bring it up close to my eyes to be able to make out the index page. All manner of strange words became legible: "voodoo"; "Etruscan magic"; "mesmerism"; "automatic writing"; "clairomancy."

"Is there anything we can rule out?" I asked. "Something we are sure Lily will not have turned to?"

"I know nothing about Lily's magical education. She could be versed in any and all magical practices. I don't think, however, that she will have used the same trick twice."

I nodded. "No wraith, then."

"I think not."

I opened the book up at random. "We must assume that what you are hearing is connected to whatever roams the factory, though, because it is quite similar to what happened to me yesterday."

"Except for the bells. You didn't hear them."

"No, I didn't. I did smell pipe tobacco, though, like the kind my father used to smoke."

August paused, frowning. "That is peculiar. Until you said that, I couldn't place why the bells sound so familiar. But I remember now . . . my mother used a hand bell to call for her breakfast that sounded exactly the same. How had I forgotten that?"

I looked up at him. "Then both of us have heard or smelled something that reminds us of our childhood?"

"Perhaps of happier or safer times. Times when things still made some kind of sense."

I nodded. "That could be how it lures us, then, whatever this thing is."

"Except that I keep hearing them, no matter where I am, while the effect wore off for you."

"When did it start?"

August sat down with a sigh. "The moment I stepped onto the factory floor, and I've heard them every day since."

I tried not to flinch. He had kept it from me for days. He hadn't trusted me with that knowledge for days.

Because you are of no importance.

I gritted my teeth.

I'd noticed a few moments of distraction, of him blinking away thoughts, but I had never imagined . . .

There was no point in dwelling on that now. We needed to find out how to stop the effect. "Well, that proves it, then. This is Lily's new nightmare at work, but it's latched on to you and not me. Perhaps because of the nature of my powers."

"There's every possibility you are right, Anne, but it doesn't bring us any closer to finding out what to do about it."

"We'll find something in these books," I said.

He smiled softly. "I'm sure we will."

We wasted no more time, and each dove into our chosen reading. The encyclopedia's text was dense, full of words I had never seen before and didn't have the vaguest idea as to what they might mean. I searched for mentions of bells or similar phenomena, but the ones I found dealt mainly with ghostly appearances, none of which had any bearing on our circumstances. Nevertheless, I jotted these mentions down on the hotel's stationery.

Every few minutes, I glanced up at August to ensure he wasn't hearing anything strange, and began to see from the slowly deepening frown on his face that he was having no better luck with his volume.

The sky darkened as the afternoon wore on. I stood to turn on some lights so that we wouldn't end up blind on top of everything else, and winced. After spending the day traipsing around London in heeled shoes, my feet were in full protest.

"Would it be too improper if I removed my shoes? I can hardly stand them anymore."

August didn't even look up from his book. "I've seen your feet, Anne. I'll do my best not to swoon."

I tossed a cushion at him, feeling immensely gratified when it hit him squarely in the face.

His shock was enough to set me laughing, chasing away—for a moment, at least—the knowledge of the death I had caused and the new one dawn would bring with it if Lily's creature was somehow able to lure one of the women into the factory.

"I'm glad to see we've progressed to the mature part of the evening," he said as he tucked the cushion next to him, but I could see a smile blooming at the corner of his mouth. "Have you found anything worthwhile in your readings?"

I glanced down at my notes. "Not unless you think the factory is being haunted by 'the spirit of a dishonored Japanese ancestor.'"

He snorted. "Unlikely. I've also had no luck. Nothing that remotely describes what we've experienced." He placed a hand at the back of his neck and moved his head from side to side. "Would you like to order supper? We can go down to the restaurant, if you prefer."

I couldn't face putting my shoes on again.

He must have read the thought on my face, because he half-smiled and said, "I'll order something."

"Oh, bless you," I said, and sat back down to continue.

Supper came and went, and still we read on.

Last night's victim suffered. There was nothing swift about her death, not with a disembowelment. It'll be the same tonight.

My hands tightened around the book in my lap, and I prayed to whoever might be listening to keep the women away. To let them heed my warning.

I sent word to Eustace that she was not to bother coming up tonight, since we wouldn't need her services. In reality, we didn't want her asking any questions. We didn't need to be thrown out of the Salisbury on suspicion of witchcraft, especially not if Scotland Yard had already heard our names mentioned in a similar accusation.

"There's nothing in this one," I said, placing the second book August had handed me on the table. "Can I touch any of the others?"

August glanced up and pointed to a book with deep blue binding. "That one should be benign enough."

I leaned forward to grab it and let out a sharp hiss as the corset cut off my breath.

August looked up, taking in my discomfort. "There's no need for you to be swaddled in all those layers, Anne. It's frustrating enough to have to read through these texts; I can't imagine what it must be like to do so in bustles and whatever other nonsense is required of you to wear in proper company. Of which I am certainly not, by the way."

My face warmed. I should have been used to his unconventional way of speaking by now, but it was still disconcerting to hear a man speak so of women's undergarments. It just wasn't done, not even in the servants' quarters.

I shouldn't even acknowledge his words, I knew that, but it had been hours and hours of compressed ribs and strangled breath. Propriety had its place, but it was difficult to honor it when my entire body ached.

I stood. I had a dressing gown I could wear over my nightdress which would be modest enough. "I'll just be a minute, then."

August nodded and went back to his reading.

It wasn't until I had stepped into my chambers and removed the rose from the small pouch of fabric I'd sewn to my dress that I realized how idiotic I'd been. Without Eustace's help, I couldn't shed even the first layer of silk, let alone undo the corset laces that ran up and down my back.

I looked at the clock on my night table. It was almost two in the morning. I couldn't call down and wake her up at this time of night, not when she had worked the entire day and had to get up to work all of tomorrow.

If I'd had a pair of scissors, I would have cut the laces myself and worried about explaining the torn dress later, but there were none. Whyever would a lady need scissors, after all?

If I walked back into the sitting room still dressed, August would ask me why and . . . I groaned.

There was no helping it.

I stepped back out of the room. "August."

"Hmm?" He was copying something from the book he held onto a sheet of stationery.

"I seem to have forgotten that I need help, uh, removing some of this clothing."

The pen he held slowed, then stopped.

"Just undoing laces and buttons. I'm not used to needing another pair of hands." I tried to sound as casual as possible, but my voice wavered.

He lowered the pen and stood. "Of course."

I turned around as he walked toward me and hoped he didn't catch the slight tremble in my hands. "They shouldn't be too difficult."

August chuckled. "I think I can handle a few knots without sending for reinforcements."

"Right. Of course."

He drew close to me and started on the laces and long line of buttons on the dress itself. I could barely feel his touch through the fabric, just a fluttering warmth on my back as he loosened the first layer, one pearl button at a time. The sweet scent that always accompanied his presence swirled around me, enveloping me while he worked his way down my back.

As soon as the silk allowed it, I undid my cuffs and tried to pull the layer off, but the corset made it impossible to tug the dress over my head. I just couldn't lift my arms high enough.

"Let me," August said softly.

He bent and picked up the hem of the dress. I felt his warmth on my bare ankles, rising up my legs and slowly to my waist. He moved with the same care I had seen him use when handling his bottles of herbs at Rosewood Manor, as if he was afraid to shatter me with the wrong touch.

The silk swished against my bare arms as I lifted them as much as I could, allowing August to completely remove the layer. He let the silk fall to the floor next to me.

The skin on my arms and down the exposed nape of my neck tingled under his gaze. Oh, how I wished for his sarcasm, now! Anything to ease the tension that was wrapped around us tighter than my laces. But he was silent as he drew near and began to undo the corset.

His soft breath traveled over my neck, sending ripples all through me. My heart crashed against my chest over and over, and I was sure he could feel it against his hands, which worked smoothly and evenly to undo the knots.

The more laces he untied, and the looser the corset got, the less breath I could catch.

"Just one more," he said. His voice was no stronger than a caress of air. His hair brushed against my neck as he reached for the set of laces at my waist.

I brought my arms to my chest to prevent the whalebone and fabric contraption from falling away completely. I had a chemise underneath, but it was as thin as onion-skin.

Once the last knot was undone and the corset was loose in my grip, August's hands stopped. He didn't move, and neither did I. It was as if the entire room held its breath.

I felt his hands hover over the almost translucent chemise that separated his skin from mine. For a long moment, he was so close to touching me, to undoing the last set of buttons that would fully uncover me and bring me closer to him, that the burn his nearness brought was painful to withstand.

A bubbling mixture of fear and anticipation overtook me.

Long, lingering caresses, Anne. Remember what I told you.

I winced as if the words had struck me.

August took a deep breath and stepped away. He cleared his throat. "You're cold, Anne. You should head on to bed. We can continue the research in the morning; there's no need to keep going now."

I didn't want to turn around, for fear that my face would betray my confused emotions, the way Lily's voice had tangled itself in my head, but nevertheless, I did. I clutched the corset tighter to my chest and turned to face him. "It's all right. I can continue."

His smile was as pale as my chemise. "Go rest. We'll start fresh tomorrow." He bent and picked up my silk dress.

"What if you hear the bells again?" I asked.

"If I feel it beginning, I'll wake you." He smoothed the fabric out in his hands.

I stepped closer, forcing his gaze to meet mine. "Will you truly?"

August's eyes glittered as if he had fire coursing through his veins. He looked quickly away and handed me the dress with a nod. "I promise."

A scream tore me from sleep.

For one bewildering instant, I was sure I was back at Rosewood Manor, the last two months erased as I leapt out of bed, my heart in my throat, and rushed to face whatever new horror the wraith had in store for us. The confusion lasted long enough for me to stub my toe on a chair that was in the completely wrong place.

The pain slammed the present back into my mind. My father's death, Lily's threat, the bells.

The shriek of shattering glass made me gasp.

"August," I said, and yanked the half-closed door open.

The lights were still on in the sitting room, making me blink after the darkness of my chamber and adding to the feeling of unreality, to the sensation that I was still dreaming.

But I knew that this was no dream.

I ran to August's room and pulled the door open.

He stood before the large, full-length mirror that was identical to the one in my room, except that this one's glass had been shattered so forcefully there was a puddle of shards at August's feet. He was frozen in front of it, clutching a blade of mirror in one hand. Blood from his palm ran down his arm to mingle with the glass on the floor.

"August!"

He didn't turn toward me. Only the slight twitch of his lips in the reflection let me know he'd heard me at all.

I crossed the length of the room. My feet were bare, but the only way to reach him was to cross the pool of glass he stood inside. I had pulled glass slivers from my flesh just yesterday. I could do it again.

As I neared, the long blade he held moved closer to his other arm, toward his wrist.

"Stop," I said, holding my hands out as if trying to appease a frightened animal. "August, please stop."

All my voice did was bring the glittering blade closer to his skin.

I summoned my power as he'd taught me, allowing it to uncoil as I lunged forward. My hands landed on his bare skin, the burn as powerful as scalding water as I released my energy.

August gasped and coughed, his eyes clearing, his face once more belonging to the man I loved. He dropped the piece of mirror.

"You promised you would wake me!" I yelled, digging my nails into his arm. "What if I hadn't heard you scream? You would be dead!"

When he spoke, his voice was hoarse, as if he had been screaming for hours. "I had no warning, Anne." He brought a hand up to cover another cough, and the marks I had left on his skin were already beginning to welt. "I couldn't do anything at all. My body was no longer under my control." He shook his head and turned eyes dark with fright to meet mine. "This is getting much, much worse."

I didn't know what to say. There were no comforting words I could offer. "Let's take care of your hand."

"It's just a cut."

How frustrating could one man be? "Just a cut? The last time you had 'just a cut' like this, I had to charge through your bloody manor to keep you from dying. Don't you think we have quite enough problems?"

Despite everything, August's lips curled into a thin smile. "Fair enough, I suppose."

I stepped out of the circle of glass, avoiding stepping on as much of it as I could, and walked into August's bathroom. It was rather similar to mine in size, but with a claw-footed bath of dark blue enamel instead of white. The porcelain tiles on the walls were also more masculine, with arabesque shapes in place of flowery etchings. The most conspicuous difference, however, was that there were no windows in this bathroom.

"Sit," I said, and pointed to a chair in the corner of the room.

While he did as I commanded, I rummaged through the drawers of the slim armoire where the towels were kept. I found nothing that resembled a bandage, but I would make do with one of the smaller hand towels. I tore strips of it with my teeth and laid them out on the washbasin's table.

"I'm sure no one in the history of the Salisbury has ever done that," August said. "Mr. Rushworth will have a fit."

"Mr. Rushworth can afford to buy more hand towels," I said, and turned on the basin's hot water faucet. I dipped one of the strips into the water until it was soaking wet. Alcohol would have been better, of course, or the carbolic acid powder that Mary kept in her kitchen for the unavoidable chopping block or carving knife cut, but this would have to do.

I draped the strips on my arm and walked over to August. "Let me see."

The cut wasn't too deep, and it had almost stopped bleeding by now, but I wrapped the wet cloth against it, anyway, followed by a few layers of dry strips, and tightened it all with a knot. My palms stung from the burns, and I was careful to avoid touching August again.

"Your powers are growing," he said as he watched my hands. "That was quite forceful, what you did back there."

"We certainly have the burns to prove it." I tucked the ends of the last strip into the rest of the bandage. "I am sorry."

"For saving my life? Because I'm quite certain that is what was at stake."

I nodded. "Whatever these bells are, they mean to kill you. Today, on the street, now this . . ." I bit my lip as I considered how best to say these next words.

"What is it?"

Out with it, then. "Lily told me that everything was about to get much worse, and that I would regret—" I stopped.

"Regret what?"

But I couldn't do it. I couldn't bring myself to tell him the truth now, not when his eyes still shone with barely smothered fear. I cleared my throat. "Helping you, I suppose. Not fleeing when the manor burned down."

He looked at me. "I sometimes wonder the same thing."

"August, you know why I'm here. You know I l—"

His eyelids fluttered, and his hands tensed into fists on his lap. His gaze lost its sharpness and its light, dulling under a sheen of internal shadows.

"August?" But I knew it was happening again.

His entire body was as rigid as marble as I placed a hand on his wrist and sent a current of power through my fingertips. As soon as I did, he gasped and returned to me.

"You heard them."

He closed his eyes. "I had no warning at all."

"I know."

"And it is happening more often."

My voice was a whisper. "Yes."

We both flinched at the sound of a knock on the sitting room door. A muffled man's voice called out, "Lord Grey, Lady Grey?"

August stood, but I stopped him. "I'll get it. If they see you with an injury, they'll want to summon a doctor, and that is not the wisest idea right now."

"One moment," I called as I walked out of August's room and toward the front door. It was only as I turned the handle that I remembered I was still only in my nightdress, but by then, it was too late.

Mr. Rushworth did his best not to look too shocked by my near nakedness, but failed as his eyes widened and color rose to his cheeks.

"I'm, uh, I'm sorry to disturb you, madam, but one of the guests was concerned about a scream they heard coming from this room. I wanted to ascertain that you and Lord Grey were well."

"A scream? How peculiar. No, we are both perfectly all right. A mirror did fall and break, however; perhaps they mistook that sound for someone screaming." I gave him my most pleasant smile.

"Ah, perhaps. Would you like someone to come clear the glass, madam?"

"That's very kind, but it can wait until the morning."

"It wouldn't be any trouble at all."

Damn his efficiency. "My husband is sleeping, and I would rather not wake him. It really can wait until tomorrow."

He bowed his head. "As you wish, madam. Neither of you were injured?"

"Thank you for your concern, Mr. Rushworth, but we are both just fine." I nodded a dismissal and closed the door.

If I had ever uttered a bigger lie, I couldn't recall it.

The night felt interminable. Hour after hour, I was aware of August's every move as I sat next to him, watching for the slightest tension, for his hands curling into fists, his tightening mouth. I fought against my own insistent exhaustion that refused to be shoved aside no matter how worried each passing moment made me.

Because it *was* happening more and more often. To the point where not even half an hour would go by without me having to drag him out of a bell-infested nightmare with my touch. I should have expected this sudden escalation from Lily's creature. I knew how her mind worked. She would be doing her utmost to show me just what a mistake I had made in choosing to stay with August, and she would continue to amplify the effects until one, or both, of us broke.

I had no idea what to do. Despite having been born with this Grounding ability of mine, I had no natural instinct about this situation. So I allowed my years of service to take over. I made sure he drank water throughout the night, that his cut was no longer bleeding, that the burns I'd caused were not too painful, that he was warm enough and comfortable on the sofa where we had decided to perch ourselves for the night.

"Enough, Anne. I don't need any more blasted pillows. Just sit down."

I did, but it was difficult to remain still and watch him struggle against this thing that could not be controlled.

It was still a bit before dawn seeped through the windows—*has another life been snuffed out, Anne?*—when I found that my touch no longer had the same effect on August that it'd had just hours before.

He had tensed next to me, his eyes clouding, and I'd grabbed his bare hand, just as I'd done for each of his fits. For one chilling moment, his skin had brought no burn to mine. It had been like touching anyone else. It was just a beat of time, and then the normal pain had returned, but that second of nothingness was enough to frighten me in a way that not even the wraith had managed to do.

Pretty soon, I realized, I would not be able to help him at all.

"August," I said when I had managed to lead him back into consciousness.

"Yes?"

I turned to look at his pale, exhausted face. He wouldn't last another night like this one—not with his sanity intact, at least, and I wasn't sure I could manage it, either.

"We need help."

NINE

I LOOKED DOWN AT THE NUMBERS WRITTEN IN August's tight script on a piece of hotel stationery, and then back up at the shop before me.

The numbers matched, but there were no signs of life, of the bustling enterprise I'd expected from an apothecary in London. I squinted to see the words etched on the glass door. *Apothecary*, it read, *By Appointment Only*. Well, I suppose that explained the lack of foot traffic.

"Ask for a Mr. Price," August had said to me before I left. "Tell him as much as you can about what is happening."

"Will he believe me?" I'd looked around August's bathroom for anything else he could use to harm himself when he next heard the bells again. I had already removed the shaving mirror and razors, all the towels, the toiletries, and even the bathtub's stopper in case he thought drowning was a good way to greet the morning. The room was, as far as I could tell, safe.

"For decades, he supplied the Brothers with all manner of magical ingredients," he'd said. "He is well aware of our abilities. I just hope he is still among the living."

I'd locked August in his bathroom and taken the key with me in case Eustace decided to enter the room despite my insistence that she take the day off. Leaving him alone in his state was not exactly the best idea, but neither was allowing him to leave our chambers until we'd found some answers.

It had taken almost half an hour to reach the apothecary's shop, my hands tightening against the note I held every time the traffic brought the carriage to a jarring halt. Images of the most horrendous nature flashed through my mind as time slipped away from me. What would I find when I returned to our chambers?

But I was finally here, and I would not waste another minute.

I walked to the door and pulled on the handle. It answered me with a dry *click*. Locked.

There were no strings to pull that would announce my presence by jingling a bell, and it was difficult to see inside the darkened store, even when I cupped my hands over the glass and peered inside.

"I'll be damned if I came all this way to be stopped by a locked door," I said. I brought a hand up and knocked.

There was no sound from inside, no movement at all, but my whole being *knew* there was someone in there. It knew it the same skin-prickling way it had known something was wrong with Rosewood Manor the moment I'd arrived.

I knocked again. And again.

I must have stood there rapping on the glass for a good ten minutes before I saw a silhouette move inside the shop.

"Mr. Price," I called out. "I need to speak to you. Please, it's an emergency."

There was a *click* as a key turned and the lock disengaged. The door opened, and a man who could not be younger than seventy appeared, his skin as creased as if it had been folded over and over like a piece of paper. His eyes, however, could easily have been a younger man's.

"Miss, my services are by appointment only."

"You are Mr. Price, then?"

"I am," he said, "but I'm afraid I cannot help you."

"*Silasi almahodin tuori,*" I said, the inflections as close to the way August had said the words as I could remember.

The man's eyes narrowed. Had I said them incorrectly, or did he not know what they meant? His lips suddenly tightened, and he stepped away from the door. "Inside. Now."

I did as I was told and entered the dark shop. It was much warmer than the spring day outside, almost uncomfortably so, not even a sigh of fresh air circulating the cramped space. For it was a small shop, made even more so by the shelves of glass bottles and jars covered in a fine layer of dust. Some of them held liquids in a range of colors, but most of them sat empty. Some bottles even had hair-thin cracks that would have made holding any liquid at all impossible. If the shop had ever been a working apothecary, it certainly wasn't one now.

The door closed behind me.

"You should not know those words," Mr. Price said.

I turned to meet his eyes. "I need your help, sir."

"They have not been uttered by a woman in centuries. It is blasphemous that you should speak them." He took a step toward me, and I couldn't help but back away, even as I back further into the darkened shop.

"I . . . I know about the Brothers."

"That is impossible," he said. "Women are not allowed to learn about the Order."

I frowned. "'With honor and power.' That's what those words mean. I know all about the Order, about the abilities the members had, about the Master, even about their deaths."

Mr. Price watched me as if he expected me to vanish at any moment, as if I were just something his imagination had conjured. "How did you come by this information? If you know that the Brothers died tragically, every single one of them, then who told you about the Order?"

I hesitated only for an instant. "Not all of them, sir. August Grey is still alive. That is why I'm here. He . . . needs your assistance. He's under some kind of curse."

Mr. Price's face lost what little pleasantness it still contained. When he spoke next, his voice was a snarl. "Of course it would be Grey revealing the Order's secrets to a woman. Not only a murderer and a coward, but now a traitor, as well." He snorted. "He will receive no help from me. Unlike him, *I* believe in loyalty."

"And I had such hopes that he would drink himself to death as his worthless father did."

I gasped and turned to face the man who had spoken behind me. He was leaning against a doorway I hadn't seen in the darkness of the shop's interior. He looked younger than Mr. Price, with an air of movement to him, like a cat waiting to spring. He had the coldest blue eyes I had ever seen.

I swallowed a knot of fear.

"He always thought he was so much better that the rest of us," this man said. "More powerful, richer, of nobler lineage.

A laugh, really, when you consider his drunk of a father and his irrational, foolish mother."

"You're one of them?" I asked.

"A Brother, yes," the man said.

"But you . . . you're alive."

"Observant of you. I was fortunate enough to slip out of the room before August decided to murder our Brethren. He and I are the only ones left. But," he said, moving away from the doorway, "the real question is why August would send you here, to Mr. Price. To have the gall to not only come asking for help—if I heard that correctly—from the very people he betrayed, but to also reveal our sacred oath to a woman."

The fine hairs on my arms prickled as a wave of power fueled by his rising anger filled the shop. "He didn't betray you. That was not how it happened, and you both know it. The Master set him up to die that night."

"And quite right, too, for turning away from the Brothers and every generosity the Master had ever offered him, including his own daughter's hand," Mr. Price said.

The man in front of me nodded. "No one has ever left the Order in all its history, and then along comes August, expecting different treatment. He should have accepted his punishment with honor." He stared at me as if trying to pick me apart, bone by bone. "And what makes *you* so special that you should know about the Brothers?"

I couldn't hold the words back any longer. "Lily Bellingham knows about the Order and about magic. She is the one behind the malady August suffers from."

"Miss Bellingham is dead," Mr. Price said.

"She is not. She falsified her death, and—"

"And even if she were not," the younger man said, as if I hadn't spoken, "she would not have the means of placing any kind of enchantment on anyone. Yes, she dabbled in magic with her father's indulgence as a child, but the Master soon put an end to that when she was old enough to marry." He waved a hand in my direction. "Women are never vehicles for the kind of power our work requires. They have limited abilities."

I gritted my teeth together.

He really believed that nonsense, and from his furious nodding, so did Mr. Price. They had not even the vaguest idea of what Lily was capable of doing, of how she had managed to harness the kind of power these men, even August, could not compete with.

She had been shoved aside to become a beautiful, glittering ornament on a man's arm when in fact, she was brimming with magic. I felt no sympathy for Lily for the horror and deaths she had caused, but to have been denied her powers, to have been forced into an unnatural isolation by her father, and to have had the man she loved reject her the way August had . . . it made the chaos I had seen inside her head more comprehensible, if not excusable.

These men were archaic, I realized. Steeped in their traditions, without the potential to change or improve.

"Neither of you will help, then?"

The younger man smiled, a scar on his upper lip stretching with the effort. "Not unless it is to help August toward a speedier death. I just hope that whoever cursed him has the backbone to bring it to its conclusion."

I shook my head. "I can see why August might have thought you were beneath him. You are."

I turned on my heels and headed for the front door.

"How dare you," the man said. His voice was as flat as water in a glass, but it wasn't his voice which worried me. It was the crackling energy emanating from him, growing in the air all around me, closing in like an invisible, stinging fishnet. I tried to take another step toward the door.

"You will turn to look at me when I speak to you, woman," he said, and a whip of power grabbed my shoulders.

That was enough nonsense for one morning.

Uncoiling my own power from wherever it slept, I shoved the alien energy back. It was surprisingly easy to do, much easier to handle than August's power, let alone Lily's. Whatever this man thought he was, the possessor of extraordinary magical abilities he was not.

I only realized my mistake when he sucked in a sharp breath. I turned to meet his widening eyes. Bloody hell, I had overplayed my hand.

"It can't be," he said.

"What is it?" Mr. Price asked.

But the man only shook his head, unable to tear his attention from me. The shield of power I had surrounded myself with pulsed like a heart around me, ready for the next onslaught.

"I've only read about them in books," the younger man said, his voice hushed. "I didn't even truly believe they existed. And to appear as a woman . . ."

"What are you talking about?"

The man nodded in my direction. "She's a Grounder."

At the utterance of that word, Mr. Price's head jerked in my direction. "But . . . but that's impossible." His eyes traveled up and down my body, taking in my small stature, my dress, the way I held myself, his disbelief growing. "Are you certain?"

"Of course I am." The man practically growled the words out. "I've studied my whole life to find one. And here one is."

My whole being shivered with the surge of anticipation coming from the younger man. A harsh internal warning set my heart pounding. I had to get out of here. Now.

"Perhaps we should hold on to her," Mr. Price said, "until we decide what to do next."

Yes, definitely the moment to make a hasty retreat. I took a step backward, my hand stretching out for the doorknob.

"Where are you going in such a hurry?"

A bolt of something hot hit my legs. I yelped in pain, tried to jump back, but found I could no longer feel anything below my waist. I scrambled to gather my power together once again, to put up some kind of defense, but another jolt of heat hit my chest, scattering my concentration.

My torso became as stiff as a tree's trunk. One more hit of power, and I'd be completely immobilized.

I did the only thing I could think of in my panic. My right hand fumbled for one of the low display shelves next to the door and closed around a glass decanter. I threw it at the younger man with all the strength I had.

My aim was true.

The decanter slammed into his head, the delicate glass shattering on contact. His concentration broke as he groaned in pain, and my limbs were once again my own.

Without allowing either man to utter even one more word, I yanked the door open and ran out into London's streets.

Half an hour later, I closed the door to our rooms at the Salisbury and finally allowed myself to take a deep breath.

After rushing out of the apothecary's shop, I had continued to run for blocks and blocks, drawing all manner of stares from bystanders as I raced past in my lady's day gown. Sweat trickled down my back under all the layers of cotton, silk, and lace.

I wiped my forehead with a hand and took a deep breath.

"Anne?" August called from the bathroom in his chamber.

"Coming."

I entered his bedroom, clutching the key to the bathroom door, and saw a full water carafe on a side table. A wisp of annoyance made me frown. I told Eustace not to come in today for any reason, and yet she had disobeyed.

My thoughts brought me up short. Disobeyed? It wasn't more than a few months ago that I had been in Eustace's place, working for a difficult employer, handling peculiar demands I wasn't accustomed to. Surely I could be generous in forgiving her mistakes when I had made plenty of them myself. Besides, fresh water was always welcomed.

I walked to the table and poured some of it into the sparkling glass next to the carafe. I slipped the key into the bathroom door and turned it.

August sat on the floor, his arms wrapped around his knees. There was such a gleam of expectation on his face that it pained me to look at him.

I shook my head.

August sighed and closed his eyes for a moment. "I should have known."

I knelt in front of him and offered him the glass of water. "They did not want to help."

"They?"

"There was another man with Mr. Price. He claimed to be a Brother."

August took the glass from me. "I thought all of them were present that awful night."

"They were. This man slipped out before the whole thing began."

He took a sip of water. "Did he tell you his name?"

"No, but he was a bit younger than Mr. Price, of medium height. He expressed obvious contempt for women."

August shrugged. "That was most Brothers. They found women beautiful to look at, but utterly unimportant in the larger scheme of things."

And you don't? You, who tossed a woman out of your life when she was no longer of any use to you?

The words stung like rubbing alcohol on a bare wound.

"He also had very blue eyes. Almost white," I continued, forcing Lily's voice back. "And a small scar on his upper lip."

"Ah. That is John Thompson, then. His family has been in the Order for generations. An insufferable man." He looked down at his hands. "But at least that is one less person I killed."

I didn't want to further burden August with the knowledge that this John Thompson had discovered what I was, but I also didn't want to keep another secret from him. One was more than plenty.

"What is it, Anne?"

"I don't know if it's important right now."

"All the same, I'd rather know."

I sighed. "They are aware of my abilities."

August frowned. "Are you certain?"

I nodded. "Thompson even mentioned the name. He knew that I was a Grounder."

August leapt to his feet, spilling half the water out of the glass, and I jerked back. I always managed to forget just how much energy he had trapped inside that thin, lanky frame of his.

"Blast it all," he said. "I shouldn't have sent you. I should have gone myself."

"Oh, yes, that would have made things much better," I said, rolling my eyes. "They would have been more than happy to serve you a teacup full of strychnine or kindly help you through a window." I shook my head. "There will be no aid from that quarter."

"Perhaps you are right," he said, "but they will be looking for you now that they know. I don't think you understand how unusual someone with your abilities is. How valuable a tool for a magician."

I looked down as a gurgle of deep, smoke-filled laughter echoed through me.

Ask.

"That's all I am, then? A tool?"

"I will not dignify such a ridiculous question with an answer. You know better than that, Anne."

Yes, of course I did. Of course.

And yet . . . what was I, really? Not a parlor maid, not a lover, certainly not a wife. He cared for me, I was sure of it—*of course you are*—but what was I doing here? He hadn't made any promises to me, and I hadn't and wouldn't ask him to do so, which meant that we could continue as we were for years. Pretending to be what we were not. Me, following after him. I loved him, yes, but was that enough?

Don't you want more than just "enough"?

"Oh, it doesn't matter," I said, to myself, to Lily's voice, to him. If we didn't find a solution to this, and soon, August and I would have no future to worry about.

"I didn't say where we were living," I continued, "or anything that might help them find us, so we should be all right."

August was silent.

I looked up and saw him standing before one of the walls, his body as stiff as the plaster.

I stood. "August?"

He lifted a hand, curling it into a fist, and slammed it into the wall.

Quickly, I walked toward him. There was nothing on his face, his eyes as empty and lusterless as the ones on Lord Caldwell's mounted deer heads. Whatever it is that made August himself had been emptied out in an instant.

Unlike the night before, when I had seen the twitch of his will doing its best to return to his body, I saw nothing I recognized in his face now.

Once again, he brought his fist against the wall. And again.

"Stop, you'll injure yourself," I said. I placed my hands on his wrists and found the same delay in the usual burn. My power surged forward unimpeded, meeting no resistance. Even seconds later, when a tepid wave of August's energy finally found its way free and crashed into mine, it made no difference.

He was gone.

He stayed gone for hours. Whatever had taken control of his body had forced him to pace the bathroom without pause. I sat beside the door listening to him, willing August to find his way back, asking a God I had never really believed in for the smallest bit of help.

I must have fallen asleep like that, against the bathroom door, because the dry *click* of the front door opening shook me awake.

"Lady Grey?"

I cleared my throat. "I'll be right out, Eustace." The pacing behind the door had stopped, at least, but I knew that if August had returned to himself, he would have called for me.

I got to my feet and walked out into the sitting room. Eustace stood with her hands folded against her lap.

"I am sorry to disturb you, madam, but I wasn't certain if you needed my services tonight."

"I do, Eustace, thank you." My smile was so tight I feared it would snap in two, but I had to maintain a semblance of normalcy or risk questions.

As she helped me undress, I did my best to ask her about her family, and her health, while waving aside her apologies whenever she pulled too tightly on the corset strings. I drew her attention away from the silence in the other chamber and the shadows under my eyes with mindless chatter that consumed the last dregs of energy I had left.

By the time Eustace retired to bed, I didn't think I could spend another second on my feet. I'd already decided to sleep in August's chamber so I could be there to unlock the door when he called. Or at least, I'd attempt to sleep. Though my body ached with exhaustion, my mind kept spinning with worry, filling my head with the worst scenarios it could conceive. And it could conceive of many.

With a sigh, I turned to get my dressing gown from where it lay on the bed and instantly felt like the floor had given way beneath me.

On the night table, as usual, sat August's rose in its glass of water.

Next to it on the table was a single fallen petal, wrinkled and bruised, its edges puckered as if by flame.

Tears burned in my tired eyes.

He had promised me the rose would bloom, unfading in beauty and strength, for as long as he was alive. And now . . .

I picked up the petal with a trembling hand. It was limp between my fingers, the color already turning from vibrant red to the dullest brown.

The rest of the flower appeared as it always did, but that did not remove the thorn of fear digging itself deeper into my heart. That single fallen petal could mean only one thing: the rose was dying.

And if the rose was dying, then so was August.

TEN

I NEEDED TO RUN, BUT I COULDN'T MOVE. MY feet kept tangling with each other; the floor had lost its hard surface and become flexible. Strings wrapped around my ankles and feet, pulling me down, down, down, until my face was pressed against the writhing floor. I couldn't draw breath. I couldn't—

"Anne."

The voice was like the sharpest pair of scissors ever made, snipping at the strings that held me in an instant, allowing me to stand.

My eyes opened to a room stained with the beginnings of a new day. I lay on the floor next to the bathroom door, where I had placed a pillow and a coverlet. I had expected to toss and turn the whole night, but it appeared my body had thought differently.

"August?" I murmured as I remembered the voice in my dream.

"Yes."

I sat up, fumbling for the key I'd left on the floor beside me, and unlocked the door.

August smiled lightly when he saw me. It was as wan a thing as the sun's dawning rays on the floor. His eyelids flickered, and I had only a moment to race to him before his legs gave out.

"August, stay awake. I can't carry you." I held him up as well as I could by placing my shoulder under his arm, but he was too heavy.

His body was so tepid against mine that I knew my touch would not burn him enough to keep him awake. Instead, I grabbed the hand that still had the cut from the shard of mirror and pressed my fingernails into the wound.

Pain brought his eyes back into focus, and his legs steadied themselves somewhat.

"Come on. It's just a few steps to the bed."

"I'm so tired," he said against my ear.

"I know. You can rest now, I promise, just a little bit more."

As soon as we neared the bed, I shifted his weight so that all he had to do was bend his legs. He eased down onto the pillow, his chest heaving with the effort to stay conscious.

"I . . . don't . . ." His voice came as if from a deep well, faint and breathy.

"Don't talk now. Just rest."

He had already slipped away again, though this time, it was only into sleep. Doing my best not to wake him—though I very much doubted that that would be so easy to do, considering how deeply and steadily he breathed—I covered him with a blanket and sat down to wait for him once more.

Relief at having him back soured into further worry as the hours ticked past and he slept on. Whatever had happened to him, it had depleted his strength in a way that hadn't occurred before. How could he help me find out how to heal him if he was either gone from his own body and mind, or so exhausted he could not remain conscious?

I spent the morning hours rereading the magical books I could touch without burning myself and still found nothing of use. I thought with longing of the pile of books in August's rooms at Rosewood Manor. They would have held the information we needed.

At midday, Eustace brought in the day's newspaper, its bold front-page headline announcing another death at Wodenhouse Mill. Lily had many faults, but she certainly kept her word. She'd found a way to get one of the women into the factory.

The guilt of it made me toss the paper aside. "It is no one's fault but hers," I murmured, but the words no longer held the conviction they once had. I refused to leave August, especially now, but I couldn't watch this continue. There had to be a way to get back inside Wodenhouse and keep investigating. Even if none of the workers spoke with me, I might still be able to find out what had been up there on the second story.

"I have to go back to the factory," I said softly.

"Not on your own, you won't," August said.

I gasped and hurried to his side. The afternoon light had dimmed enough for me to require the bedside lamp to see him.

"Hi," I said with a smile. "I'm sorry if I woke you. How are you feeling?"

"You are not going to the factory alone, Anne."

He looked more like himself. Some of his normal color had returned, and his eyes held the familiar sharp glint of intelligence that could be so easily cut. If I hadn't seen it myself, I wouldn't have believed that that spark could be swept away so effortlessly, leaving behind nothing but a shell.

"There's been another death," I said. "If I could just get inside again, I might be able to find something that could help us understand what's happening."

"And have you forgotten your last foray to the second story? The one that almost ended with your skull sliced in two by a sheet of glass?"

"I'll be more careful."

August sat up. "You are not going alone."

"Well, it's not as if you can come with me," I said.

His lip curled into a half-smile as he turned to look at me. "You are still not going alone."

I sighed. I didn't want to argue about this now. "How are you feeling?"

"Better." He cleared his throat and looked away. "How long?"

"You were asleep for about eight hours, and, uh, gone for most of yesterday."

He exhaled and closed his eyes for a moment. "A day and a half. Lost."

"What are we going to do?"

With one of his sudden gusts of energy, August flung the blanket aside and got to his feet. "A banishment."

I frowned. "Like we did for the wraith?"

"Not quite. We'll have to widen the boundaries of the banishment, since we know nothing about this creature except for the person who cast it. Which is, considering last time"—he shook his head—"ironic, I suppose. We'll perform the banishment directly on me."

"But is that safe? I mean, won't that do something to your own powers?"

He brought his hand up to his shirt's collar, which I only now noticed was standing wide open. "It shouldn't, but it's impossible to know for certain with magic. Still, it is the only thing I can think of that might have some effect."

August walked to the ornate desk by the window and took up one of his dark cravats. He tossed the fabric around his neck with the ease of years of practice and began tying it. Seeing him act as normal as he ever had released the tight knot right in the center of my chest. He looked healthy, stronger even than he had at Rosewood Manor. Perhaps I had been wrong about the rose. Perhaps it had meant nothing more than a malfunctioning enchantment.

"I am going to need a few items for this. Most of them should be simple enough to find," he said as he smoothed the fabric out, "but the last one could be a problem. Is this on straight?"

I nodded. "Surprisingly so. Why would the last one be a problem?"

"It's a rare enough crystal that I know of only one shop in all of London that used to carry it. If you walk into that store and ask for one, heads will turn, Anne. As I am sure you have gathered by now, women are not entirely welcomed in the world of powerful magic."

"Yes, the point has been made."

His eyes were fixed on mine. "Your gender alone will draw suspicion, but that is not all. The men who run the shop are not Brothers, but they know everything there is to know about magical crystals. That means that they also know about everything that can affect them, like Grounders. They won't take too kindly to one walking through their collection of precious crystals, a simple touch away from destroying their wares."

"I am not planning on announcing it," I said.

"No, but can you manage to restrain your hands from touching anything at all? It is not, if I recall correctly, something that comes naturally for you."

My mouth opened, but I couldn't think of anything to say. He was right; my hands did often seem to have a mind of their own. That tendency had gotten me into trouble more than once at Caldwell House, and it had almost killed me at Rosewood Manor.

August's eyes widened at my silence. "Nothing, Anne? Not a single rebuttal? I'm shocked by the civility."

I crossed my arms. "And I am shocked you can recognize civility."

He smiled. "Right, well, just be sure not to touch anything. That includes the crystal we need. Assuming, of course, that the shop is even still on its feet and the owners don't laugh you out into the street before you can tell them what you would like to purchase."

"Yes, sir," I said with a half-curtsey so badly performed it was shameful even to me. I was certainly out of practice. "I'll grab my handbag and call for a carriage."

August glanced at the tepid light coming in through the window. His smile, which had grown brighter at my feeble attempt at mock reverence, slipped away as quickly as the hours of the last day and a half had drained from his life. "It'll be dark soon, and the shops will be closing. Tomorrow will have to do. I suppose I'd best write the items down in case I'm not myself in the morning."

The weight of reality returned to the room like a heavy fog.

I walked over to August's side and encircled his thin arm in mine. His taut muscles relaxed under my touch, though I hadn't even thought to call my power forward. I leaned my head against his sleeve and willed him to stay with me.

Together, we watched the night arrive.

"A crystal, ma'am?" Timothy said, cocking an eyebrow like he had never heard of such a ridiculous request in his short life.

"Yes." I opened the piece of paper August had given me last night and pointed to a rough drawing he'd made in ink. "It looks like this, with beveled edges just like these. It's a dark green color, but it doesn't shine too much."

The boy frowned at the drawing. "Ain't never 'eard of one that don't shine."

"This is a special crystal. One I very much need." I glanced up and out of the alleyway in which we stood, one street away from the shop. It would not do to have the owners see me.

As August had said, most of the items had taken less than a couple of hours to gather. A black hand bell was common enough, as was chalk, a piece of strong rope, and a dropper bottle. All I had left was this crystal.

"What's it called again?" Timothy asked.

"Moldonite. But you don't have to worry about remembering the name. It's all written here." I handed him the piece of paper with the crystal's drawing, the name of the stone, and, beneath it, the Brothers' oath written in the language of magic. "You just hand this piece of paper to the man behind the counter and he will help you."

I hoped.

He looked down at the words. "And that's all?"

"He will ask you who the crystal is for, and you must tell him that your master sent you to buy it. Don't mention any names, no matter how much he insists, and be sure to ask to see the crystal before handing him the payment. If it doesn't look like this, then it is the wrong one." I bit my bottom lip. "Can you do that, Timothy?"

Perhaps this was asking too much of him. He was just a boy. But if not him, then who?

I'd thought about the best way to acquire the crystal as I waited for any bit of sleep I could gather the previous evening, and this was the only possibility. It was too risky to go myself, and the few people we knew in London would have asked more questions than we wanted to answer. Except for Timothy. He could easily pass as an apprentice or a servant sent out on an errand, and though he couldn't read the words on the paper he held, he was a bright boy.

And apparently, a courageous one, too, since there was no hesitation at all as he pocketed the purse full of pounds I'd given him and turned toward the street. "Of course, ma'am. I'll get what you need."

I held my breath and watched him walk out of the alley and into the muddied streets. He strolled with absolute confidence, as if this were an everyday errand and not one that had spun through my head for hours the previous night.

"Please, please, please," I said under my breath as he disappeared from sight.

I leaned against the brick wall of the building behind which I was hiding and forced myself to calm. He would be able to get the crystal, and I would be able to head back to the hotel and unlock August from the bathroom. We would do the banishment and perhaps . . . yes, perhaps he would be all right.

My hand brushed the hidden pocket where the rose usually lay and my mouth tightened when I remembered I didn't have it with me. I'd left it behind, too afraid to jostle it around the entire day.

The needling voice of doubt that had followed me all of last night and all of this morning had returned.

What if the banishment didn't work?

Trying to see through that possibility was like trying to stare directly at the summer sun. I had no idea what we would do, then. Even if I left August, as Lily had demanded, she had already made it abundantly clear that she would continue to haunt him for as long as he was alive. Which, if the rose now perched in a glass of water on my night table was any indication, would not be for much longer. Leaving him would not keep him safe.

It would help the women at the factory, though.

I shook my head at myself.

No. I couldn't do it. I couldn't just leave him.

Laughter from the street pulled me away from that blinding thought. I frowned at the familiar sound.

"And then I told her that if she did it again, I'd put ink in her morning tea."

Two sets of female voices spun off into giggles and left me with no question whatsoever about what it was I was hearing. One of those voices was Elsie's.

I pushed away from the wall on instinct, ready to run across the street and embrace her. There was so much I had to tell her, about everything that had happened at Rosewood Manor, about my father, about August, about my abilities, about our current nightmare.

That stopped me. Lily was looking for anything she could use to punish me and force my hand into leaving August. If she realized how much Elsie meant to me, that she wasn't just someone I had worked beside for years, but was as much of a sister as I would ever have, nothing would stop her from harming her.

I took a step back, drawing further into the shade of the alleyway. Moments later, she and another young woman I didn't recognize, walked by. Neither saw me where I lurked among the shadows.

It felt like a hand had wrapped itself tight around my heart when I saw her. Elsie looked the same as always, her golden hair tucked into a rather messy bun and her simple day dress already swarming with wrinkles though it was only noon or so. I smiled. She never could keep it pressed for more than an hour.

Both of them were out of uniform and looked to be in no hurry, so it had to be their half-free day. Perhaps the other young woman, the one now saying something so apparently amusing Elsie had to lean on a wall to keep from falling with laughter, was the person who had replaced me in the household. Who now shared a room with Elsie.

It should have given me comfort to know that she was happy and not alone, but the laughter and chatter only brought into stark relief what I was doing, skulking in an alleyway in the middle of the day. She lived her life in sunlight, while for months now, shadows had been my home. We were so far removed from one another, she could have been in a different country instead of just across the street.

Maybe one day, if all of this ended, I might be able to embrace her and tell her everything that had occurred since we last saw each other.

But not today.

A sudden, booming yell made Elsie and the other woman turn their heads to the other side of the street.

In the direction of the crystal shop.

The clatter of running filled the alleyway as a blur of movement raced through the opposite street.

"Ma'am!" Timothy yelled, waving at me in panic, and without stopping. "I 'ave it! Come on!"

He had the crystal! But there was no time to celebrate, apparently. I didn't think twice about it. I picked up my skirts and launched into a run after him.

"Stop!" a man yelled. "Thief! He's a thief!"

I heard a shocked, "Anne?" from behind me, but I forced myself not to glance in Elsie's direction. All I did was keep my eyes locked on the small figure weaving himself at an in-credible pace through the cluster of people on the sidewalk, his bare feet sure on the muddied stones while I cursed at my heels.

Pedestrians all around me turned to look. It was common enough to see a waif of a boy careening down a crowded street, but not a woman dressed as I was. Ladies did not run, they sauntered, and here I was, my skirts flapping, my carefully coifed hair coming undone, beads of sweat trickling down the sides of my face. It would have been amusing in other circumstances.

Timothy sprinted into the middle of the street, bringing coachmen to a confused halt and only narrowly avoiding the wheel of a carriage. I followed him through the chaos of angry men and panting horses, my chest heaving as I tried to keep up. Only when I had made it to the opposite side of the street did I risk a glance back.

The man pursuing us—one of the shop owners, I assumed—was still giving chase. He was agile for a man who looked not a day younger than fifty, but the commotion on the street had forced him to slow down. He was much larger than Timothy and I were, and it wasn't as simple for him to maneuver around the carriages as it had been for us.

"Ma'am!"

I looked up and saw the boy waving me forward.

"This way!" he called as he took a corner at full speed.

I followed, praying that I wouldn't collide with anyone. He led us into a side street, which, though less crowded, was also narrower.

"Pardon me," I said as my shoulder bumped against a man carrying a sack of vegetables well past their prime, if their smell was any indication.

He muttered something I didn't catch before he continued on. I turned away from him, looking for Timothy's small figure, but he was no longer in front of me. Fear chilled the sweat around my collar.

I looked all around me, drawing further stares with my frantic movements, but he had disappeared. I walked to where the street came to a walled end, two branching side streets leading off of it.

"Timothy!"

There was no answer. He had probably run on while I was distracted by the man with the vegetables. But I had no idea which street he'd taken.

"Bloody hell," I said, and smacked one of the walls with my palm.

A woman passing by gasped at my curse, but I had already lost time trying to be polite.

Left or right. He could have gone either way, and I had to make the decision now, before the man chasing us saw me. He'd been following my skirts long enough now to have realized that Timothy and I were connected.

Both streets looked the same, but I chose the one on the right, which had more people walking through it. They would at least provide a bit of cover from the shop owner. The last thing I needed right now was to be dragged into Scotland Yard for stealing.

I turned, ready to start running again, when a hand reached out from the wall in front of me and grasped my arm.

I couldn't hold back my squeal of surprise.

It took me an instant to recognize what I was seeing. A section of the wall in front of me had shifted inward, revealing half of Timothy's face. I blinked in surprise. I'd heard about these kinds of passages in London, but I had never seen one before.

"In 'ere, ma'am."

I didn't stop to think whether my dress, with all of its voluminous volume, would fit, but squeezed myself through the narrow space, pulling at my skirts so that Timothy could replace the piece of wall before the shop owner saw.

The darkness was absolute.

"Timothy?" I stretched a hand out, tapping the air to get a sense of the dimensions around me.

There was a soft hiss, and the glow of a lamp dispelled the darkness. In front of me, Timothy smiled and stood on the tips of his toes to place the gas lamp he held on a wooden ledge nailed next to the door.

"Life saver, this," he said, nodding to the light. "I would 'ave cracked my 'ead open at least a dozen times runnin' through the tunnels without it." He reached into the pocket of his stained short trousers and pulled something out. He held his closed hand out to me with a grin that would have looked right at home on a woodland imp, and slowly uncurled his fingers.

The crystal was the deep green of holly leaves. It didn't shine or glitter, not even when Timothy held it up to the lamp and turned it from side to side. It was as if it had trapped the light, catching it in its beveled surfaces and swallowing it whole. But its power was palpable. I felt it against the roof of my mouth, on my tongue, metallic like blood.

"It's the right one, ma'am?"

I smiled. "Yes. This is what we needed."

"Good, because I didn't want to 'ave run all this way for nothing.'"

"Why did you take it? Was it more expensive than I anticipated?"

He shook his head. "No, ma'am. The owner wanted to know who my master was, as you warned me, and I told 'im it weren't none of 'is concern. Didn't take too kindly to that, saying 'e wouldn't sell it to me without my master comin' in person. I acted all contrite like, and asked 'im to show me the crystal, so I could at least make sure it was the right one before draggin' my master there. As soon as I saw it was the same as the drawin', I swiped it out of 'is 'ands and took off."

He held the crystal out so I could take it.

I draped a handkerchief I'd brought just for this moment around the moldonite and enclosed all of its surfaces in the fabric.

Timothy watched me with a frown.

"I don't want it to get scratched after all of your efforts to obtain it," I said.

He shrugged, but even in the dim light, I saw the slight reddening of his cheeks. "I've done it plenty of times. For food and such. Just ain't never done it with somethin' like this."

Ensuring that my skin would not touch the crystal at all, I took it from his hands. It was much heavier than I'd expected, solid as a brick, but only a quarter of its size. I slipped it into the hidden pocket where August's rose should have been.

"'ere, ma'am. It weren't needed." Timothy held out the pouch of bills and coins.

"It's all right. Keep it," I said. "You earned it."

The boy's eyes widened in an alarming manner. "All of it, ma'am?"

"Yes, all of it." Although I didn't know the exact sum August had placed inside the pouch, I did know that it was substantial. More than enough for him to live for years without having to sell a single newspaper. Money meant nothing to August, and not even this large a sum could make even the slightest of dents in his fortune, but it meant everything to Timothy. His life could be his own now.

He hesitated for only a breath, and then took the pouch. "Thank you, ma'am. If you ever need 'elp, you can depend on me."

"I'll keep that in mind." The knowledge that I could count on someone in London, even someone who was not a day older than ten and who ran the streets barefoot, was a relief I hadn't expected.

My breathing had returned to normal now that the immediate danger had passed, and I allowed myself a look around. The gas lamp's light spilled shadows on every wall as it flickered with a current of air. The passage expanded behind us, a maw of darkness that could lead anywhere.

"Where are we?" I asked.

"Tunnel, ma'am."

"It looks large."

Timothy nodded. "It goes down to the underground rails. Walk straight for 'alf an 'our and you be under the Thames."

"Really?"

"Yes, ma'am. A bit narrow, that passage, but there ain't no train runnin' through it or nothing anymore. It's a nice walk."

Just the thought of being under all that water, with only a few cement walls keeping the river from my lungs, left me gasping for air.

"I use this tunnel all time, ma'am, whenever I need to outrun someone. None of the coppers know about it, and we're all careful to keep it secret-like." He suddenly frowned, an expression that added years to his face. "You won't tell, will you, ma'am?"

I smiled. "I'm quite good at keeping secrets. Besides, we all need an escape route now and then, don't we?"

ELEVEN

AUGUST WAS STILL HIMSELF WHEN I RETURNED to the hotel, but the rose had lost another petal. The sight of it on my bedside table sent me spinning back into the maelstrom of worry I had somewhat managed to escape during the distraction of my task. Having to acquire the items for the banishment had taken most of the afternoon. We couldn't waste another moment.

"Bring that chair here," August said, pointing to the one by the small table in the sitting room.

I placed it in the space we had cleared in the center of the room. August had already called down to whoever was in charge of such things and announced that we would not be requiring Eustace or any other services for the evening; it would not do at all for someone to walk in and see the two sofas pushed back toward the walls, the intricate carpet rolled up and out of the way. Mr. Rushworth appeared to be a pleasant man, but even a pleasant man might be tempted to be less than kind if faced with the unexpected redecoration of his rooms.

"Are there any magical words I need to say?" I asked.

"No. I can do all of that on my own this time. This banishment is so broad it can be done successfully without a Grounder. It would be beneficial to have another magician here, especially since it's a banishment I will have to do on myself, but that is not an option. What I need you to do, Anne, is to ring the bell at specific times throughout the ritual, because I won't be free to do it myself. The crystal will do the rest."

I frowned. "What will you be holding?"

"Nothing, but my hands will be bound behind my back with the rope you brought."

I blinked. "Whatever for?"

"There is no way to predict what will happen. Obviously, someone or something is shoving me out of my own body and mind, taking control, and whatever that is, it will not be content to just passively be evicted."

"You think something possesses you during your . . . spells?"

He dragged a side table closer to the chair. "I don't know, Anne, but how else would you explain what occurs each time I hear those blasted bells? I lose control of everything that is innately me."

Mr. Keery's face, as I had seen it that last time, flashed through my mind, his eyes empty of humanity, his arms flaying at the flames he had set upon his own body. I shuddered.

"I'll sit, and you can tie my hands behind the chair. You'll have to hold the paper with the magical words so I can read them, and the bell with the other hand." He handed me the piece of stationery where he had copied over the intricate words. "I hope you know a few strong knots."

August sat down and placed the hard-won crystal on the floor at his feet. Then he looked up at me. Worry must have been etched into every line of my face, because he smiled. "Everything will be fine, Anne."

"Oh, you're clairvoyant now, are you? Great, for a minute there, I was worried that you might, I don't know, disappear from your own body forever, or maybe die tied to a chair. But as long as you assure me that everything will be fine, I can just kick up my heels and relax." I grabbed the rope and walked behind him, glad for an excuse to turn away.

August lifted his arms and crossed his hands behind the chair's back. The rope shook in my grip under the weight of fear and frustration. How was it possible that we were here once again, the two of us alone and facing what could easily destroy us?

I had lived for far too long in domestic service to not know a few sturdy knots by rote, but I paid special mind to them now. No matter what happened, he had to be unable to get out of that chair.

August had remained silent as I worked, flinching only once when my bare skin brushed his. I stepped away from him when the last knot was tied.

"Try to get loose," I said.

He twisted his hands back and forth, but could barely move them. Short of standing and smashing the chair against a wall, which Heaven knew could very well happen if he lost control, August was stuck.

"Well done, Anne," he said.

I walked back in front of him and sighed. "This could be a disaster, couldn't it?"

"It could, yes."

"But we have to try."

He nodded.

I picked up the paper with one hand and the black bell in the other. "Right, well, no point in delaying it, then. When do I ring the bell?"

August looked up at me. "I'll nod each time."

"Fine."

He took a deep breath and, without further warning, launched into the layers of lace-like words, each one a glistening thread that thrummed against me as he spoke. My skin tingled at their sound, but I held my powers tightly against me. I could not allow them to interfere this time.

Long seconds passed before he nodded, without looking away from the page in front of him. I rang the black bell, and August flinched before his logic caught up with him. This was an altogether different bell than the one that had started all of this. This one was very real.

The crystal at our feet began to glimmer a deep, moss green.

The words continued, twining around each other, growing stronger and faster, so that I had to tighten my reins on my power even more to keep them from lashing out.

The crystal grew brighter with each repetition of the slippery words, with each instance I rang the bell, until it stained the paper I held with its green light.

August closed his eyes and lowered his head. Had that been a nod? His lips were parted, but no further words came out. I waited a moment to see if he would continue or demand I ring the bell, but the only thing that told me he was even still conscious was a soft swaying of his head from side to side.

Not even the sudden tensing of his entire body prepared me for the scream, however.

It was a violent sound, as if someone or something were tearing August's head in two. The fear and pain embedded in it paralyzed me as nothing before had ever done.

He jerked his head back as his eyes flung open and locked on me.

"Stop it! Make it stop!" His voice was contorted with pain.

The paralysis fell off me like a cloak. I dropped the paper and the bell, and placed my hands on the only place where his bare skin could meet mine: his face. My powers had built themselves into a wave, and I allowed them to crash over August, but something was wrong. I knew it the moment I touched him.

The heat was draining from his skin, and quickly.

"What's happening?" I called, but his eyes had lost focus.

His skin cooled, his features slackening from the ravages of pain. Even his heartbeat, which I had felt pounding in his temples under my hands, slowed.

I knew there was little chance that he could still hear me, but I tried anyway. "August, how can I help?"

I almost leapt backward when his eyes shifted and locked on mine.

His lips curled into a smile that prickled my skin with its foreignness. Whatever it was in front of me, it was not August.

I did step away then, and his smile widened.

"Come now, Anne, there is no need to look so alarmed. I'm quite all right. Better than I've ever been, come to think of it." It was August's voice, but there was a sibilant quality to his consonants that I had never heard before.

The impostor chuckled.

"Where's August?"

"My dear, I think you are a bit confused. Whoever do you think I am?" He swayed his head from side to side, as if keeping beat with music only he could hear.

"Bring him back," I said. "Right now."

The impostor only smiled, twisting August's face until it was unrecognizable.

I hadn't the slightest clue what I should do. On impulse, I bent to grab the piece of paper that contained the magical words, along with the bell resting next to it, but he was faster. The impostor struck out with his foot and hit my shin with such strength that my leg buckled under me. I gasped in pain and shock. Whatever had taken hold of August's body placed his foot on the paper and dragged it backward, out of my reach unless I wanted to risk coming much closer to him.

"None of that, now. All of that chanting is nothing but a bore, and why should I be bored when there's a lovely woman like you in the room with me? This thing between us has all been much too chaste." He cocked his head to the side in such a familiar way, it sent a bolt of pain searing through me.

"I think it's time we got to know each other a little better, don't you?" He shifted in the chair and tried to get his hands loose with a sharp pull. When the rope didn't budge, he did it again. And again.

I held my breath, afraid I'd hear the snap of the ropes. *Run*, my whole being screamed. *Get out of here before he gets loose.* But I had to make sure he couldn't escape. If he did, August would be lost to me forever. Whatever had possessed his body would take him directly to Lily; directly to his death. I knew this with the same certainty with which I knew my own name.

So I watched him strain against the ropes until drops of blood began to spatter the floor beneath the chair. I wanted to scream, to smash something over the impostor's head so that I didn't have to watch it hurt August, but all I could think of was the way his skin had cooled against my hands. He had slipped away within seconds and was replaced just as quickly. His body had moved on its own last time, free from his consciousness, but this full replacement had never happened before. It chilled me to think of what it could mean.

"You might not be good for much," the impostor said, his chest heaving with the unfruitful effort, "but you do know how to tie a knot." He burst into a hissing laughter that cut like glass.

"What are you?" I asked.

His unnatural, wide smile returned, his lips pulled back to reveal his teeth. "It's a secret."

"Tell me."

He turned his head to the ceiling and began to hum. It was a tuneless, discordant sound.

"Tell me, or I will—"

"Will what? Try that quaint banishment again? I've never heard a more pointless thing in my life, and I have lived for centuries. There, happy? I've given you at least one piece of information. But really, that crystal, that . . ." He paused, turning inward as he rifled through August's head. "Moldonite. Yes, moldonite. It could be a piece of paste for all the good it's going to do you. Oh, and you went through such trouble to get it, too. What a shame." The impostor laughed.

I ignored the taunting and focused on the information it had revealed. It said it had lived for centuries, doing to others what it was doing to August, I supposed, but it hadn't known what the crystal was. How was that possible? Surely someone would have tried a similar banishment throughout all of those years.

"Anne's mind is wandering," it said, the hiss of its voice sending a chill down my spine. "But I know exactly what will keep it right here." It leaned forward in the chair. "You see, I have complete access to August's thoughts, and an absolute multitude of them have to do with you. Would you like to hear them?"

I held my breath.

"Of course you would," the impostor said. "Shall I begin with what he thought when you first met, or reveal what he felt as he helped you undress? There is so much to choose from!" It chuckled, the sound ending in a violent exhalation of air.

I took a step backward. "Enough," I said.

"Don't you want to know of all the lustful images that crossed his mind while he undid your corset strings? How much he wanted to run his hands down the length of your bare skin?"

"I said, enough!"

Tears of frustration burned in my eyes. These were August's private thoughts, his and no one else's. His to reveal when and if he desired, not to be flung at me like blades without his permission. As much as I had wanted to know what was going through his mind after our embrace at Rosewood Manor, I would be betraying him, and me, if I listened to these twisted words.

My powers roiled, fighting to break free from my tenuous grip, but I couldn't allow that. There was no knowing what effect my abilities would have on August's body when flung at him at their full strength.

"Don't be such a bore, Anne," it said. "Let's try something else, then. Perhaps you'd like to know what he really thinks of you. Not of your pretty face and young body, which is tempting enough, but of *you*. Don't you want to know how ridiculous he thinks you look dressed as a lady? Or how many times he's bitten his lips to keep from laughing at you? How much he wishes he could just drain your powers out so that he no longer has to drag you behind him everywhere he goes?"

The impostor was lying. There was no reason I should believe it. It was just doing what it could to hurt me.

"I see you need proof. Fair enough." It paused for a moment, once more searching through August's mind. "Oh, I know! That ghastly dress you chose, the one with the rotting leaves on it. When you put it on before the ball, August thought, and I quote, 'Lord, I'm expected to have her hanging from my arm in that dress? Half the ballroom will be doubled over with laughter, and the other half will think her a madwoman.'"

If someone had driven a carving knife through me, it would have hurt less than those words did.

I did warn you.

No. He couldn't have thought that.

It sounds exactly like something he would think.

He couldn't have smiled down at me the whole night while entertaining those thoughts. I would have seen it. I would have felt it.

I didn't.

Her words rang through my mind like my own set of ghastly bells, banging louder and louder against the sides of my head.

No, she hadn't. And if someone as clever as Lily had fallen for his lies, what chance did someone such as I have?

Suddenly, I couldn't catch my breath. I was shaking, my back and legs covered in sweat so cold I thought I'd never get warm again.

"Oh, the truth is finally breaking through. He could have any woman he wants, Anne. My dear, sweet Anne. Why, oh why, would you ever think what he claimed to feel for you was real? For you, of all people?"

A small groan left my mouth.

I turned away and ran the last few steps to the door. Flinging it open, I raced out of the room and slammed it closed. My hands trembled as I placed the key in the lock.

I covered my mouth with my hands to prevent the sobs that shook me from escaping.

Standing in the Salisbury's luxurious and bright corridor, the same despair I'd felt on those last few days at Rosewood Manor dug its frozen claws into me once more.

A modicum of calm finally returned to me after I'd finished the second cup of tea.

I sat in the hotel's café, ungloved, wearing no hat, my eyes swollen from crying, and tried not to feel the weight of the stares I drew from the patrons and passersby around me. My head throbbed, but it was nothing compared to the ache that had begun in my chest, a ball of it that seemed to grow by the second.

I didn't know what to think or what to do. I had to return upstairs, but I couldn't make myself move. If I went back, I'd have to confront August, I'd have to ask him about what the impostor had said, and I was afraid, so afraid, of the truth.

What would I do if he had been lying to me all along?

Shifting the teacup away, I leaned my elbows on the table and cradled my head with my hands. It wasn't something ladies did, but exhaustion made that knowledge much less important. I wasn't a lady, anyway, whatever my clothes might claim. I couldn't keep behaving like something I'd never be.

"You look like you are carrying an awful weight, my dear."

I glanced up.

A woman wearing the finest blue silk walking dress I'd ever seen stood in front of the table at which I sat. The thin lines around her mouth and eyes told me she was around Lady Caldwell's age, but there was none of my old employer's tight severity in her face. On the contrary, a soft smile made her face appear wide open, welcoming.

"May I?" she asked, nodding to the empty chair that faced me.

"Yes," I said, a croak of a sound.

Her smile widened, and she sat with a whisper of silk on silk. "Thank you. It does get lonely in hotels, doesn't it? Even in one as grand as the Salisbury. I haven't spoken to a soul all afternoon." Slowly, she tugged her gloves off, one finger at a time.

"Would you—?" I cleared my throat and tried again, motioning to the silver platter I'd not touched. "Would you like a scone?"

"Not at all, but thank you. I've had my tea already. You just looked so awfully sad, I couldn't help myself from coming over. I hope I'm not being too intrusive."

I shook my head.

"Is there anything at all that I can do?"

The kindness in her voice scratched at the thin layer of calm I'd managed to weave around myself. It tore.

I pressed a hand to my mouth again, but even that couldn't stop the sob from spilling out into the room.

"Oh, my dear!" the woman said.

Her hand was all at once covering mine, her skin warm, and real, no energy within it reaching out for me. It demanded nothing from me. I couldn't remember the last time that had happened.

She squeezed my hand, but made no attempt to halt my tears, nor did she urge me to remove myself from view.

So I cried until I could hardly breathe, in a café at the Salisbury, while a woman who hadn't even given me her name held my hand.

Everything poured out of my in those tears. Every lingering horror from my time at the manor, my feelings for August that I'd compressed and compressed for months, my guilt for my father's death and what was happening at the factory, my fear of the future I couldn't see, and the limb-numbing panic at what was happening to August, at the truth I would find once I made it back to our rooms.

I was like a full decanter overturning, spilling everything within me onto that table.

"You know," the woman said, when my tears had almost stopped, "there are all manner of awful things in this world, and I think that, despite your youth, you've seen a number of them. Horrors that I am sure I know nothing about. But there's something my mother always used to say to me when I was young, and I would like to share it with you, if you wouldn't think it inappropriate of me."

I couldn't help but smile. She'd just watched me crumple over a café table in the grandest hotel in London, and *she* was worried about being inappropriate?

I wiped at my eyes with the cloth napkin I'd spread across my lap. "Please."

She gave my hand another squeeze. "Well, my mother used to tell me that no matter how awful things were, how alone, how frightened I was, I could always depend on one person. Myself. My own instincts. Whatever nonsense I had to live through, I could always count on my own good sense to know the truth. To find true north, if I'm not too trite about it."

I looked up at her, and she smiled.

"I know. It sounds silly. I thought so, as well, the first time she said it. But over the years, I've found those words have carried me through many an unpleasant moment." She lowered her voice. "We're taught to depend on the men in our lives, but we're clever enough to figure the truth out ourselves, aren't we? We know when something doesn't feel quite . . . right."

Her words were like sliding a needle into a cramped muscle.

All at once, I could breathe again. I could think again.

Not quite right.

No, none of this was right. Not a moment of it. Not from the instant I'd first listened to Lily's venomous words and allowed them to burrow inside my head.

Had I doubted August before that? No. I'd wished for more, for the closeness we'd had that last night at the manor, but I'd been sure of him. I'd known true north. It was only when her madness had seeped into me the way her creature had seeped into August that everything had become distorted.

It was my turn to clasp the woman's soft hands.

"Thank you," I said, and was surprised to find that I meant it with my whole being.

That surprise brought with it a scalding shame, for I realized I hadn't expected kindness or anything but frivolity from this woman. From the moment I'd seen her silk dress, I'd laid judgement on her.

I felt my cheeks burn. I'd just done what I'd hated my employers for: deemed a person unworthy because of their class.

Yes, the hands I held had surely never seen a day of work, but did that really matter? Did that make her any less than I was? No. She and I were no different. Not at all. She might have been born into wealth and status, while I'd been born to wield a dust rag and a broom, but she had seen someone in need and had done what she could to help. As I would have.

No, there was no difference at all.

And there wasn't any between Lily and me, either, whatever she might claim. We had both struggled against our chains, hadn't we? What if hers had been golden? They were chains, nonetheless.

For one heartbeat, one furious second, I saw Lily for what she was. Someone so hurt, so torn, that the only thing that kept the threads of her life together was her hate.

And despite everything she'd done, to me, to August, to my father, to the women at the factory, I understood.

I couldn't forgive, not ever, but I understood.

She was keeping herself alive the only way she knew how.

Blinking the remnants of tears away, I clasped the woman's hand tightly. "I am in your debt. Truly. I won't forget your kindness."

Her smile was like a lamp's light cutting through fog. "Think nothing of it. We must all do what little we can to help each other. Who knows when we ourselves will be in need of a bolstering word?"

She stood, and I released her hand. "Whatever you are struggling through, I know that you will beat it. You have that look about you."

"That look?"

"Of someone who refuses to give in." She smiled again and made a fist. "Keep firm hold of it, whatever it is. Never let it go."

With a small dip of her head, she turned and walked away in a swish of silk.

August was sitting as I'd left him, his hands bound behind the chair. His head, which he or the impostor had lowered against his chest, rose when I entered.

It took me less than a second to know that August, the real August, had returned.

He had never looked as ill as he did now. His pallor was accentuated to such a degree that it appeared like he had lost all the blood in his veins. His eyes were the only thing with life in them, and they stared at me as someone dying of thirst might look at a glass of water.

"I'm sorry," August whispered with what was left of his voice. "I didn't know that would happen."

I wanted to go to him, but I hesitated to draw closer. Though the hesitation lasted only for a moment, it was enough.

August flinched as if I'd struck him.

"You believe its words, then? You believe the horrors it said?"

I held my silence and watched as his eyes lost what little luster they'd had in them.

Forcing myself to gather my scattered senses, I walked over to him. My hands shook as I placed them on the ropes around his wrists and began undoing the knots. They continued to do so when the burn I expected at touching him was no more than a mild warmth.

I unwound the rope. One side of it was drenched in blood from where it had scraped his skin raw.

"Lily said more to you that night at the ball than you've told me, didn't she?" he said. "I've . . ." He gave a shudder that shook his thin frame. "I've felt a change in you since that night, like you're listening for something in my words, or just beneath them. I think it's why you asked if you were only a tool to me." He didn't turn, but held himself very still. "I'm right, aren't I?"

I took a deep breath. It was time to face this, then. "Yes. She told me you were using me just as you'd used her, and if I'm honest, she made a compelling argument."

He turned so quickly to look at me that I felt a ripple of fear, but I could still see August in those light eyes, not that other being.

"After every awful thing I've done, all of the damage to Lily and all of the deaths that damage brought, do you really think me so cruel, so heartless, that I'd do the same thing to you?"

I held his gaze, watching his eyes search mine with that the same bright fear I'd seen in the factory glinting within them.

He's pretending. He's lying.

I shoved aside Lily's voice, or my voice wearing her cold finery, and called up the stranger's words instead.

Find true north.

"No, I do not really think that," I finally said.

He exhaled sharply.

"But I did. For a moment, after that creature said those horrible things, I did." I rubbed my forehead. "It's not easy to understand, August. Any of this. You cannot fault me for wondering if I am only at your side because of my powers." I shrugged. "You cannot fault me for wondering if you'd have even noticed I existed without them."

August closed his eyes and shook his head. "I have been so stupid, Anne. There is so much I have wanted to say, to explain, but I kept telling myself that I would do so once this was all over, once we'd reached some semblance of normalcy. So many times since we arrived here, I thought I saw worry and hesitation about our future in your face, and still I said nothing to assuage those fears. I was just so sure that you knew how I felt . . ."

He rose to his feet and had to grip the chair to steady himself.

"August," I began, but he lifted a hand.

"No. Please." His voice flared with energy, his eyes glittering with something I could only guess at. "There's something you need to know. The only proof I can provide that the vile words you heard come out of my mouth never came from my thoughts."

The anxiety in his face was impossible to ignore.

I nodded.

"If I could, I'd show you what I'm about to say like I did at the manor, but I'm afraid I don't think I can manage even that. Whatever this is, it's chipping away at my powers."

To hell with his powers, whatever this was chipping away at *him*.

He ran a hand through his hair and started again. "You know a little about my mother, from what I showed you, but you do not know that she was ill long before the consumption that carried her into the grave."

I frowned.

"They call it hysterics, but I'm not sure that that is an accurate name for what she suffered. She was . . . changeable.

That's the only way I can describe her. One day, she would spend hours with me, running through the manor's grounds, laughing at every rose I made bloom right out of the air, and the next, she'd be locked in her chambers, refusing to come out or to admit anyone, including me."

He spoke of it lightly, but I could still hear a jagged tear of hurt in his voice that had survived all of these years. "Father managed, for a while, keeping visitors from the house on the days when she was at her worst, but there was one evening when I must have been about seven, when there was a ball at the manor. Mother wasn't at her best, and Father told her to remain in her rooms for the night. He had gotten into the habit of locking her in on the days when she couldn't keep still, when she hardly slept and spoke so quickly that no one could understood half of what she said, but that evening, it slipped his mind."

August's jaw tightened.

This is what he'd referred to, then, when he wasn't sure that the bells were Lily's doing. What must he have thought, what must he have remembered, when I'd had to lock him up in his bathroom? The fear that must have coursed through him at the possibility that he was losing his senses, just like his mother.

"You don't have to do this," I said, softly. "I'm sure it can wait until you've rested."

"No. I want you to understand just how . . . how monstrous what that creature said really was. This is the only way." He turned away from me. "Around midnight on the night of the ball, I left my own chambers to watch some of the dancing. The ballroom was in a part of the house that you never got to see, Anne, because the wraith had already taken possession of it, but it had small glass windows along the sides which were for the servants, so that they could watch for the depletion of refreshments without having to step inside the room. I used these windows to look in whenever I could."

His shoulders and back were taut, as if each word he said pulled at his skin.

"I was one of the first to see Mother walk into the ball-room. She had dressed in one of her mother's old gowns, something that was at least fifty years old, which fell off her shoulder because she was much slighter than Grandmother. I can still see her so clearly, the dress dragging behind her, lace panels half-detached from the skirt. She . . . she kept tangling her shoes in them, reaching out to people to steady herself. And the guests, who belonged to the wealthiest, most power-ful families, who were of the highest breeding, pulled their arms away. Laughed at her or turned from her completely, as if she didn't exist. Not even Father did anything to help her."

The pain in his voice was the red of a new wound.

I walked toward him and placed a hand on his arm.

"It was Ms. Simple who finally came in and helped her out of the ballroom. Imagine, Anne, dozens of fine people doing nothing while my mother asked for help in the only way she knew how, and it was Ms. Simple, someone who'd been a parlor maid, then, who had provided it. I still remem-ber the hate I felt as I watched. The way it had transformed all of those beautiful gowns and all of the dress coats I'd been admiring into gaudy costumes. All of those smiling faces into cruel, high-bred monstrosities."

More hate.

It was so obvious, now, that I couldn't imagine why I hadn't realized it before. This hate had been there the night of the Lyceum's ball, disguised in biting sarcasm, and it had been there in the memories he'd shared with me at Rosewood

Manor, in every word he'd spoken to the Master, to the Brothers.

He, too, had held on to that hate to keep from unraveling. He held on to it still.

"I know that there is no reason for you to believe me," he continued, "when you know all too well what I did to Lily. But I would have burnt the words out of myself if I'd ever thought such terrible things as that creature spoke of."

True north.

I slid my hand down into his. A fist tightened around my heart when his touch created no raging fire on my skin. "I believe you," I said.

He turned to look at me. "I've made such a mess of things, Anne. I've been so cold and distant, when I wanted to be the opposite and just didn't know how. Of course you doubted me." He breathed in deeply. "But I won't waste another second. I don't know how much longer I will be myself, or how many other chances I will have to say this."

"August—"

"No, Anne, I need to say it. You deserve to hear it from me, not have it be used as a taunt."

My heart was beating so quickly, I could feel it on the tips of my fingers.

August shrugged again and smiled, a genuine smile the likes of which I hadn't seen in days. "I love you, Anne Tinning. As complicated as everything has been since we met, what I feel for you, what I've felt for months now, is simple enough."

There was no hesitation on my part this time.

I kissed him. It was the only answer I could coherently form to his confession. A flare of heat rose between us for an instant as our lips touched, as his arms wrapped around me, but it was too quickly smothered by Lily's newest revenge.

He pressed his forehead against mine and smiled, but it was a pale, weak thing. He looked so tired, like he would shatter into pieces right in front of me.

"We should try the banishment again," I said. "Perhaps it can still work."

"It's not strong enough. Neither the moldonite nor the magical words will do anything more than anger whatever this being is. I've never felt anything like it, Anne. It was as if I were being skinned alive."

"Did you hear the bells?"

"Yes, but they were hundreds of times louder, deafeningly so. And then the pain began, and I couldn't fight it. I tried, but the creature shoved me out of my body effortlessly. I could hear and see everything, but I might as well have been dead for all the good that did." He shook his head. "I don't know what we're going to do."

"We'll manage," I said.

"I'm not so sure anymore."

I pulled away and looked at him. "So, you're surrendering? Just like that?"

"No. Never. But I can't picture a happy ending this time, Anne. Can you?"

I tightened my grip on his hands and tried to call up the memory of the woman at the café, her smile, the softness of her words. Her confidence that everything could be solved.

And I held on to that memory, even as the image of the rose in my room, its petals falling silently and drying into dust, seared right through its center.

TWELVE

"THERE ARE TWO MEN WANTING TO SPEAK with you and Lord Grey, madam," Eustace said the following morning. "They say it is urgent."

I sat up on the sofa, blinking the sleepless hours of night-time vigil out of my eyes. It had been a tense, if uneventful, night.

"Did they say what they want?"

"No, madam, but . . ." Eustace stopped, uncertainty tightening her features.

"What is it?"

Her voice was a whisper when she spoke again, as if anyone could be listening through the walls. "I think they are from Scotland Yard, madam."

I clenched my jaw. I'd known they would come asking questions soon enough, with everything the factory workers must have told them, but if there had ever been a more inopportune time, I'd never encountered it. August had spent the night as himself, but there was no guaranteeing that that would continue for much longer, and if the police saw him as I had seen him yesterday afternoon . . .

I stood. There was no avoiding this. "Tell them to come up in fifteen minutes, Eustace."

"Yes, madam. Would Her Ladyship like me to bring up some tea at that time, as well?"

"No, that's all right. I don't expect they will be staying very long." I hoped not, at least.

"Of course, madam." She curtsied and slipped out the front door as quietly as she had entered.

With a sigh, I walked into August's chambers. The curtains were still drawn, even though it was gone eleven in the morning. I tapped lightly on the bathroom door. The sound of moving water swished through from the other side.

"Is everything all right, Anne?" August called.

"It's Scotland Yard. They're here to speak with us."

More violent splashing. A moment later, the door opened and August stood in front of me, his hair wet and as black as a crow's wing, his hands just finishing tying the knot on his dressing gown. He looked so young like this. Like someone who should be worrying about placing his name on a debutante's dance card, not fearing each moment, waiting to lose control over his own mind and body.

"I told Eustace to allow them up in fifteen minutes, but maybe it's best if I see them in the restaurant or in the café downstairs on my own."

August walked to the armoire. "I won't leave you to face them alone." He pulled out trousers, a crisp shirt, and a dark coat.

I turned away. Heat rushed to my face as I heard August remove his dressing gown and begin to dress. Despite the intimacy we had been flung into since the beginning, it was difficult to keep from feeling embarrassed at knowing his state of undress.

"And if something were to happen?" I asked.

"I don't know. We'll just have to hurry the conversation along and hope that I can remain myself for its length."

Ten minutes later, August and I sat side by side in front of two Scotland Yard detectives, one who looked as if the last mystery he had solved was that of how much the human body could consume without bursting, and the other looked as if he was about to fall asleep on the sofa.

"Detective Whitby, we are more than happy to help in any way we can, but frankly, I am not too sure why you are here," August said. He looked completely at ease, with a slight, reassuring smile on his lips, while I felt like bolting out of the room.

"It is awfully kind of you to receive us in your chambers, Lord and Lady Grey," Detective Whitby said. His jowls moved like uncooked dough with every word. "You must be aware of the disappearances and deaths that have occurred at the Wodenhouse Mill."

"Yes," August said. "An awful affair."

"Quite right. We had another woman turn up dead yesterday, and another one this morning. We questioned the factory workers each time, and your names were mentioned. We have to follow up on all leads, you understand, but it is all routine."

August nodded. "Of course. My wife and I can answer any questions you might have."

I did my best to smile, but it couldn't have looked like anything other than a grimace.

Two women dead, and I could have saved them both. I bit the inside of my lips and clasped my hands tighter together.

"Wonderful," Detective Whitby said. He nodded at the other man, who pulled a notebook and pen from his coat pocket. "Let's begin, then, shall we? We had a witness state that Lady Grey was able to perform some sort of unnatural act while at the factory."

I glanced at August, who smiled thinly at the detectives.

"And you believe such nonsense? I'm surprised, gentlemen."

Detective Whitby shrugged. "Of course not, sir. The factory women claim it to be true, but we all know how prone the female sex is to hysteria."

I clenched my jaw to keep from speaking. It would not do to allow my tongue free rein now. As if guessing my thoughts, August took my hand and squeezed it.

"Of course," he said, his voice tight. "But if you do not believe them, I'm curious as to why you have chosen to visit us."

"We are questioning everyone who has had any recent dealings with the Wodenhouse Mill and, according to Mr. Lovett, the two of you were particularly interested in the disappearances," the detective said.

Blast it. "Yes, detective, we asked about the disappearances," I said.

The man did not bother to even glance in my direction. Even after years of service, being ignored in that manner was still a blow to my pride. This really was how ladies were treated, as well, then. About as important as pieces of furniture.

"My wife is right. We were curious about what had occurred in the factory, and since we were thinking of investing in it—"

The other detective, who had not said a word until now, sat up. "That's not quite accurate, sir. Mr. Lovett shared that you were not, in fact, looking to invest, but were there exclusively to learn more about the disappearances. That is the truth, is it not?"

August's smile widened. "It is what we told Mr. Lovett, yes, but it is not quite the truth. I invest carefully, and I did not want to be pressured into financing the wrong factory. We had heard about the missing women, and we knew that the foreman would try to convince us nothing had gone amiss in order to get our support. We proved it, as well, since he revealed everything he'd been working to conceal as soon as we told him we were not there to invest in the factory."

August's hand tightened around mine in a spasm, making me catch my breath.

"And now, gentlemen," he said, standing, "if you would excuse us, we have a very long day ahead of us."

He wavered on his feet, and I took hold of his arm to steady him. With a moan, August's hands went up to his head, as if trying to block some horrid sound out.

"Gentlemen," I said, leaping to my feet. "We'll continue this another time."

Detective Whitby frowned. "Is your husband ill?"

Wonderful, *now* he realizes I existed. "I'm afraid so."

"Is it catching?"

August's torso folded in on itself as a scream tore its way through him. I gripped him tighter to keep him from falling.

These men needed to get out of here, now, before it was too late. I grasped the detective's last words.

"Yes, the doctors think it could be highly contagious. I suggest you leave the room immediately," I said. "And it would not be an exaggeration to tell you to wash your hands as soon as possible, perhaps even burn your coats and shoes."

Both men leapt to their feet as if the sofa had caught fire.

"What illness is it?" Detective Whitby said, hurrying to the door.

"A tropical disease, from when we traveled to India. Very rare, it seems. We didn't know of it until the symptoms began a couple of days ago." August's arms became rigid under my hands, and I knew that he was slipping away. "Gentlemen, I urge you to leave this instant," I said.

They hurried out of the room with apologies and other mutterings I did not pay attention to. My whole being was focused on preventing August from hurting himself as wave after wave of pain overtook him.

"Anne," he said from between clenched teeth, "get out. Get out now, before it's too late."

Another scream sliced through the room, loud enough to shake the window panes, and was chased by an icy silence that frightened me even more.

"August?"

His chest rose and fell in a pant and his skin had lost every bit of warmth it had still held.

"August, are you there?"

Much too quickly for me to react, he grabbed my wrist and twisted it. His nails dug into my skin deeply enough that I felt blood rise to the surface.

"August, stop!"

The pressure only increased, until I feared that he would snap my wrist in two. Where had this strength come from? With my free hand, I did the only thing I could think of and slapped him, hard enough to hurt my own palm. The shock of it made him loosen his grip for a moment, but that was all I needed.

I backed away quickly.

"Stupid girl." It was the impostor's voice again, all sibilance and coldness. "You should have listened to him; you should have left when you could."

In a blur of movement, it was in front of me again. Whatever was powering August was much faster than he was, much stronger, moving in sharp, rapid jerks that revealed just how inhuman it was. I recognized nothing in the face I loved so well, all traces of the man I loved gone.

"Tell me what you are," I said as I continued to back away. I had to think of a way to incapacitate it before it cornered me. If it managed to grab hold of me again, I wasn't sure I could get loose a second time.

"I think not," it said with a chuckle. "It's satisfying to watch you struggle, Anne. It's . . . exciting."

I didn't see it move. I blinked, and it was suddenly just a breath away from me. It grabbed my shoulders and shoved me back against the front door, slamming me against the wood. The pain was immediate, spreading from my head down to my ribs, robbing me of all breath. Before I could recover, before I could even think to reach for the doorknob and flee from the room, the impostor pinned my arms above my head.

I gasped and fought to get loose, but though it held me with only one hand, the strength behind that grip was unnatural. It was like trying to shift a block of marble.

"This is enjoyable, isn't it?" the impostor murmured as it watched me struggle.

"August!"

"You are a bit slow, Anne. August is not here anymore, and I'm not sure I'll allow him back at all. It is too amusing to have you all to myself."

With a yell, I kicked out in the hopes of landing a knee to its groin, but it shifted on its feet, easily evading my efforts. I tried again, but it pressed its own legs against mine until I couldn't move a single muscle.

"You are quite the fighter. I do like that."

"Stop it. Let me go!"

The imposter smiled. "Oh, but there is little chance of that, dear, sweet Anne."

I couldn't stop a whimper from escaping my throat.

"You know, I realized after our last little visit together that this is all rather one-sided, don't you think? I've aired a few of August's secrets, but you have not shared a single one with him. And we both know that there is something you've been keeping from him, isn't there, Anne? A rather important piece of information about your chat with Lily that you left out, I think. One you even held back from him yesterday, after he'd uncovered his heart to you."

My breath snagged. No, August couldn't know this.

The impostor leaned in, until its mouth was a hair's breadth from my ear. "Shall we tell him?"

"Please," I said, knowing it would do no good. "Please don't."

It chuckled, a dry, rasping sound. "Yes, let's. Because the poor boy has been drowning in guilt at all of his secrets, while you've ferreted away the fact that Lily gave you a very generous option. One that could have saved your life as well as those of all the women at the factory. All she required of you was that you leave August. Oh, but you couldn't do that, could you? So you didn't, no, of course not. And you couldn't tell him, either."

As tears doubled my vision, I tried to kick out again, but all my muscles did was twitch beneath the impostor's weight.

"These past days," it continued, "as the two of you have struggled uselessly to battle something you cannot even name, I have killed women, disemboweled them, because of your *great* love for him. Secrets and more secrets," it hissed. "You two really are a pair."

A flare of sudden anger ripped through the layer of fear that had been smothering me.

I spat in the impostor's face.

It jerked back, and its eyes, which until now had still looked like August's, lost all semblance of humanity. The pupils expanded, turning the light eyes I'd looked into for months into pits of oily darkness.

I saw only a blur of movement, and then a cement hand squeezed my throat closed. My mouth gaped open, tried to draw breath, but it was no use.

"Bitch," it said, and there was not a single thread of August's voice left.

Panic came swiftly, rolling over my senses and my thoughts, leaving me as frightened and confused as I had been when the wraith pushed me into its black fountain. Only this time, August was not here to help, and perhaps never would be again.

After everything we had been through, everything we had fought through, was this really how it would end? Breathless in the hands I loved, but which were no longer familiar?

A sudden memory of August's face, *his* face, not the abomination in front of me now, flashed through my mind as the pressure in my lungs increased.

"Concentrate," he said, his voice wavering as he nodded to something glowing in front of me. "Nothing else exists. Remember that."

Oh! It was the candle, the one I had spent so many days staring into, trying to snuff it out with my powers.

"Concentrate," he said again. "Concentrate now!"

His shout cut through the memory and into the present, puncturing the panic.

I blinked, and this time, I didn't just snuff the candle out: I ripped it apart.

All at once, I could feel everything. Every muscle in my body, every strand of hair on my head, every grain of earth stories below me, every patch of cloud above me. It was an onslaught of sensations that seemed to pause the world.

My heart's beating slowed, and the need to breathe, the gut-twisting call for air rushing through my lungs, disappeared.

Beneath my feet, the ground began to shake. The rumble of it, of stone rubbing upon stone, of splintering wood, was louder than anything I'd ever heard before as each vibration coursed through my bones.

My eyes caught every detail of August's coat in front of me, of his hair. Behind him, through the large windows that allowed the morning light in, cascades of feathered bodies glinted as they fell to the London streets below, just as they had on my seventeenth birthday.

There was a difference, however. I felt it thrumming through me. I hadn't just erased their power to fly, not this time; this time, I had pulled that power into myself, absorbing it as soil absorbed water.

Tendrils of me extended outward, climbing past the ceiling and roof and into the sky, down through the hotel's foundations and into the bare dirt like roots. I felt the city and everything in it pulse in rhythm with the blood in my veins.

I saw everything: the woman across the Thames scolding her children for muddying her floors; the banker in Westminster tossing a crumbled cracker at a handful of pigeons; the beggar in soot-stained clothes singing in Covent Garden; the rats scurrying through the underground tunnels in search of something to chew.

And the being in front of me. The being that was neither human nor animal, that was not August, or anything recognizable. I felt it, too. The chattering of its limbs and the rancid-meat smell of its cold skin.

It would not kill me. Not today.

Without conscious thought, I pulled on all of London. I gathered the energy from all of those people and animals I saw, from the electricity humming through the buildings, and even from the roiling Thames, and held it in a mass of light at the core of my being.

The impostor flinched when it sensed the change in me, but it did not react quickly enough.

I released all that pent-up energy, slamming it into the center of August's body.

The hands around my neck loosened and fell away as the force of the strike sent the impostor flying backward.

I gasped, gulping in air, the connection between me and everything in the city snapping as the world rushed to return to its normal pace. The floor stopped shaking, the birds stopped falling, and my throat burned with each delicious gulp of air.

The impostor's eyes rolled back. It, and whatever bit of August still remained, collapsed to the floor, its head hitting the wooden boards with a thud that made me wince

"Aug—" I started, but could not finish. My voice slipped away from me as my knees buckled. Sweat trickled down my face and back, and my consciousness seemed to be draining away from me with each of my heartbeats. The room dimmed more and more, pulling me into warm, watery darkness.

I must have fainted, because I woke with my face pressed against the floor, one of my arms asleep under the weight of my body. For a blissful instant, I could not remember who I was or where I was, just that I was still alive, if a bit sore. With a groan, I sat up and shook my prickling arm out to bring feeling back, and that's when it all returned. Like a collection of slaps, memories rushed at me, cold and hot at the same time.

"August," I tried to say, but my voice cracked into shards. Not even during the worst of Rosewood Manor had I felt this tired, this worn down. Everything ached, but my throat was the worst. Each time I swallowed felt like swallowing needles.

I turned my head as cautiously as I could to avoid sending my neck's raw skin screaming.

August, or at least his body, lay prone against one of the sofas, his head turned away from me. It reminded me so much of how he'd looked at the foot of the black fountain that last cursed night that I had to look away.

What if I had killed him? I had never felt the kind of power I had flung at August's body, and if it had a limit, I didn't know it yet. I hadn't been thinking of controlling it or measuring it; I had just thrown it at the impostor without thought for anything other than my survival. For all I knew, it could have stopped August's heart and fed on its energy the way it had fed on everything else in the city.

Placing a hand on the doorknob above me, I pulled myself up. My head buzzed as it sometimes did when I'd missed one meal too many, but I dug my nails into my palms to stay upright.

Fear coiled around me as I walked the few steps to where August lay. Could I ever forgive myself if he'd died by my hand?

Kneeling, I turned him onto his back. His face was the color of ash, but his chest rose and fell with breath. I exhaled in relief.

I pressed my back against the sofa and stretched out my legs beside August. There was no knowing how long it would take for him to regain consciousness, or if it would be he who came back at all, but I wouldn't leave him to puzzle out what had happened on his own. Not that I had much inclination to move my limbs or do anything more strenuous than breathe.

Closing my eyes, I readied myself for the wait.

Two hours later, August, the proper August, looked up at me from the floor. I knew it was him and not the impostor without a moment's doubt, but my insides still clenched with nerves I would have died rather than admit to out loud.

It was he, however, who sat up as if I had burned him and scrambled backward.

"Get away, Anne."

I sat up, as well. "I'm sorry if I hurt you, August."

The shock and fear in his eyes only increased. "Are you daft? I'm not concerned with you hurting me. Did you forget that I almost succeeded in strangling you just a little while ago?"

"It's been about two hours, actually."

He slammed his hand down on the wooden floorboards. "It could be two years, for all I care! You should have locked me up while I was unconscious, or left, or done something to protect yourself from me. Do you not realize the seriousness of what we now face?"

"Of course I do," I said softly.

"I couldn't stop it, couldn't stop my own hands, no matter how hard I tried. I would have killed you, and yet, here you sit, as if waiting for me to wake from an afternoon doze!"

"You didn't, however. Kill me. I am still alive. And if I could protect myself once, I can do it again." Feeling as carved out and empty as I did, this was more conjecture than fact, but it would have to do.

His eyes landed on my neck, which I knew was already alive with bruises.

"God," he said and lowered his face into his hands.

All I wanted was to walk over to him and embrace him, to hold him for as long as I could before he left me again, but that would have made things worse. Instead, I waited for August to steady himself.

Finally, he looked up at me again, and I knew what he was going to ask even before he spoke.

"Did Lily really make you that offer?"

"Yes."

He sighed. "Why didn't you tell me?"

I swallowed and winced at the stab of pain. "You would have forced me to leave."

"Yes! Of course I would have."

"And I wouldn't have obeyed, so we'd be right where we are now. I didn't leave you at Rosewood, and I won't leave you now." I lifted a hand to stop his words. "We shouldn't be wasting time arguing, August. We have to find a way to end this. For you, and for the women at the factory."

I waited for him to continue, to try to convince me to leave, but he didn't. He watched me in silence for a few seconds before lowering his eyes to the floor.

"And how do we do that?" he said. "We still don't have any idea what it is that possesses me."

I frowned at how easily he'd given in. Had I finally made him understand, or was he just too tired to fight?

Either way, I suppose it didn't matter.

"Perhaps I can harm the creature with another surge of power. It looked somewhat concerned when it felt the energy build up the way it did."

"It would have been a fool not to have been concerned. That was an astonishing amount of power you raised, Anne. I was tucked away in some corner of my own mind and still I felt its waves. The building shook, didn't it?"

I nodded. "Mr. Rushworth has been busy giving orders for the past couple of hours. I could hear him yelling all the way up here about shattered chandeliers."

August sighed. "I'm not sure that it harmed the creature, however. I can still feel it in here, slithering through my head."

"I can try again," I said. "Perhaps try to raise even more power this time, even if I have to draw energy from every single breathing thing in this city. I felt it, August. There is so much more I can access."

His eyes looked into mine, as piercing as they had always been, and just as impossible to read. "Perhaps you are right. We might have been so distracted with trying to know what it is we have been battling, that we have missed the obviousness of the situation. We might not *need* to know, when we have someone with the kind of power you have, Anne."

A sliver of hope broke through the shell of despair that had been hardening around me. I nodded. "If I can learn to harness it, augment it the way I did today, then I think it is worth a try."

"You can fasten me to the chair again, to be safe, and then take the time you need to pool your energy. It might work."

I nodded. "I need practice. I don't know if I can just tap into it whenever I want."

"Yes." August stood. His jaw tightened with pain at the sudden movement, but for the first time in days, I saw him animated. "There is something that can aid you with that. The Master told me about it, though he was dubious as to its efficacy. It's a concoction brewed from an oriental herb that is meant to enhance certain kinds of powers, including the ones you possess. I have never used it, but I remember the only place where it could be purchased."

My eyes widened. Why hadn't he mentioned this sooner?

"It might be useless, but I see no harm in trying now. Do you?"

"Of course not." I stood, as well, brushing the wrinkles and the horror of the last few hours from my skirts. "Where do I need to go?"

"Do you know the Limehouse district?"

"I know of it, though I've never been there. It's where the Chinese live, isn't it?" I had heard of the opium dens, of men and women straggling out of smoke-filled rooms, half submerged in the soporific effects of that otherworldly substance.

August nodded. "Only the Chinese know the secret of this potion, and it is one they closely guard. They do, however, sell bottles of it for a hefty price."

He pulled out a thick wad of pound notes from his coat and handed them to me. I knew even without counting them that it was an exorbitant amount. "It's a good thing that money is no object, isn't it?" There was an abundance of bitterness in his voice.

I readied myself while August wrote down the address in the Limehouse district, as well as the name of the potion we needed.

"It might be best, Anne," he said as he stepped into the bathroom in which I would have to lock him again, "if you hired a coach a few streets away from the hotel. A lady asking to be taken to this part of town could draw attention, and we do not need to invite further concern from Mr. Rushworth."

"Of course."

Until now, August had kept his distance from me, ensuring that I was just out of reach in case the impostor returned with as little warning as the last time. But as he handed me the folded piece of paper, he took my hand in his. There was hardly any warmth to his skin.

"Promise me you'll be careful," he said.

"August, I'm sure—"

"Promise me."

His eyes glittered in a feverish manner I did not like. Perhaps it would be wiser to stay with him, to send word to Timothy and ask him to go find the potion. My mouth opened, but I hesitated. That would take much longer than if I went myself, and the one thing we didn't have to waste was time.

"I promise," I said, and forced a smile. "I'll be back soon with what we need."

He nodded. "Go."

I locked the bathroom door and left our rooms. Avoiding the lift which, although bordering on magical, was still slower than my own two feet, I hurried downstairs and slipped out one of the ground floor's side doors to avoid running into Mr. Rushworth.

The pavement around the entire hotel was a graveyard of birds. Despite what I'd felt earlier, I had hoped they would have shaken off the effect of my powers, just as the crows had on my last birthday, but these feathered bodies were empty. Robbed of life.

I had done this. I had killed them.

The reality of it threatened to overwhelm me, but I would not allow it. When all of this was over, I would have plenty of time to try to understand what happened here today, how I could have caused all of this destruction, but right now, August needed me.

I did as he had suggested and hailed a coach far enough away from the hotel that no one would run back to Mr. Rushworth with the gossip of my destination.

"Limehouse district, please," I said as I pulled the coach door open.

"Are you sure of that, miss?"

I clenched my jaw. Just once, I would have liked not to have my every word questioned because of my gender. Would he second-guess a male passenger? "Yes, Limehouse district. Salamander Street."

He frowned. "Never heard of that street, miss."

"Just take me to the neighborhood. I'll find it myself." At any other time, I would have felt a pang of guilt at speaking to someone in such a brusque fashion, but right now, I was too preoccupied to worry about being unkind.

The coach rattled down street after street, taking corners hard enough to compel me to stretch out a hand for balance. I didn't care. The faster the coach went, the sooner I could get what we needed and hurry back to the hotel.

I knew we had arrived when the façade of many of the shops bore their names in both English and the intricate Chinese lettering that was as detailed as August's magical language. The attire of the people on the streets was also different. Some of the men wore loose trousers that looked quite a bit like pantaloons with matching long-sleeved shirts. They had their heads covered with cap-like hats, and their hair was a dark ink line against their backs. The women wore dresses loose enough that they did not reveal even an outline of their shape, with some type of silk trousers beneath them that hid everything but the tip of their small, black slippers.

I did my best not to gawk. As someone born and raised in London, I had encountered my share of different ethnicities, but I had never seen a Chinese person outside of the encyclopedias Lord Caldwell kept in his library and which Elsie and I had spent afternoons perusing instead of polishing the wooden cabinets as ordered.

The coach drew to a stop beside a building with no English lettering on it at all. The driver knocked on the roof, signaling that we had arrived.

"This is Limehouse," he said, while I struggled to step out onto the street without tangling my skirts in the wheels or between my own two feet.

"Thank you." I handed him his fare. "Could you wait here until I come back? I don't know how long I'll be, but I'll pay you handsomely."

The driver looked me up and down in a manner that would have earned him a slap had he been within arm's reach. He said nothing.

"I'll pay you a pound in advance," I said. I did not want to risk not being able to find another coach in the area once I was done with my errand. "And another pound for every ten minutes you wait. You'll be resting your horse and still earn more than you would from regular fares."

He thought about it for an instant, and then nodded. "I'll wait right here, then, miss."

"Good. I'll be back as soon as I can."

After handing him the pound, I walked down a street chosen at random. There were no signs displaying names—or at least, none that I could understand—and the people weaving around me looked cold, keeping themselves at a large distance from me.

Enough, I told myself. *They are people just like everyone else. I need help and I'll have to ask them for it.*

"Hello," I said to the nearest person, a young woman carrying a basket of laundry. "Could you help me?"

She glanced at me, but immediately lowered her eyes when she took in my gown and my hair. Blast this finery. It would be much easier to ask for help wearing my maid's frock.

Or perhaps it was the bruises around my neck that I had forgotten to hide before running out of our rooms that frightened her. Oh well, it was too late to worry about that now.

"Do you know which way Salamander Street is?" I asked.

She looked like she would have liked nothing more than to bury her head in the freshly pressed sheets she carried.

"Please," I said. "It's really important that I find it." I took a step closer in my eagerness. The woman said something

I couldn't understand and turned away from me. In a few steps, she had disappeared into the crowd.

No matter. I would try again.

And I did, again and again, encountering mostly the blank stares or the shaking heads of people whose language was a labyrinth of sounds, and who most likely thought the same thing about mine.

A knot of fear and worry tightened in my stomach with every minute I wasted, with every person who shook her head at me or shrugged his shoulders at the street name. Something pulled at me, urging me to hurry, though, rationally, I knew that August was as safe as he could be, even if the impostor had taken over his body again.

With a deep breath, I crossed the street toward a group of men speaking in front of a store. As I neared, enticing smells, sweetly aromatic but with an edge of something spicier, reminded me that I hadn't eaten since before Scotland Yard had disturbed our morning. My hunger would have to wait, though.

"Pardon me, could you help me?" I said.

Most of the men glanced up and looked away as if I didn't exist, but one of them, a man in what looked to be his sixties, met my eyes.

"I will do my best," he said. "How can I be of service?" His English, though lilting in accent, was perfect.

I smiled. "Thank you. I need to find Salamander Street. Would you happen to know where it is?"

The man frowned. "Salamander Street, in the Limehouse district?"

"Yes."

He turned to the group of men who still looked everywhere but at me, and said something in their native tongue. More frowning and shaking of heads.

"I'm sorry, but none of us have heard of that street. Are you sure it was in this neighborhood?"

"Yes." From my pocket, I pulled out the note where August had written the address and showed it to him. "See? Perhaps the street has another name now. The person who gave me this hasn't been in London for almost a decade, so it could . . ."

My voice trickled to a stop at the man's shaking head.

"I've lived in Limehouse for almost thirty years, and I have never heard of Salamander Street. I'm afraid that the person who wrote that is mistaken, or has lied to you."

I looked down at the paper in my hand. For the first time, I noticed how shaky August's handwriting was, how uneven. There was a blot of ink on the page at the start of the street name, where the pen had rested a beat too long, as if . . . as if . . .

As if he had been thinking up a name to write down.

Wintery truth enveloped me, robbing me of breath.

My feet were moving before my head could even begin to make decisions, my pace quickening on its own into a full run back to the waiting carriage. Blurred faces turned to look at me and the flurry of panic that surrounded me like a net.

"Take me to the Salisbury," I said to the driver and yanked the carriage door with so much force it caused its hinges to squeak.

"One mome—"

"Now!"

I slammed the door shut and pressed my hands to my face. How could I have been so stupid? So utterly idiotic?

The carriage lurched to life, and all I could do was sit very still as my heart tried to escape my chest, and will wings onto the horse in front of me.

THIRTEEN

EVEN AS I SIDE-STEPPED THE BIRDS' CORPSES
that still gaped with sightless eyes at the sky above the hotel, I
knew I was too late. I felt it like an ache deep inside me.

I hurried past the Salisbury's front room, where eyes
landed heavily on my clammy, heated face, my wrinkled
skirts, my shaking hands, and ran up the four sets of stairs.
The luxurious clothes I wore could not erase the strength from
my legs from years of trailing up and down Caldwell House's
stairs; not even the corset could weaken me any longer.

Our chamber doors were unlocked.

"August!"

The sitting room was empty and silent, as if all the violence of just a few hours ago had never occurred.

My vision seemed to narrow as I opened August's bedroom door, becoming a pinpoint that could only focus on
what lay before me.

The bathroom door, cracked open. The chair I had left for him to sit on splintered beside it.

"August," I said again, but I knew that it was pointless. He was no longer here. "No."

I ran into the bathroom, unwilling to accept the emptiness of the rooms, and saw it on the sink's edge: a folded piece of paper.

My hands shook so much I had to hold the note with both of them to be able to make out the words.

Anne,

There is too much to say, and I don't have much time before you return from the address I have given you. I hope that you will forgive me someday for lying to you, and for what I am about to do. I can find no alternative. After this morning and everything that it brought with it, it is clear that I am putting you, as well as all of the factory's women, in mortal danger by remaining at your side. I know you and your stubbornness well enough to realize that you will not leave of your own volition, so I will do it for you.

I have settled the bill at the hotel, and I have left you all the pounds I have on me in the case on my bed, along with a signed note bequeathing the rest of my fortune to you. Present it at the Bank of England at Threadneedle Street here in London, and you will be given access to the entirety of the Grey estate. I have no heirs or remaining family, except for you, my wife in everything but name, so no one will contest it. If the bank insists on a marriage certificate, say that it was burned with all our possessions at Rosewood, and if they need a witness to verify the validity of the claim, Mr. Rushworth can help.

You will never have to work another day of your life, Anne, and you can live however and wherever you please, free from the grip of Lily's madness. There's not much I can do to make up for the horrors I have brought into your life since we met, but I can do that, at least.

I pray, with everything within me, that you will understand why I must leave your side. I do not have much time left, and I cannot, I will not, watch myself kill the woman that I love. Forget about all of this, Anne. Forget about me, Rosewood Manor, and Lily Bellingham. Her revenge will soon be complete, and you will be able to go on with your life as if none of this had ever occurred. Like waking from a nightmare.

The only thing I regret is that I did not get the chance to tell you once more just how much I love you.

Yours always,
August

His name blurred and disappeared under the weight of the tears I had been fighting back since I'd rushed into our rooms. I could neither carry them nor fight them any longer. A sob rose through me, growing an edge of blades as it left my mouth and twisted into a scream.

Memories of our time together, at the manor and in these very rooms, of his face, of his smile, sped through my mind faster and faster, unbidden, until I had to press my fore-head to the cool bathroom tiles in order to draw breath again.

Grief spiraled through me.

He was out there, alone. He would have gone somewhere secure, from where he could not escape when he was no longer himself, somewhere he would die. On his own. Without an-other kind word from anyone who cared about him. Where Lily would find him and finish what she had started.

I slammed my hand against the tiles.

You have that look about you. Of someone who refuses to give in.

The soft words chased off the darkness in my mind like a feather duster through a cobweb.

Yes. Exactly. That's who I was. Who I would always be. Someone who refused to give in.

Lily would go after August. She would not be able to resist being there when his end came.

So I had to find him, never mind what he said in his note. I had to finish this, once and for all, even if it meant taking on both Lily and her creature on my own. One way or another, this madness had to stop.

"Madam."

I whirled around to find Eustace at the bedroom door, trying not to look at the damage all around me. "I'm sorry to intrude, but Mr. Rushworth asked me to see if you required anything." She frowned. "Is everything all right?"

"Yes." I suddenly knew exactly what I needed to do. I couldn't stay in these rooms a second longer, not without August. "Could you pack my luggage?"

"Of course, madam."

"I'll be leaving in a few minutes."

She nodded and hurried to my bedroom.

Now that I had decided to leave, it felt like the best possible decision. I didn't belong here, and I wouldn't belong at any other of the hotels that London had to offer. This woman who walked in lace and silk and was waited on for her every request was not me anymore than I was the person who'd worn a uniform and polished silver. And it was high time I understood that.

I walked over to August's bed and picked up the case heavy with money. The signed affidavit was tucked into one of its pockets, ready to provide me with everything I would need for the rest of my life. But what I wanted wasn't pounds. It was August, and my father, and the shadowy figure of my mother, and Elsie. All the people I had ever loved.

I knew, then, with as much certainty as I had ever known anything, where it was I needed to go.

Had it been just a few months ago that I had stood in this same courtyard, watching birds fall from the sky to my feet? The calendar claimed that it was so, but with everything that had happened since then, I felt as if I hadn't seen this place in decades.

I had waited until full dark before stepping out of a hired carriage with my suitcases and walking down the street to Caldwell House. Once the horses had clopped off and around the corner, I abandoned all but one of the cases, tucking them behind a shrub. I didn't need all of these gowns, but perhaps someone who did would find them.

I'd been well aware that I would not be able to climb over the walls surrounding the house in my corset and skirts, so I'd used the courtyard's gate instead. It was supposed to be locked as soon as the sun set, but no one had bothered with it in years. The gate itself hadn't been officially utilized since I could remember. The only reason I knew it still opened at all was because Elsie and I had used it once or twice to enter the house after curfew on our half-days off when we'd lost track of time. That, and a shimmy haloed by smothered giggles up the iron trellis right below our bedroom window, and we were back inside, no one the wiser.

There was no chance I could climb the trellis now, however, and even if I did, Elsie was bound to have a new roommate who would likely waken the entire house with a scream if a stranger climbed into their room.

I pressed my hand against the rose in my pocket as was my habit before remembering that it had now lost all but a handful of its petals. "I'm sorry," I whispered to it and removed my hand. I would have to find a safe place to store it.

But first . . .

I picked up a pebble of substantial size, one that would not break the glass, but which would make enough noise to rouse Elsie, and threw it at my old bedroom window. Too late, the question of what I would do if she now slept in another chamber swept through my mind.

Holding my breath, I waited. Elsie had always been a light sleeper, as most maids used to being woken at all hours were, but there was no movement. Nothing but my pounding heart cracked the silence around me.

I threw another pebble, harder this time, clenching my teeth at the sound which echoed through the courtyard.

"Come on," I whispered.

Seconds later, a dim glow of light appeared in the room. Not the crisp electric light that flowed throughout the rest of Caldwell House, but the inviting warmth of a gas lamp.

It bobbed and wavered as whoever I had roused walked to the window.

I prepared myself to run if anyone but Elsie appeared. Even when she did, her hair a golden bird's nest framing her pale face, my muscles were so tight with nerves that I almost bolted for the gate, anyway. Her eyes narrowed until she recognized me, when they instead widened.

I motioned for her to come down and hated myself for it. This could get her dismissed from her position. She could lose the only home she had ever known, her income, and her makeshift family in one fell swoop if someone saw her. If the same thought crossed her mind, she didn't bother with it, as she disappeared from the window without hesitation.

The path she had to take to reach the courtyard was carved into my head: each floorboard prone to groaning, each stair step that enjoyed squeaking in disapproval, each door that needed almost daily oiling to keep it quiet.

Any one of them would betray her.

I waited in the darkness and tried to justify why I had not gone to a hotel.

There was a flutter of movement at the door leading from the kitchen out into the courtyard, and Elsie's face looked out at me. In a moment, she had stepped into the night and was running barefoot to where I stood.

"I knew I'd seen you!" she said as she flung her arms around me without preamble. "I knew it!"

She smelled like sleep and the lavender soap every servant at Caldwell House was allotted, propelling me back in time to when everything was much simpler. When all I'd had to worry about was the next day's dusting. I squeezed her tighter, burying my face in her tangled hair.

"Elsie," I said. "I'm so happy to see you."

She returned my embrace for a moment more before smacking my arm with her hand.

I pulled away. "I know. I'm sorry about all of this. I wouldn't have come here and risked your position if I—"

She smacked me again. "I don't care about that. Why did you disappear? I sent three notes to Rosewood Manor and they were all returned, and then you ran away from me the other day. I didn't know what was wrong. I was so worried."

"I know. I'm sorry. So much has happened since I left, things you'll be hard pressed to believe. Everything has changed."

For the first time, she looked at me fully, taking in my dress, my hair, the glittering jewels dangling from my ears. The bruises on my neck that the silk scarf I had thrown around it couldn't quite conceal. "I can see that."

"It's a very long story, Elsie."

She nodded. "Come on."

I grabbed the suitcase I had dropped at my feet and followed her.

Elsie led us back into the kitchen. It looked just as I remembered it, Mary's voice hanging overhead like a cloud of confectioner's sugar, the memory of the scullery maids' scurrying feet imprinted on the floorboards.

She removed her set of keys from her dressing gown's pocket and headed to the cellar door. "It should be safe down there for now. No one has a need for anything in the cellar but the wine and that won't be required until tomorrow night."

I trailed after her down the stairs, wincing at every creak. "I could get you into serious trouble."

She shrugged. "We'll worry about that later. Right now," she said, shifting two wooden crates that rested in a corner of the cellar and perching herself down on one, "I want to know why you are dressed in the kind of clothes we have cursed over while ironing."

With a sigh, I lowered my suitcase and sat down next to her. "You won't believe me."

"Try me."

So I told her everything. From my arrival at Rosewood Manor to the moment I threw the pebble at her window and every second of horror and wonder in between. I described August to her and what he meant to me, ignoring the pain in my chest as worry at where he was surrounded me once again; I told her what he had done to Lily, and the price he was paying for it.

I spoke until there was nothing left to say.

Elsie kept her silence until I was done, her eyes always on mine, her face a tangle of emotions. I had planned on giving her an abridged version of what my life had become for the past few months, but once I started speaking, it all spilled out. Every unbelievable truth.

As I watched her, the only sister I would ever have, struggle to understand my words, I wanted to take it all back. What if she thought me mad? I couldn't prove much of what I had told her. I couldn't move a chair with my powers like August had done that night in his chambers when he'd revealed his truth to me, and although I had fine clothes on my back and a suitcase with more pounds in it than either one of us had seen in our lifetimes, it was more plausible that I had stolen them than that a lord had given them to me. All I had was August's letter to show her.

The silence stretched and stretched.

"It's . . . astounding," Elsie finally said.

"I know. Here," I said, and brought out the letter from one of the suitcase's crevices. "It's not much proof, I know. I could have easily forged it myself, but it's the only thing I have."

Elsie lifted an eyebrow. "You don't have to prove anything to me, Anne. Whatever would make you think that I don't believe you, you silly thing?"

"You believe me? Everything I've told you?"

"Of course I do."

I sighed with relief.

"I always knew that there was something unusual about you," she said. "Animals always flocked to you, even when we were infants, and I never felt safer and more at ease than when I was in your presence. It all makes sense, now. Besides, you have never lied to me, so why would you start now?" She sat up in eagerness. "But Anne, to have a lord declare his love for you, oh, it's like something out of an Anne Radcliffe novel!"

I smiled. "It is a bit, isn't it?"

"He must be so handsome. I can just picture him."

"He is, though he is much too thin." The smile on my lips faded as I thought of August's troubled face the last time I had seen him. Ragged with fear and worry. "I have to find him, Elsie."

She nodded. "Of course you do, and I'm going to help you."

"I can't ask that of you."

"Nonsense. We'll start tomorrow morning, bright and early."

"But what about Mary and Lady Caldwell? Surely they'll miss you if you disappear."

She shrugged. "I'll tell them I'm ill and have to see a doctor. Maud, the girl who took your position, can handle things for a day. You should also ask that boy, what was his name?"

"Timothy."

"Right, you should ask him to help."

"Yes, I've thought about that. He knows more of London than either one of us."

"And he knows what your lord looks like, too, and I do not."

I glanced down at my hands. "I have to ask another favor, Elsie."

"Tell me."

Sighing, I gestured at my gown. "I'm going to need something more mobile than these damned skirts. They're beautiful, but an absolute nuisance to walk in, let alone traipse all over the city. Besides, I've noticed that being seen as a lady makes everything more complicated. They don't have it nearly as easy as I imagined."

She lifted an eyebrow at me.

"It's just that . . . people question your actions less if you're dressed like a maid. They assume you're running an errand for your mistress."

Elsie shrugged. "I suppose, though you won't hear me pitying Lady Caldwell. At any rate, Maud wears most of your old clothes, but she doesn't fit into your skirts. I have some spare pieces, too, that I can do without."

"I'll pay you for them, so that you can buy yourself some new ones."

She frowned. "Anne Tinning, the day you pay me for anything is the day my cold corpse is buried next to my long-departed mother."

"But I want to help."

"You have, by coming here and letting me know that you are still alive and well. What use do I have for money?" She waved my words away and stood. "I'll go fetch the clothes, and we can plan how we'll find your lord."

"Be careful," I said.

She lifted her eyebrows. "As if we haven't snuck around the house like this a hundred times before. You've gone soft in your old age, Anne."

I smiled. "Perhaps I have."

Or perhaps, I thought as she closed the door behind her, I knew too well what becoming involved with August and I could bring down upon her head.

Elsie ushered me out of the cellar in the minutes before dawn, before Mary had dragged herself up to begin the day's bread.

I felt light in the maid's uniform we had pieced together, with none of the heavy fabrics or layers upon layers of cloth to lift and tuck out of the way with every step. And, if nothing else was right in my life, at least I no longer had that cursed corset squeezing the life out of me. Elsie had even surprised me by smuggling a kitchen knife into the cellar.

"I couldn't think of anything else that would work as a weapon," she said.

"But Mary will notice it's missing. You'll get into trouble."

She shrugged. "It wouldn't be the first time I've lost cutlery."

Trying not to think too much about the consequences Elsie would face if all of this was discovered, I tucked the knife's familiar weight into one of my skirt's pockets.

Now, waiting around the corner from Caldwell House for Elsie to appear, I patted it through the cloth. In the other pocket rested August's rose. It had lost more petals in the night, and I had debated long over whether I should leave it behind in the cellar. In the end, I couldn't bring myself to do it. It was the only real connection I had to him now.

Elsie appeared in her street clothes, which already looked as wrinkled as if she had been wearing them for two continuous days straight.

"Sorry I kept you waiting. Mary and Mrs. Smythe had about a million questions each as to why I hadn't let them know I had a doctor's visit today."

"Mrs. Smythe is still the housekeeper, then?"

She nodded. "That woman is planning to outlive God, I think."

We headed to Covent Garden, first, but saw no sign of Timothy among the numerous barefooted urchins.

Each second that passed as we hired a coach and rode through the tangled streets to Wellington Street in Westminster, to Timothy's other preferred haunt, was a weight against me, pulling me further away from August. What if the boy wasn't there? It wasn't as if he needed the money from the newspapers any longer. And if he wasn't there, what would I do? There were entire sections of London I had only heard of in passing, and many more that I probably didn't even know existed at all. It was the same for Elsie. To find August, who knew the city intimately from his years with the Brothers, we needed someone who had lived his entire life on these streets. That person was Timothy.

Finally, I spotted him, standing with two other boys about his age who carried piles of newspapers. His arms, however, were empty. He was gesturing wildly, hands bringing to life some exploit I had not been privy to, eliciting laughter from his companions in guffaws that were audible even from the carriage.

"Stop! Stop!" I called out, slapping the coach's ceiling with my hand.

"It's the middle of the street!" the driver said.

"I don't care. Stop now!"

With a curse he didn't bother to hide, the man reined in the horses. I was out of the carriage before it had even stopped completely, never more grateful of my maid's corset and skirts than I was as I ran through the street. A symphony of shouts and neighs sprang up as vehicles had to be forcefully stopped to avoid trampling me. I hardly noticed.

Timothy turned at the commotion and waved a hand when he saw me. The smile that mirrored the ones plastered on the other boys' faces faded slowly. With a few words, he dismissed his companions and started toward me, the smile now completely overtaken by a frown.

"Ma'am, what 'appened to your fancy clothes?" he asked when I reached him.

"Never mind that. Timothy, I'm sorry to spoil your day, but I'm afraid I need your help again."

"My 'elp? Somethin' else you need me to buy?"

I shook my head. "Not this time. I need to find my husband. He's somewhere in the city, but I haven't the slightest idea where to begin."

The boy frowned. "You lost your 'usband?"

"It's quite a long story, Timothy, but he's been ill, and he thought that the best way to protect me was to leave the hotel where we were staying. It's important that I find him as quickly as possible. He should not be alone when he is this sick. Do you understand?"

"Sure do, ma'am. You have my 'elp, of course. When did 'e leave?"

I sighed with relief. "Yesterday afternoon."

He shrugged. "He could be anywhere, then. Probably he ain't even in London anymore."

"I'm sure that he is. He wouldn't risk a long trip in his condition, not now that it's getting worse and could put people in danger."

"Blimey," the boy said. "It's that bad, then."

I nodded.

Timothy looked around, as if taking in where he was for the first time. "London is big, ma'am. It could take days without some idea of where to start. You'll need more 'elp than just me."

"I have another friend who's going to search as well, but I don't have any other acquaintances is the city. Certainly no one who knows it like you do."

Timothy's cheeks reddened at my words. "Well, the day's passin' us by standin' 'ere chattin'. Would your 'usband go to any familiar places?"

"No. He would avoid those at all costs to stop me from finding him. He has to be somewhere where even a man as wealthy as he is can become invisible, somewhere he can be alone and go undisturbed."

I saw the beginnings of a thought glittering to life in Timothy's eyes. He nodded once, the movement heavy with determination, and pressed his hat more firmly down on his head.

"Let's go find your 'usband, then, ma'am."

I waved to Elsie, who stood by the carriage's side, motioning for her to join us.

The race to save August's life despite his own infuriating self, to find him before Lily did, had just begun.

The hours unspooled themselves one after the other until the last lace-like edge of sunlight disappeared from above the city's buildings.

We had nothing to show for all that spent time.

The three of us had separated to cover more ground, Elsie with as vivid a description of August as I could give her pulsing in her mind. We'd trekked through neighborhood after neighborhood, asking pedestrians, coach drivers, shopkeepers, and anyone else who would listen if they'd seen August. He would have stood out, the wealth of his clothes, the pallor of his face, the thinness of his frame. All of it creating the unique man I'd fallen in love with. Someone had to have seen him hailing a driver or walking through the streets, and yet no one had.

I'd had to force Elsie to return to Caldwell House when the sun set to avoid Mary sending out a search party for *her*, but even if I could have snuck into the cellar behind her to gather some rest for another day of searching, the mere thought of sitting still knotted my insides. It wasn't particularly safe to be out in the night on my own, but the tightness in my chest from the collected hours of anxious worry wouldn't allow me to even consider being caged in.

Timothy was still out there searching, at least. He had insisted on it when we had reunited at our designated meeting spot in front of the Lyceum. He had promised to run straight to Caldwell House if he had even the slightest bit of information. If anyone could find August, it would be him.

And if he couldn't? What would I do then?

With a groan and a wish that my mind would hold its tongue for just a few minutes, I stood from where I hid in the alley leading into the Caldwell House's courtyard and began to pace. I couldn't leave the house's vicinity in case the boy returned with news; there was nothing I could do but wait.

And I did. I walked from one side of the alleyway to the other, over and over, until my feet grew numb. Time passed, but I paid it no heed.

Not until I heard the slap of footsteps on pavement racing toward me.

"Ma'am!" Timothy called out, paying as little heed to the sleeping homes all around us as I had to the hours that had swept me by. "I found 'im, ma'am!"

Something in my chest cracked open at his words, and the urge to cry forced itself upon me.

Saving those tears for a more opportune moment, I ran toward Timothy and took hold of his shoulders. "Did you see him? Was he safe?"

The poor boy gulped in mouthful after mouthful of air. He had been running for a long time, if the flush of his face and the sweat on his brow were any indication.

"I . . . didn't . . . see . . . 'im . . . ma'am," he gasped out.

"Catch your breath. It's all right." I reined in my impatience, when all I wanted was to take off running.

He shook his head and continued. "Someone saw 'im yesterday. Remembered 'im." He wiped at his forehead. "Tall, thin, dressed fancy-like. 'andsome, but odd."

I nodded. "Yes. Where did they see him?"

Timothy looked away from me, then, a rush of color that had nothing to do with his exertions rising to his cheeks. "It . . . it ain't a nice place, ma'am. I don't like to go there, myself."

"It doesn't matter. Just tell me."

"Whitechapel, ma'am. One of the less reputable 'ouses."

I swallowed. I should have known. August was too clever for his own good. He had gone to the place where men of all classes and backgrounds would go in search of a loose woman, where no one would notice or care about a well-dressed man asking for a room as long as his pockets rang with the silver jingle of coins.

Except someone had noticed.

"Do you know the exact house?"

"Yes, ma'am."

I nodded. "Let's go, then."

Timothy stopped me with a hand on my arm. "You can't go there, ma'am! It ain't proper for a lady like you."

"I'm not a lady," I said. "I'm . . . well, I'm not sure what I am, but I need to get to August as quickly as possible. Please help me, Timothy. Please."

The boy's face was tight with indecision.

"I can't let him die on his own."

"'e's dyin', ma'am?"

"Yes."

I swallowed tears at the sudden understanding that, yes, that was exactly what was going to happen. Unless a miracle occurred, he was going to die from the curse that had taken root inside of him, and I would be damned if I wasn't going to at least be beside him to hold his hand. Lily would not take that away from me. From us.

Timothy nodded as all hesitation left his features. "This way, ma'am."

I took his small hand, prepared to be guided away from everything I knew and led into the very bowels of London.

FOURTEEN

THE FIRST THING I NOTICED WHEN WE ENTERED the Whitechapel district was the smell. All of London lived under a fog of varying degrees of unpleasant odors, depending on the season or even the time of day, but nothing in my entire life had prepared me for the stench rising like vapor from these streets. The wet smell of sewer mixed with the scent of rotting garbage to create an almost tactile division between the rest of the city and Whitechapel.

Timothy glanced up at me as I pressed a hand to my nose. "You shouldn't 'ave come, ma'am."

I shook my head. "I'm all right. Lead the way."

We entered Dorset Street. There were people everywhere. Children sat at street curbs tossing anything they could get their hands on under the few carriages that made it into the district, while women with stained skirts and bodices of such garish colors they were visible even at night walked from one corner of the sidewalk to the other. One such woman yelled an obscenity at her apparent competition across the street, who answered in kind.

A man lurched out of a pub on our right, singing in a harsh voice that sounded as full of coal-dust as the air was. Even though I had never been in the presence of someone properly drunk, I knew immediately that this man was well into his cups.

"See somethin' you like?" he said when he caught me staring.

I averted my eyes as Timothy pulled at my hand.

We sped up, passing more and more people, some slumped on piles of clothing, gathering what bits of sleep they could right there on the street, others extending hands so encrusted with filth they no longer resembled human appendages, and children so thin their eyes seemed to be three times their normal size.

"Fancy a kiss?" a woman said to us as we passed. She leaned against a doorway from which loud voices spilled out. Her skirts were lifted high enough to see her calves. "Ever been with another woman, love? I can promise you a good time."

Heat rushed to my face, and I quickened our pace even more.

"Don't pay no mind to them, ma'am," Timothy said.

I nodded. "Of course not."

"It's just over there," he said, and pointed to the last building on our left. "Ms. Addington's establishment."

My heart pounded. After almost two days of worry, I could be just steps away from August.

"Ms. Addington rents rooms by the hour," Timothy said when we were finally before the building's entrance.

"You'll pardon me, ma'am, but a certain kind of woman uses these rooms."

I swallowed and nodded. Prostitutes were a fact of life in a city as large as this one, but it was one thing to know of them and quite another to come face to face with them.

My thoughts must have been plastered throughout my features because the boy placed a hand on my arm and said, "I can go in on my own and see if your 'usband is there."

"No, it's all right. We'll go in together, unless you prefer to go home."

He shook his head. "No chance, ma'am."

I smiled as much as my nerves would allow. "Do we knock?"

"No need. Not in a place like this, ma'am."

He reached out and turned the doorknob that was discolored from being touched by so many hands.

The door groaned itself open, revealing an interior that was more like the inside of an animal's mouth than that of a house. I frowned at the darkness that was interrupted by folds of curtains in deep reds and golds, and by the flickering of distant candles that flung even more shadows against the walls. Electricity had not made it this far down into London, it seemed.

Timothy and I stepped inside and closed the door behind us.

Though there weren't any people in sight, the energy of dozens of individuals brushed by me the moment I crossed the threshold, tugging at my hands. So much anger radiated through the air I could taste its metallic residue on my tongue. My powers picked apart what I felt, searching for the familiar touch of August's energy, but I couldn't separate it from the rest.

"Lookin' for someone special, girl?" said a voice ragged like a hem.

I flinched at the sound. I hadn't seen anyone around us.

"We're looking for Ms. Addington," I said.

The person sniffed. Whether they were a man or a woman remained to be seen, since the hoarse voice revealed nothing. "Should 'ave come three hours earlier. Ms. Addington has been imbibin' since the early afternoon, so if she's awake, it'll be a bloody miracle."

"Nevertheless," I said, "could you be so kind as to show us where we might find her?"

A shadow in the vaguest shape of a woman moved to our right. "Listen to 'er. Polite enough to charm the angels. Wastin' your time, 'cause there ain't nothin' but us devils 'ere." She snorted. "But I'll take you to see 'er 'ighness, Mistress Addington, if you want. This way."

My eyes had adjusted to the darkness by now, and I could make out the woman's silhouette as she led us through a corridor swamped with all manner of voices coming from unseen rooms. We entered what would have been a kitchen if every available surface had not been covered with empty bottles and the remnants of meals that were now just feasts for the flies, including the table in the center of the room, over which another woman was slumped.

"There she is, 'er royal 'ighness. Told you she would be no use to you."

"Ms. Addington," I said, taking a step closer to her. Not even a twitch from the woman. "Ms. Addington!"

"You'll need more than that to wake 'er. She once slept through a fire after drinking as much as she's 'ad today. Singed the 'air right off 'er 'ead."

Timothy walked up to Ms. Addington and shook her with enough force to move the table beneath her. She gave no indication she had felt it.

"Is she alive?" I asked.

"Aye, take more than a few cups to kill that one."

I wanted to reach out and slap Ms. Addington into consciousness, but even if I managed to rouse her, what would that accomplish? She would be angry, and might end up throwing us out of her house.

Instead, I turned to the woman who had led us here.

"I need to know if my husband is here. Is there some ledger or something I can look through?"

The woman's eyes widened. "So that's it, then. Looking for your 'usband in a place like this." She snorted. "If 'e is in this 'ouse, it means 'e don't want to be found."

My hands clenched into fists at my sides. We were wasting so much time! "I just need to know if he's here. There has to be a way for Ms. Addington to keep track of her tenants, especially if she rents rooms by the hour. Can she read and write enough to keep some kind of tally of who's paid and who's not?"

The woman leaned against the kitchen's doorway. "What's that information worth, then?"

"How much do you want?"

She thought for a moment. "Fifteen shillings."

I reached into my skirt's pocket and took out a handful of coins. I grabbed hold of a guinea and held it up. "Here's twenty-one shillings, which I will give to you as soon as you show me a ledger or any other list of who is staying in this house."

The woman's eyes had acquired a glitter as soon as I'd pulled out the guinea, and she straightened up. "She keeps a ledger of sorts. Can't say if it's accurate or not."

"Show it to me."

She walked over to the kitchen's pantry door and pulled it open. Pans clattered out, along with the rancid smell of vegetables long past ripe. She tossed a notebook stained with unidentifiable substances onto the kitchen table, where it landed just a breath away from Ms. Addington's unconscious form.

I grabbed it and opened it. Lists of names and numbers were scrawled across each page in a handwriting that was surprisingly neat.

I flipped to the last few pages, scanning the names, unsure if August would have even bothered to use a false one. There were no Greys or Augusts on the list, but there was one entry toward the end of the last page in which the space reserved for a name was blank with a note next to it that said, "paid in full for a month."

Everything in me vibrated at those simple words. It had to be him.

"Can you tell me which room this means?" I said, and pointed to a column which contained the cipher, "2-3-left."

The woman sniffed. "Not all of us are gifted with the power of lit'racy."

Of course, I should have known. I nodded and told her what Ms. Addington had written.

"That means second floor, third room to the left."

Timothy took off before the woman finished speaking, and I was close on his heels, both of us sprinting up a set of the shakiest stairs I'd ever seen. Every step threatened to send the whole structure down to the ground in a pile of sawdust and termites, but I gripped the banister and propelled myself upstairs. If the whole thing collapsed after me, so be it.

If the downstairs was dark, the second story was tomb-like in its gloom. There was only one window in the corridor and it had not seen the right side of a duster in decades.

In seconds, I was standing in front of the third door on the left. Without hesitation, I knocked twice, as loudly as I could, and then paused to listen.

There was no movement from the room's interior that I could discern.

"August," I called out. "It's me. Open the door."

"Sir," Timothy said. "It's Tim, sir. We've been searching for you the 'ole day."

Still nothing. Anxiety gripped me in its claws.

I banged on the discolored wood. "Open the door, August." Nothing but silence. "August!"

From behind us, I heard the squeal of an old hinge followed by a chuckle. "You lost?"

"They certainly look lost."

I turned and had to quickly avert my eyes from the two young women wearing nothing more than corsets and pantaloons.

"Maybe she's one of Madame Rachelle's new girls," one of them said.

"With a son? She'd never employ her."

"Perhaps he's her customer."

Their laughter struck the hallway like lightning, causing more doors to open, more scantily clad women and men to peer out of their darkened rooms.

"Nah, it's a maid. Look at 'er outfit," another woman said. "Come to fetch your master 'ome?"

"Making sure 'e's not buggering someone else, probably."

More laughter.

I ignored my burning cheeks and lifted my eyes to face them. "I'm here for my husband."

"'usband! Look at 'er. She's younger than me own daughter," the only man in the group said. He looked me over, tracing me from the tip of my scuffed shoe to my sweaty brow.

"That's why 'er 'usband is 'ere, then. Too young to know a man's doodle from 'is finger."

"Wouldn't mind 'avin' a go at 'er meself, though," the man said.

The woman on his arm laughed. "Of course you—"

"Have any of you seen him?" My eyes traveled from face to face. "I will pay a pound to the first person who can give me real information."

That quieted them at once, and they all exchanged glances. Eagerness blinked out of each of their faces.

"I seen him."

The voice came from the darkest part of the corridor, where I hadn't even noticed that there was a door. A girl, for she could be no more than fourteen, stepped out of the shadows and into the dusty bit of candle light seeping out of the open chamber doorways. She was in the same state of undress as the rest of them, but instead of making her look like a fully grown woman, it accentuated her youth.

The other tenants appeared just as surprised as I was to see her, like they had forgotten she existed. They shuffled and sniffed in disappointment that they were not the ones who would earn the reward.

"A tall man, yeah? Very pale and thin. With dark hair," the girl said.

I nodded. "Yes, that's him."

"He ain't there now. A woman came into his rooms and took him away with her."

Her words burned through me. I was too late.

"It was maybe two hours ago," she added. "I came out into the hallway because she knocked on his door a long time. I ain't never seen someone as beautiful as her, like something out of a dream."

Or a nightmare. "He let her in?" I asked.

"He must have at least unlocked the door, because she just turned the handle and walked in." The girl frowned. "Though, now that I think about it, I heard him shout at her to get out, to leave him alone. There was a lot of yelling, mostly from him."

"Wonder what she was doin' to 'im, then," one of the other women said, eliciting harsh laughter from the rest of the group.

"That's enough," Timothy said. "It's 'er 'usband."

"It might be her husband now, but if he left with that other woman, he won't be for long." This created another ripple of laughter.

I clenched my jaw until I thought I would crack my teeth.

"Can I have my pound now?"

Blinking, I focused on the girl once again. "Of course. One more thing, though. Did you hear where they were going? Perhaps the woman said something?"

The girl shrugged. "Not that I know."

I handed her the promised pound and did what I could to smile. "Thank you."

She motioned with her hand at the doorway behind me and Timothy. "If you need help getting into the room, I can do it for a guinea," she said.

"You have a key?"

She smiled for the first time. "Don't need no key."

"That ain't fair!" the man in the group said. "I can open that door just as good as she can. Better, even."

I ignored him and nodded to the girl. "Deal."

She walked to the door and pulled out a pin from somewhere in the folds of her dark hair. Kneeling, she inserted it into the keyhole with such ease and familiarity that there was no question she had done this numerous times.

The man continued mumbling behind us, but the girl paid him as little mind as I did, focusing instead on the thin bit of glittering metal in her hand.

There was a dry *click*, as if the door had cleared its throat, and she smiled. With a twist of the knob, the door creaked open to reveal a room lit only by a thread of moonlight sliding in through a hole in one of the curtains.

"Thank you," I breathed. I handed the girl the guinea as I stepped into the room.

If I'd had any doubts that August had stayed here, they dissipated as soon as I caught his warm scent of spiced rose. Beneath this familiar smell, however, there was something darker, less pleasant, like flowers that have been left in a vase for too long.

"That's enough of you lot," Timothy said to the group of people behind us. "This is a private affair b'tween a 'usband and a wife." He followed me in and closed the door behind him, much to the muttering of the disappointed spectators.

The only physical remnant of August's presence rested on the single chair in the room. His coat, tossed aside and forgotten.

"Look, ma'am," Timothy said, pointing to something on the bed.

It was another note, but I saw as soon as I took a hold of it that it was not in August's slanted hand, but in the same one as the invitation to the ball we had received so many days ago.

Lily's.

Dearest, sweetest, loveliest Anne,

If you are reading this, then you have been most clever, though not clever enough, since I have found our wounded knight before you. It is not entirely your fault, of course, because I have eyes all over this great city and you, alas, do not. Nevertheless, I commend you for being a good sport, and to demonstrate that I am a gracious victor, I will allow you to see our darling August once more. Isn't that kind of me?

Come to the Wodenhouse Mill as swiftly as your petite, scuffed little feet can carry you. I'm afraid I cannot promise you that you will walk out alive, but isn't the chance to look into your loved one's eyes one last time worth the risk of death?

Come, prove to me that love can indeed conquer all.

Lily Bellingham

I should have felt an avalanche of emotions. At the very least, I should have felt fear, since I would be walking into a mortal trap that Lily hadn't even bothered to disguise. But I was surprised to find I was calm—relieved, even. I no longer had the maw of uncertainty open before me. Now, I knew precisely where August and Lily were, and what I had to do. The confusion I'd felt back at Rosewood Manor and again throughout all the days at the hotel was gone. All I had to do was get to Wodenhouse Mill, and whatever had to happen would.

I just wished I'd said goodbye to Elsie.

"Ma'am?" Timothy said. "What's it say?"

I cleared my throat and prayed that the shadows in the room would help me hide the truth. "Oh, just that my husband is fine. There is no need to worry." I forced a smile and folded the letter over.

Timothy looked me full in the face, his eyes narrowing. "But 'e's sick, ain't 'e?"

"He says he feels quite a bit better and is waiting for me back at the hotel. He consulted a doctor in these parts, that's why he had to leave for a day, and he was worried that I might not deem it proper." I chuckled. "Men, always doing things backward."

Timothy's frown deepened. "Just up and left without a word?"

"Now, that was my mistake, I'm afraid. He mentions something about a letter he left on his bedroom table, and silly as I am, I didn't see it." I sighed. "I am so sorry, Timothy, for putting you through all of this. I overreacted."

He stared at me without a word.

Please don't ask anything else, please just let all of this go, I repeated to myself over and over.

There were so many inconsistencies in my story, but it was the only thing I could come up with that would stop him from following me to the factory. And that, I could not allow. I'd be damned if I put one more person in danger.

"I'll pay you for your time, of course," I said to distract him from the chain of thought he might be following.

The boy shook his head. "No need. I was 'appy to 'elp."

"You're sure?"

"Yes, ma'am."

I bent down so I was at his height. "You have been invaluable, Timothy. I truly do not know what I would have done without you all of these days. I doubt that I will see you again—" I bit my bottom lip and hurried to cover my slip. "I mean, at least not on this visit. My husband and I are meant to leave London in just a day or two, but I wanted to make sure you knew how much what you've done has meant to us." I hesitated. "Would it be all right if I gave you a hug, as a goodbye?"

The boy swallowed. "Of course, ma'am."

I embraced him, pulling him tightly against me. I gritted my teeth against the sudden onslaught of sadness that prickled in my eyes. If I knew anything about Lily, it was that she would do her utmost to kill me in that factory, and that she was strong enough to succeed, no matter how much I fought back. Which meant that, yes, this was quite feasibly the last time I would see Timothy. I only wished that I could have embraced Elsie once more, as well, but there was no helping that now.

"Keep yourself safe, Timothy," I said, and stood up straight again.

"Yes, ma'am."

"Go on, then. Go get some sleep. I'll let my husband know how much help you were."

The boy nodded and opened the door. He was about to step out of the room when he turned to face me once more, his face as serious as I'd ever seen it.

"Be careful, ma'am."

I opened my mouth to tell him not to worry about me, but he had already taken off, rushing headlong into the darkness of Ms. Addington's establishment.

FIFTEEN

WODENHOUSE MILL WAS A DARK STAIN AGAINST the night sky.

I chose a spot away from the main road and climbed over the metal fence, tucking my skirts between my legs to avoid tangling them up as I swung myself over to the other side. The kitchen knife, which was still in my left pocket, dug into my leg and made me gasp. I had to be more careful. I wouldn't want to do Lily's job for her, after all.

I landed on the dirt road leading up to one of the factory's side entrances. I didn't know if it would be open, or if I would be forced to use the front doors and walk straight into an ambush, but then again, did it really matter? Lily would be prepared for me no matter which entrance I used.

There was no sound from inside the factory, but I could feel that it was not empty, either. The building pulsed like a vein with energy, so much of it that the skin on my arms puckered as if with cold.

The side door's handle turned under my hand and opened silently.

The smell of wet, upturned earth and that same unnatural warmth I'd felt in the previous visits enveloped me, pulling me into the building. I put up no fight. Not yet, at least.

As if it had a life of its own, the door closed behind me with a surprisingly soft and well-oiled *click*, erasing the only bit of light the moon had provided for my steps.

As I waited for my vision to adjust, I listened.

The factory breathed, a large beast filling itself up with air, with my scent. There was no question that Lily and whoever or whatever else was in here with her knew of my presence. Was August conscious enough to pick out my energy, too, among all of this darkness?

After a minute, I realized that I couldn't stand around forever waiting for my eyes to pare some light out of my surroundings. The time for action had come.

I walked forward, my hands feeling around me for any sudden obstacles, but if I remembered correctly, I was in an empty, narrow corridor that led to the main factory floor.

As I neared the end of the passage, a subtle glow seeped through the blackness, throwing the nearest looms into stark relief against the opposite walls. I narrowed my eyes and tried to see if there was anyone near me, but all I could make out were shadows. I walked closer to the source of light.

It was a single candle hovering in midair at the very center of the factory floor. Its flame flickered with unseen breezes, but the candle itself did not move.

A low laugh made me gasp.

"A bit trite, I know, but effective, wouldn't you say? The lone candle in a dark room." Lily slipped out of a mass of shadows the way a snake slips out of its skin. "I am so glad you were able to make it, sweet Anne. Truly."

"You'll forgive me if I find that a bit hard to believe," I said.

She smiled. Even now, after everything that had occurred, Lily's beauty still stunned. "You should believe me, Anne. I cannot think of a more satisfying night than the one I have planned for us." She lowered her head a fraction.

From behind her, more shadows moved and separated, becoming unique bodies. Women. And they weren't standing just behind Lily, either. The soft swish of skirts came from all around the factory floor.

I turned. I was completely surrounded, with no exit left to me, the gloom and the figures bringing in a flash August's memory of the night the Brothers had died.

"This is my army," Lily said, motioning around her. "I think you'll find some familiar faces among them. Here, for example"—she nodded to the figure on her right—"is someone you know very well."

With no more than a look, Lily guided the suspended candle toward the woman and brought the light up to reveal her face. My eyes widened.

It was Eustace.

"She is a model servant, is she not?" Lily said. "As soon as I knew you and dear August were coming to London, I realized that you would have to stay at the Salisbury. Where else can you find the kind of finery a lord is accustomed to? Inserting Eustace into the staff was easy enough, and having her assigned to your chambers was easier still. Mr. Rushworth's mind is quite susceptible to forceful suggestions, as it turns out. With Eustace in place, I could monitor both of you with no effort on my part, and what was most important of all, I could continue to weaken August without his knowledge."

My skin chilled at her words. "Weaken him?"

"But of course. I needed to lower his defenses so that my creature could root itself into his being. A tasteless powder in the decanter of water Eustace brought up to your rooms every day and the deed was done. It had no effect on you, alas, because your powers are very different from his, but I do dare say it did quite a number on August. Without that daily enchantment, he might have slipped from my creature's grasp as easily as you have." She smiled. "Though that will all change tonight."

The room vibrated with energy, with anticipation.

"And then there's Ingrid, of course. You remember her."

The candle floated to another figure, revealing the woman I had tried to help at the factory, the one who had reacted with such fear to my powers.

"Quite an actress, wouldn't you say? She was essential in commandeering the uprising against you and raising suspicion with the police. Oh, and these two were the ones supposedly disemboweled." She laughed. "We did put on a good performance. You must at least agree with that."

Her hand became a knife as it sliced through the air, commanding the candle from shadow to shadow, faster and faster, revealing faces I knew, faces I had seen right here in the factory working at the looms, or in shops around London, faces that had smiled at me or nodded to me on the street.

"It's taken me less than two months to create this empire of women, Anne. Can you guess why? No? I will tell you." Her skirts whispered as she walked nearer. "You may know from our dear August that I was forbidden from becoming one of the Brothers, despite being more powerful than the whole lot put together. Because women have no powers. That's what we are taught from the moment we have use of reason. All of us, just poor defenseless beings always at the mercy of a man's kindness. Powerless, subservient, naturally inferior beings."

Her laughter rang out through the factory floor like cracking glass, echoed by all the other figures.

"Imagine it, all of these women carrying magic within them with no one to show them how to wield it until I took it upon myself to do so. Until I gave them a chance to finally prove just how much they were worth."

Lily's eyes blazed as the candle spun with increasing speed all along the circle of figures, lighting each face for only an instant. With each of its revolutions around the room, a tail whip of power slapped against me, causing my pulse to race faster.

"A woman," she continued, "is certainly not powerful enough to raise a creature from the depths of Hell, to have it do her bidding night after night, to twist someone's life into a nightmare from which he cannot escape. It is simply not heard of."

She chuckled and brought the candle to a stop.

"But I was rather pleased with the way my newest creature worked," Lily said. "It's an intriguing process that it takes its victims through, wouldn't you say? First enchanting them, lowering their defenses enough to dig itself a nice burrow inside their bodies and minds, and then casting them out completely, leaving the burrow devoid of anything but the most basic of locomotion. Ready to do its master's, or in this case mistress's, bidding. Not the best choice for a quick punishment, but I've never been very fond of those, anyway. They don't hurt nearly as much as they should."

I'd had a rebuke perched on my lips, but those words stopped it.

It was well hidden in her voice, but I'd heard it. For the first time, I'd heard it. A thread of pain.

Because she would know about that, wouldn't she? She would know about the kind of hurt that seeped in a drop at a time. She had lived with it for years.

The thoughts that had filled my mind as I sat in the Salisbury's café returned to me now, and I knew what I had to do. I owed it to myself.

I owed it to her.

"Miss Bellingham. Lily," I said, lifting my hand when she made to speak. "May I say something?"

An undulation of laughter wove around the room at my question, but it didn't touch Lily's lips. It was like she'd sensed the way my thoughts had shifted.

She watched me for an instant, her eyes trying to dig grooves into my head, before nodding.

I held her gaze. "I know that there is nothing that will change your mind about any of this, so that is not my intention. I am not asking for anything. I suppose, then, that this is mainly for my benefit, to clear my conscience when it comes to you."

Her eyes narrowed.

I took a deep breath and began. "For a while now, I've thought of you as if you were . . . uh . . . as if you were that image that burned at the manor. I've taken you at your surface, you see, your beauty and the hate you have for August, and for me. It made it easy to lay the blame on you when that was all you were."

A slight frown marred her ivory forehead.

Was I doing the right thing? Would this just make her angrier? Oh, but I had to say it. Even if it had the opposite effect I hoped it would, I still had to say it out loud.

I swallowed. "Even when I was in your memories, and felt all of the hate, all of the damage within you, I still failed to recognize one crucial thing, until just a couple of days ago. I realized then, that you had truly loved August as much as I do. And that he had tossed you aside."

She rolled her eyes, but I took a step closer.

"No, of course, I'd *known* that and yet, somehow, I hadn't understood what it meant, what it felt like, until you gave me a taste of it. I know I should hate you for it, and for everything else, but I find it harder to do now, Lily."

Her frown deepened.

"Because that kind of doubt and betrayal, it's a bit like what you've called upon August, isn't it? It finds a way inside of you, makes its home inside your head, and shoves you out of it until you can barely recognize which thoughts are your own anymore." I smiled softly. "You lose sense of where true north lies."

Lily's jaw clenched, as if she were trying to bite back a scream.

"I lived with it for just a few hours, lived with that kind of pain, and I could hardly bear it. I cannot imagine carrying its weight for years. As you have. Alone. How can I bring myself to hate you for wanting to punish the person who did that to you, who so selfishly unraveled your life? I love August, but that's not easy to forgive, even for me." I shook my head. "You deserved better, and the people in your life failed you. All of them."

The candle hovering between us shook.

Out with it, then. Didn't someone who'd been so hurt deserve at least some kindness, regardless of whatever monstrous actions that hurt had provoked?

"You won't believe me, but I am sorry. And I admire you for being someone who doesn't give in." I shrugged. "I needed you to know that, for whatever it's worth."

Something in Lily's face shifted, wavered, and I saw a flicker of the young woman—the girl, really—August had so harmed. She looked so young. She had so much to say!

Lily breathed. Her lips parted.

Eustace leaned in and whispered something in her ear. In an instant, the ivory mask covered her face once again, smothering that other version of her I'd only caught a glimpse of.

"Those are sweet words, Anne," she said, nodding to Eustace, who broke the circle and slipped farther into the encroaching darkness. "But you're right. I don't believe a single one of them."

I searched her face, but this was the unreachable Lily once more. Had I really expected anything else?

Eustace reappeared, and behind her was another figure.

August. Or what was left of him.

The change was shocking. His whole body exuded an emptiness that I'd only seen once before, in the wax works at Marylebone Road created by Madame Tussaud.

Everything that made him himself, his mannerisms, the sharpness in his gaze, the very essence of his being, was gone. I didn't need to look at the rose in my pocket to know that the last petals had fallen off and that all that was left were its thorns.

Lily pointed to a spot inside the circle, and August's body obeyed, coming to a stop exactly where she had indicated.

"August," I said, and hurried to his side. Some of the women surrounding me shifted, anxious for whatever revenge Lily had promised them they would be able to perpetrate on me. It didn't stop me. Let them do their worst. I would not be kept from saying goodbye.

"Can you hear me, August?"

I touched his cheek with a shaking hand and felt only the coldness of death on his skin.

"August," I whispered, and wrapped my arms around him one more time. I sent my powers in a reckless search through the husk of the man I loved, tentacles tapping every corner of his being to find something, anything, that was still him.

"It is a wondrous change, is it not?" Lily said. "I wish I could do the same to you, but alas, I just do not have the time to watch you lose your mind."

I held my breath. Not at her words, but at a flicker, like a spark coming off a piece of flint, brushing against my face where my bare skin touched August's chest.

"August," I said once more, as softly as I could. "Are you there?"

"That is quite enough of this silly romance for one evening." Lily moved her hand and August's body stiffened against me.

"No," I said, and held on tighter. "Please."

Lily flicked a finger and August grabbed my wrists, pulled me away. I tried to break away from his grip, but it was impossible.

Had I only imagined that he was still there? Why could he not hear me?

He turned away from me at Lily's bidding and walked to her side, his eyes coming to rest on a point somewhere above my head.

"I find this new August much improved, I must say, though I am sure you do not agree," she said. With a smile, she brought her hands up to her chest in a surprisingly girlish gesture. "But there's no time to speak of that now, not when the exciting part of the evening is finally beginning."

As she spoke, the circle of women tightened, each figure linking hands with the person next to her. Lily stepped backward into the spot left vacant for her and took Eustace's and Ingrid's hands into her own, completing the circle. August remained immobile inside the circle, exactly where Lily had left him.

A ripple of power surged through the room and pushed me backward a step. I called up my own energy, but it was not enough to shield me from the combined efforts of Lily and her women.

From somewhere above me came a thundering crash followed by quick, scraping steps that sounded like someone was walking on knife-edged stilts.

Lily said one word in the twisted language of magic. One word, and the world seemed to crack in two.

A scream like a shrieking kettle, but ten times its volume, preceded the squeal of tortured metal as whatever unholy creature they had called upon raced through the corridors upstairs, coming closer.

Coming for me.

"I do hope you enjoy my little beast. It's been anxious to meet you in its own form." Lily smiled. "We'll be leaving you, now, but be assured, sweet Anne, that we will all follow your struggle most attentively. Even if there can be only one conclusion."

As I watched, Lily and the rest of the women eased back into the darkness from which they had come, disappearing from sight.

"Wait," I said. "Please, take August with you!" They couldn't leave him like this, unable to move on his own, defenseless.

Laughter clashed with the resounding steps of the creature Lily had conjured up.

"I thought it would be more romantic if the two of you died together," she said. "You should be thankful I am kind enough to grant you that."

"Lily, please!"

The only response came from the candle, which stopped its midair hovering and fell to the floor. The sole source of light in the factory was suddenly snuffed out.

My eyes widened in the darkness, trying to gather any bit of light that might remain, but I was utterly blind. And the creature drew nearer by the second.

I refused to be killed while spooked into immobility. If I had to die, I would do it fighting, for my life and for August's.

Arms out, fingers vibrating with fear, I took a step toward where I remembered he stood, and another, ignoring the ever-closer threat. At last, I touched August's arm.

"Let's go," I said, and took his hand. It was cold and limp, his fingers refusing to curl around mine, to respond in any way to my touch. "August, we have to move. Now."

I pulled on his arm, but despite his slight frame, he was rooted in place. There was no shifting him from where Lily's last order had left him.

A hiss slithered into the room.

Whatever this creature was, whatever monstrousness it had in store for us, it was now on the factory floor.

I dug my nails into August's hand until I felt the slickness of blood on my fingertips. "We are going to die in a matter of seconds," I whispered. "This thing is going to kill the two of us right here, where we stand, because I am not leaving you here alone. If you're still in there somewhere, and if you ever loved me, help me, please!" I pulled on his hand again, but moving stone would have been easier.

The sound of blades scraping the wooden floor echoed through the large room, making it impossible to tell how near this thing that hunted us truly was.

Hot, angry tears spilled down my cheeks. Lily would win, then. She would be rid of us both in mere moments, not even allowing August and I a proper goodbye. What did the living statue in front of me care of my kisses or words?

There was a sudden tingle on my fingertips.

My first thought was that it was my reaction to fear or nerves, but the sensation grew until it felt like my fingertips, still wet with August's blood, were on fire.

I felt August's familiar power race down his arm and leap out into the room. A gust of warm air swept my hair back as every candle throughout the factory, even the one still tipped on its side on the floor, lit up at his unspoken command.

And just in time to reveal the horror in front of us.

It could have been called a gigantic black spider if it had had less appendages, and if those appendages had not narrowed down into glittering, knife-like ends. It had glistening jaws from where fangs as long as my arm protruded and eyes, all half-dozen of them, burned with hunger, with the anticipation of the kill. I recognized the malice in them. It was what had stared at me from August's eyes when his hands had wrapped around my throat.

Each flickering candle flame shone off its ink-black carapace as it lifted itself on its hind legs.

The sight of it immobilized me for an instant. Which was exactly an instant too long.

The creature swiped one of its front legs in my direction, missing me by a hair's width, but shoving August backward so violently he remained upright only because one of the factory walls was there to stop the fall.

"Run!" I screamed, though I knew that it was pointless. Perhaps he could hear me, but he had used whatever bit of strength he had left to give me sight.

The spider-like horror rounded on August. This had been what had haunted him, what had taken control of him; those monstrous legs had carved him out of his own head and left an almost empty shell it could maneuver at will from the safety of this factory, from its den.

Thick threads of saliva dangled from its jaws as it approached August's immobile figure.

"No, goddamn it!"

I picked up the first thing I saw, a spool of white thread as large as a pot, and threw it at the creature with as much force as I could muster.

It turned with the kind of speed reserved only for pursuits in nightmares.

With a gasp, I took off running, my only thought to get it as far away from August as I could. I raced through an aisle of floor looms, not daring to look back. Not that I needed to when I could hear its hissing breaths close behind me.

Too close behind me.

I took a hard right and felt one of its legs slice the air in the very spot I had just vacated. A shriek of hissing fury rang through my head, making my teeth ache and my vision blur.

My legs slowed without my consent and in spite of the mortal threat behind me. I grabbed on to the nearest loom to push myself forward, but I felt as if my legs were submerged in something viscous, like mud or bog water.

Fear called on my instinct and that instinct drew my powers forward. I felt the warmth in my chest rise and spread through me, neutralizing whatever the creature's voice had done to me. My vision cleared, and I shook the torpor from my legs.

The creature screamed again, the sound as violent as its words had been when it had taken control of August's voice, but I was already racing away from it, ducking behind looms, throwing everything I could grab behind me. Though it was a gigantic target, nothing I flung at it did more than bounce off its black shell. I had no idea how to kill it, if I even *could* kill it. All I was hoping for was to slow it down enough so I could think.

I heard the whiz of air before I felt the hot sting of the blade against my back. I cried out at the pain that bloomed across my body, radiating up and down, inside and out, until it seemed that all I had ever felt and all I would ever feel was this agony.

My knees buckled, and I knew if I allowed myself to fall, there would be no getting back up, not with this kind of injury. I lifted my eyes, and what I saw brought an idea crashing into my head.

Biting my lips to keep from screaming, I ran to the largest loom on the factory floor. It stood surrounded by crates full of cones of thread in all manner of colors, crate piled upon crate, effectively blocking the loom off from the rest of the room. The machine itself was as wide and tall as a four-poster bed, and it had thousands of white threads stretched tautly to its huge beams, ready to create bed sheets or dining linen. It would not stop the creature, but it would give me a few moments to come up with a better idea.

I slid underneath the loom as I had seen the children do, my back stinging enough with every move that I thought I would lose consciousness. One of the creature's blades sliced at my ankles again, but I was quicker this time, and yanked them under the temporary cover of the loom. Tangles of thread brushed against my face and against my injured back, but I ignored them. Not for the first time, I gave thanks that I was roughly the size of a child in stature and slimness, so that I could pull myself out from beneath the loom on the other side.

Behind me, the creature shrieked in fury that it couldn't get to me, but it didn't despair for long. With a leap that shook the whole factory, it jumped onto the loom. The machine creaked under the unexpected weight, sudden large splinters of broken wood stabbing the air like thorns. One of the beams cracked in two and the threads, so long under continuous pressure, snapped like whips outward.

Thousands of thin threads collapsed and spilled every which way.

The creature roared and moved a leg forward, which immediately became ensnared in the threads. It tried to free itself with another frantic shift of limbs, but only managed to tangle itself deeper and deeper in the white nest at its feet.

I knew it would figure how to shift its bladed appendages enough to cut clean through the thread, but I was not about to wait around for that. With its shrieks of anger and frustration in my ears and my wound dripping blood onto the floor with each movement, I ran to the door that led to the second story. I didn't want to leave August behind on the ground floor, but I needed to find a weapon of some kind, anything that would at least wound the spider-like horror and let us run out of here.

My hands shook from the pain and the blood loss as I turned the knob.

It was locked. Of course it was locked. I kicked the door, slammed my fists into it, but it would not budge. There was a crash from behind me, the loom splitting apart while the creature at its very center, legs still entangled, jerked and pulled with all of its strength. I watched an appendage hack through a handful of white thread in an instant.

I was running out of time.

I swept my gaze around the factory floor for anything large enough, flammable enough, or sharp enough to use, but all I could see was thread and gears, woven cloth that could not be of any use to me.

Anne.

The voice came as if from centuries away, muffled, and faded like parchment, but I would have recognized it anywhere.

Anne, August said again in my head, drawing my eyes to where he still stood locked in place by the creature's power. I followed his unblinking stare.

Something across the floor's length was alight with the reflection of one of the flickering candles. I narrowed my eyes and realized what it was: the largest pair of shears I had ever seen. They sat on a stool in front of a spinning wheel.

I didn't stop to think if I could possibly reach them in time, if they had been sharpened recently, what I would do with them if I did reach them, or even if I could wield something that looked like solid bronze. I just ran.

The wound across my back burned with the movement, sending waves of blackness across my vision.

Behind me, the loom broke apart completely with a bone-like crunch.

I had a head start, but I wouldn't for long.

The creature screeched, and I heard it launch into a chase that brought it much too close in just two or three of its giant strides. I wove around another row of looms and turned just in time to see the long-legged horror climb right over the top of them, leaping from one machine to the other with ghastly agility. Its feet slashed through taut threads like it would slice through my skin if it caught me.

I didn't see the cart full of unspun wool that had shifted toward the center of the aisle until I had already slammed into it. It knocked all breath from my chest and brought another vicious flare of pain from the wound on my back. For a moment, I thought I would lose consciousness, and that would be it, Lily would have won. But it was the creature's own screech, the shattered-glass quality of its voice, which brought me back from the edge of darkness. It cut into my head too loudly to ignore. I shook the faintness off, shoved the cart away from me, and ran on.

The glitter of the shears was closer now. I didn't dare hope to kill the creature with the blades, but if I could grab hold of them and shove them at its torso, or better yet, at one of its eyes, I was sure I could do some damage. Perhaps surprise it enough to lop off an appendage or two. Anything that would give me an advantage.

If I could just get there, get them in my hands . . .

I ran for millennia, the metallic glimmer like a lighthouse beam calling me in. It was a straight run to the spinning wheel and finally, finally, my hands closed around the cool surface of the shears.

That's when I felt that something was wrong. A sudden silence and stillness had fallen behind me, as overwhelming as the creature's cracking voice had been. I spun around.

Nothing but broken looms met my gaze. No creature. Nothing racing toward me.

I'd thought having a giant spider chase me was frightening, but this abrupt nothingness was even worse. Where had a being of that size gone in the seconds it had taken me to grab hold of the shears?

Lifting them at chest level, I pointed the blades out, waiting for the creature to crash down in front of me. My heart was the only sound in the entire factory floor.

It began with a numbing sensation in my feet and hands.

Unlike the first time it had happened, I recognized what it was at once, and shook my head, trying to clear it.

The heat of a perfectly lit fire lapped at my limbs, relaxing my muscles, the comforting heat spreading through me like wine. My grip on the shears slackened.

"No," I said with the bit of voice I could summon from the embrace that had begun slowly squeezing me. I did my best to summon my power, but it slid from my grasp, as slippery as an earthworm.

But . . . why did I need it? My mind fought to remember.

The sweet smell of pipe tobacco rose around me and brought with it images of my father's hands as he prepared his nightly indulgence. "It's all right, Anne," he said, and smiled.

I couldn't help but smile back. Was it? I couldn't recall if everything was all right or not, but my father had said it and he was never wrong. It was so good to see him, too. How long had it been?

The warmth had spread all through me, and it was rather nice. I had been afraid of it a second before, but why? It was more than pleasant; it was the kind of warmth that only came from the best down duvet, or a just-filled bath.

"That's it," my father said. "Good girl."

My hand opened and the shears tumbled out. I heard the clatter of the metal against the floor as if from underwater. But it was all right. Everything was all right. If only my heart would stop pounding, pounding, pounding, and if the sound behind it, attached to each beat, would cease . . .

I was too tired to worry about it, though. More than anything, I wanted to sink to the ground right where I was, curl up in this heat, and sleep. It would be heavenly. Surely, then, my heart would quiet down.

Something slid down to dangle in front of me, something long, black, and glittering in the candlelight. A leg, was my first thought, but why would a leg drop down from the ceiling at Caldwell House? Or . . . was I at that other house? Rose . . . something. I couldn't remember which one I worked in now. My father would know.

The leg doubled as I watched, then tripled, multiplying and multiplying, until a dozen of them dripped like ink in front of me, lowering themselves slowly to the floor. *How very peculiar*, I thought, and blinked.

Another wave of tobacco scent swept the slight curiosity away. I couldn't bring myself to worry about anything now, not when my father was nearby after so long without seeing him. I had to tell Mary and Elsie. But later, when I felt less tired.

My eyes closed of their own accord. My thoughts stilled. From somewhere in my head there was a hiss of words, but they were so far away, too far away, and if I listened, they would break through this warmth.

Discomfort.

I felt every slack muscle in my face fight as I tried to frown. What was it?

The sudden sensation increased, sharpening, but I couldn't tell where it was coming from. It surprised me to notice that I couldn't really feel my hands, or most of my body, in fact. Except for that growing pain, pulsing and pulsing, but where?

A gasp fluttered like a bird in my throat as my right thigh lit up with pain. It was impossible to ignore, not when it felt like it would eat me alive if I didn't do something to stop it.

My right hand twitched, but didn't budge from where it hung at my side.

Deeper pain flared, and my hand finally jerked to stamp it out, pressing against my skirt where something burned. Following only the instinct to stop the pain, every movement as heavy as if I moved through some sort of sludge, I reached into my pocket.

Fire met my palm.

Sharp heat, like a needle held over a flame, cut into my flesh and I remembered. The rose in my pocket.

August's face flashed through my mind, his power beating in my hand. I squeezed my fist around the flower's stem, around the rose which had no soft comfort left, which had only pain to gift me. But weren't its thorns as essential as its petals?

My skin screamed with the pain as blood began to pool in my palm, as my body and my mind began to roar back to life bit by bit.

I knew that I was out of time.

I remembered the shears at my feet, but they couldn't help me anymore. They were too far away. I couldn't run, either, or call upon my powers, not with a body that was still not wholly under my control. Despite everything, despite every effort, I would die right here where I stood, and so would August.

And then the answer came to me with the sharpness of a slap.

Still gripping the rose's stem in one hand, I slid my free one into my left pocket. I opened my eyes a slit, just enough to see that the creature had bent its multitude of legs so that its jaws were level with my face. If it had noticed the slackening of its power on my mind, it showed no sign of it as it softly hissed, its fangs dripping with anticipated victory. I stifled a shudder and took hold of the only defense I had left.

Elsie's kitchen knife.

I pulled it out of my pocket with as much speed as my returning muscles would allow, lifted it up high above me, and with the strength that came from years of carving entire chickens and slicing into roasts, I plunged it into one of the creature's many eyes.

It was like stabbing into an egg, the brief crackle of the outer shell giving way to the gooey interior.

The creature screeched in surprise and fury, but I didn't hesitate. I yanked the knife out and plunged it into the next eye.

Behind me, August gasped as if he had been holding his breath for days. A harsh cough tore through him as the next eye burst open.

The monstrous being reared back and I lost my grip on the knife, which remained caught in the last bleeding socket I'd managed to puncture. One of its legs lunged at me. The bladed end cut into my shoulder before I could jump out of its path, the strength behind it shoving me to the ground. I scrambled backward, but all I could see were blades, bringing my death on their glittering edges.

August's voice resounded through the factory floor as he called out in the twisting language of magic.

The creature's scream cracked in half as his power tore it apart in an instant, limb from limb, its middle splitting open like rotten fruit. It hovered upright for a breath, its remaining eyes locked on me, and then collapsed with a crash.

I held my breath, half expecting it to rise again, to feel the final cut of its appendages in my skin. But there was no movement, no sound, just the absolute stillness of death.

"Anne!" August called, and his voice cut through that stillness like the sweetest ring of a bell. In moments, he was kneeling at my side, running his eyes over my face and body, taking in my wounds. "We need to get you to a doctor."

I met his gaze.

"Anne?"

Despite the scratches and bruises on his face, he looked more like himself than he had in a long time. The sharp light in his eyes had returned, dispelling the shadows that the horror now dead on the cement had placed within them. It was August, my August, once again.

I smiled and wrapped my arms around him. All the worry melted from my limbs under the biting heat of his skin on mine. He was fully here, with me.

"You were immobile . . . I thought it was going to kill you," he murmured in my ear.

"It was looking very possible for a moment."

The burn increased, swallowing the pain from the cut on my back and shoulder as his arms tightened around me. "I didn't know what to do to wake you up. The creature was so focused on you, it relaxed its grip on me enough that I was able to slip a bit of my power out to reach you. It was the only thing I could think of."

"And it worked," I said, pulling back to look at him as I brought the rose from my pocket. It was in full bloom once more, petals as red and glistening as the blood that still seeped from the thorns' puncture marks in my palm.

August smiled. "I was hoping it was still in your pocket. Thank God it was."

"It was the only thing connecting me to you when you left. Do you think I would have forgotten it?" That brought back the fear and anger I'd felt at reading his note, and I couldn't help myself. I smacked him in the arm forcefully enough to make my already injured hands sting. "Never do that to me again. Not ever."

"You would never have left, and I couldn't keep putting you in that kind of danger."

"I don't—wait." My eyes widened at the one crucial thing I had forgotten. "Where's Lily?"

"She's gone. She and the rest of the women left as soon as that . . . thing had you cornered."

I frowned. She hadn't stayed to watch the culmination of months of planning? She was that convinced that we would both die that she didn't feel the need to verify it? The news should have been a relief, for she would think us dead now. We would be able to leave the city, perhaps even the country, without the threat of her revenge looming over us. I should have been laughing and celebrating, but a grim grain of doubt had settled in the pit of my stomach. Lily was not someone who left ends un-tucked.

These thoughts must have been scrawled on my face because August nodded. "It is rather worrisome."

My mind poised itself to spiral down into unease, but I halted it. Perhaps Lily did have more in store for us, but for right now, right this minute, we were both alive and together. After what we had lived through these past few days, that was enough for me.

"Come," he said, offering me his arm. "Let me help you up."

I groaned and winced my way into a somewhat upright position with his support. My dress had tacked onto the wound along my back, so that each movement shifted the cloth and sent spasms of pain along my body.

"Perhaps you shouldn't move," August said. "I'll go in search of a carriage."

"And leave me here with the carcass of that creature? I think not."

"You're too injured, Anne."

I waved his words aside in conscious imitation of his own familiar gesture and leaned forward. I pressed my lips lightly on August's. He made a small sound in the back of his throat as I deepened the kiss and brought his hands to my shoulders in a, honestly, rather weak attempt to continue protesting. Less than a heartbeat more, and those same hands had slid into my disheveled hair and brought me closer, both of us ignoring the scorching pain until we could bear it no longer.

I reveled in that sting, because I knew what it meant to lose it.

The crash of a door slamming open against a wall was what separated us. Voices spilled into the factory floor, along with the bobbing light of lamps, as we stumbled to our feet.

"Quickly!" said one of the voices—a man's.

My muscles tightened as August took a step forward, standing between me and whoever it was headed our way.

Six people ran through the door separating the factory floor from the foyer, four of them people I would have given quite a lot to have never seen again. August's sudden tension next to me revealed the identical nature of our thoughts.

"That's 'er!" Ingrid yelled, and pointed in my direction. "She's responsible for everythin'!"

"What?" I began. "I don't—" My voice caught in my throat in shock.

"She killed the girls from the factory!" said Eustace, standing beside Ingrid.

"That's absurd!" August said.

The only two strangers in the group, both of them in the uniform of Scotland Yard, turned toward me. "You'll have to come with us, ma'am," one of them said.

August stepped fully in front of me now, blocking the constables' way. "What proof do you have? You can't just take their word for it."

"We have proof," the constable said. "A pendant belonging to one of the missing girls was found among her belongings at the Salisbury. We understand she is your wife, sir, but she needs to come with us."

My belongings? I had taken everything with me when I left the hotel. No, this wasn't happening. It couldn't be.

"She ain't even 'is wife," Ingrid said. "She's been stayin' under a false name with this man, whom she lured 'ere to kill for 'is fortune."

August's fury radiated like a miniature sun. "How dare you make such allegations? She is my wife, and she has nothing to do with any disappearances, and certainly not with having lured me anywhere."

I felt as if I were looking at everything from high above, as if it were occurring to someone far removed from me.

"Then what are the two of you doing here at this time of night?" Eustace said.

"That is none of your concern."

"Her real name is Anne Tinning."

I turned to look at the two other men who had remained silent until now. Mr. Price gave me a tight smile. "After you left so abruptly from my shop, I made it my business to inquire about you. With Mr. Thompson's help, of course. What we found was rather interesting."

Next to him, Mr. Thompson's almost colorless blue eyes glittered. "For example, we learned that someone in the last household you worked at was killed. That cannot be a coincidence."

Mr. Keery's face flashed through my mind as I had last seen it, burnt raw and tight with pain. I closed my eyes against the image, but it could not be erased. How had they found all of this out? Had they been working with Lily all along?

"We didn't want to see anything happen to you, August," Mr. Thompson continued, "not after our history together, so we told these fine constables everything we knew." His smile never reached his eyes. "And we arrived just in time to prevent a disaster, I see."

His gaze shifted to look past us. All of our eyes followed.

The spot on which the lifeless body of the creature had crashed down was now empty, no evidence remaining of its existence. The bloodied kitchen knife I had wielded rested on the bare floor. Whatever magic had given that monster physical presence had swept it away and with it, any explanation we might have had for the disappearances and deaths.

"I'm not a police constable, but this is all very peculiar, wouldn't you say, Mr. Price? It seems to me that we came to August's rescue just in time." Mr. Thompson smiled at

Eustace. "Thanks to this lady's quick thinking in coming to fetch us, of course."

The implications of this were staggering. Eustace must have followed me the day I went to the apothecary and had told Lily about my visit and hasty retreat. It had been foolish to assume that she would not have kept herself apprised of all our actions. That day, I had handed her another way she could hurt us without even realizing it.

The second constable stepped forward. "We must take you in, ma'am, pending an investigation. There is too much evidence against you."

"You will do no such thing," August said.

"I'm afraid I must insist, sir." The two constables stepped toward me.

I felt August's powers roil, gathering force, waves of energy tumbling over each other. The air felt heavy and charged, like the slightest movement would set it on fire. Eustace and Ingrid exchanged a glance with Mr. Thompson.

As powerful as August was, he wouldn't be able to take on three magicians at the same time, not after the expenditure of energy that killing the creature had required of him. And even if he could, what would that accomplish? We would have the entirety of London's police force searching for us if we escaped, making us prisoners of our own fear anywhere we went.

Both of us had lived under the weight of fear long enough.

I took a deep breath and placed my hand on August's sleeve. It was time to do what I did best. What I was born to do.

"Back away from him," one of the constables called out.

I ignored the order and sent a rivulet of calm up August's arm, allowing the power to caress his cheek, to flutter through him. It was a soft puff of energy, and his magic tried to smother it, but he had taught me well. As if I was smoothing out wrinkles on a piece of cloth, I found every bit of resistance in him and undid it.

August turned to me. His eyes pleaded with me, begged me to stop.

"It's all right," I whispered. "I'm sure we will sort this all out."

The lie was harsh in the air between us. It was obvious that Lily had planned this in case the creature did not succeed in killing us both. She had left nothing to chance. The evidence would be where she needed it to be to best damage me, and her influence and power were enough to close my cell door with resounding conviction.

"Anne . . ." His voice disappeared under the weight of what he wanted to say.

"I know." I gave him a smile and stood on my toes to kiss his cheek. Would I ever get to do that again?

"Step away from him, miss. I won't say it again."

Forcing down every feeling that screamed for me to stop, I walked over to the waiting constables.

"Anne Tinning, you are under arrest." The first constable brought out a pair of dark handcuffs. "Hold out your hands."

"Is that necessary?" August said.

The constable met my eyes. "Hold out your hands. Now."

I swallowed and did as I was told. The metal snapped shut over my wrists with violent finality.

"She's injured and needs a doctor," August said. "It is her right to be given proper care."

"She will receive the care she deserves. You, sir, will also be questioned, so if you had any plans of leaving the city, I would change them."

"Oh, do not trouble yourself with that," Mr. Thompson said. "We will make sure he remains in London."

I winced at the violence those words promised.

The constable nodded and pulled on my hands. "Let's go."

The two men flanked me on each side, their grip tight on my upper arms as they led me down the factory floor toward the front doors.

I bit back tears. If ever there had been a time for them, it was now, but if I allowed them to fall, I wasn't sure I would be able to stop the panic from rising fully to the surface.

I strained to look back at August.

Mr. Thompson and Mr. Price had already drawn near to him, circling their prey. But August's eyes were not on them. They were on me.

I was leaving him as I had found him all those months ago: swallowed by guilt and grief, and wholly alone. Only this time, I had no means of helping him. I didn't even have the means of helping myself.

It was unlikely that I would see him again, so I smiled and hoped it didn't look like a grimace. His lips thinned, and he made as if to start after me, but one of Mr. Thompson's hands curled around his arm and stopped him.

The constable on my right jerked me back to face the front.

"Those men mean him harm," I said. "You have to protect him—"

"Be quiet. He is no longer your concern."

They led me through the entrance to the foyer and as much as I tried, I couldn't hold the tears back anymore. The world blurred. The lamplight in the constable's hand swung as he opened the front doors and shoved me into the waiting darkness.

The last thing I heard before the Wodenhouse Mill's doors slammed shut behind me was Lily's low, shadow-filled laughter, chasing me into the night.

The End

ACKNOWLEDGEMENTS

A number of people have helped get this novel out to you and I'd be remiss if I didn't thank them, however briefly.

Thank you to Cal Spivey, for the insightful comments that propelled the story to a better version of itself, as well as to Kisa Whipkey for carefully smoothing the manuscript up for publication. A big thank you to Ashley Ruggirello, not only for the deliciously gothic cover but for believing in Anne and August's story from the beginning.

A big thank you as well to my family, for giving me silence when I needed it.

And finally, perhaps most importantly, another massive thank you to anyone who took the time to read my words.

ABOUT VALENTINA

Valentina Cano was born in Montevideo, Uruguay but now makes her home in the swampy land that is Miami and dreams of London. She is a student of classical singing who spends whatever free time she has either reading, writing, weaving, or spinning wool on her antique spinning wheel.

She first began writing poetry to combat severe depression and has continued on to push her own personal boundaries of comfort and truth. Her works have appeared in numerous publications and her poetry has been nominated for the Pushcart Prize and Best of the Web. She has two chapbook out, Winter Myths, and Event Horizon, as well as her debut novel, The Rose Master, which was published in 2014 and was called a "strong and satisfying effort" by Publishers Weekly.

She is represented by Christopher Schelling at Selectric Artists